The Colour of Shadows

The Colour of Shadows

Gawain Barker

ISBN-13: 978-0-9876430-1-8

Cover design & Imprint
bushbrother

website
thecolourofshadows.com

for

my FNQ mob

CONTENTS

By Christ, You Can Blue

Cairns 1965

The little blonde lead singer danced like a randy dandy savage. He was tearing up the joint! The girls all wanted to root him; most blokes wanted to bash him. But how bloody good was the lead guitarist? With a cigarette permanently parked in his mouth and a pick in his blurred fingers, he played aggressive, fast, dirty; making a wild, go-and-get-stuffed noise that Seth hadn't believed possible.

Drunk on the long-necks of NQ lager he'd knocked back outside with his brother Alex and his mates, Seth reeled with amazement. No radio station or LP had prepared him for this! Straight from the guts, the boys in this band meant every note they played, and from their looks and attitude it was obvious that they just didn't care if anyone else liked it or not.

Cairns would never be the same – hell, he'd never be the same! An unknown world had just opened up, full of things he wanted like crazy to feel. This music was shouting in his ear a truth he was so ready to know.

The drummer ducked another bottle. Idiots spat at the singer. A lot of blokes had come along tonight to just give these interstate bands some curry. The police didn't care – they were up the back, laughing with the doormen.

A fold-up chair skittered across the floor and bounced off the stage front. A girl slipped over. A bloke lent down as if to help, but flipped up her skirt instead. His mates laughed. Seth quickly pushed through, got the girl up and she turned the air blue, swearing at the jeering men.

Real fans were dancing up the front; flash young fellas in good denim and corduroy pants, their girls wearing fashion boots and groovy patterned skirts. But a pack of mongrels kept pushing and tripping them. Seth blinked in disbelief, overwhelmed by his rage. This was the best bloody thing he'd ever seen and these bastards were ruining it!

A nong in a grimy cowboy hat grabbed at the guitarist's ankles. The guitarist kicked him in the chest. With a roar of outrage, the nong and two of his mates began to climb onto the stage. The guitarist, puffing on his cigarette, kept playing and just sneered down at them like the god he was.

His gun-fighter cool was incredible, but this wonderful man was about to get well and truly bashed. These bastards would go for his hands, his fingers; smashing them into useless pegs. Seth knew with every atom of his being that he had to stop that from happening. His brother had told him to keep his head down, but Alex knew bugger-all about rock and roll.

Seth grabbed one bloke, threw him on the floor. He then put three piledriver punches into the next one's head and he fell from the stage edge into a heap. The first fella, his eyes as mean as cat shit, got up, and Seth put him down for good with a match-winning kick to the goolies. The third twit started chucking punches and Seth dropped his head. The bloke's fist hit his thick blonde skull. Snap, crackle and pop! The bloke shouted; snatched his fist back, and Seth knocked him out with a sugar-train left between the eyes.

Other bastards waded in, and Seth, with his back to the stage, began to fight in earnest. He was sixteen and nearly six foot tall, not afraid, but mighty angry. It was one thing not to like the music, but trying to stop it, or others from enjoying it, was not on. Not by a long shot.

With the beautiful noise of The Purple Hearts in his ears, and a sea of sweating shouting faces in front of him, Seth dished out a perfect flogging. It all went lightning fast, and impossibly slow too; time just a trick of the mind, and when he heard the guitarist start ripping out a solo – he knew it was being played for him.

For infinite seconds the two of them merged perfectly; guitar and fists in unison, the notes and punches creating something glorious, something pure. Oh my gosh, thought Seth, would life ever be this good again?

Just when it started to get hairy, with too many blokes to fight, Alex and his hard-case mates, the Macs, were there, knocking and shoving blokes away. As the melee dispersed Seth caught his breath. The band had stopped playing and he turned towards the stage.

A nasty middle-knuckle-out punch drove into his left kidney. Gasping with pain, he spun around, fists rising to face his assailant. It was his big brother Alex, glaring at him like a demon.

Seth felt something sting his eyes. Fair bloody go! He'd just had the fight of his life; acquitting himself in a massive barney. Any bloke would be well stoked at what he'd done. Any brother would be proud. But not his.

See, Alex always started things, always held the reins too, and his word was law. But Seth knew he'd done something good and important here; something bigger than himself.

It was a wonderful feeling. A good reason to be.

"Get the hell out of here," said his brother.

Seth defiantly ignored him, lent back on the edge of the stage and looked himself over. His knuckles were skinned; stinging, and bugger, there was blood on his good white shirt. It wasn't his, but what would Mum say?

"Hey! You there! Hey thank you!" yelled a Pommy voice behind him. Seth turned. It was the singer – talking to him! The little bloke grinned broadly and then called to the guitarist, "Hey Lobby – look! Here he is! He's just a kid."

The guitarist came over and smiled down at Seth.

"Good onya!" he said. "By Christ, you can blue!"

Then he looked out over the room and shook his head.

"You fellas are crazy up here."

The Rainbow

Cairns 1980

Seth could smell the gun. Over the motel-room pong of Glen 20 disinfectant came a sweet whiff of Ballistol. It must be newly borrowed, or recently stolen, because the three skinny pricks standing there didn't look like they knew how to wipe their own bums – let alone clean a gun.

Going toe-to-toe with these bastards wasn't a problem. It would take Mick and him five seconds to put them on the deck. But in this little double down the back of the Rainbow Motor Inn, a gun could be a real hassle.

As though tired, Seth massaged his forehead, and began to move slow and casual across the room.

"C'mon Aaron, let's not muck around," said Mick. "We sorted this all out before. You show me the money – here in this room – then we go for a drive."

"Nah. You show us the dope first," said Aaron.

Mick's lenient smile faded; his hands became fists.

Next to the wall Seth stifled a yawn, turned his head and spotted the gun. Under Aaron's loose shirt, it looked big.

"Mick, let's go," said Seth. His tone of voice was a code his mate instantly understood.

"Aw, you're joking!" said Mick to Aaron. "What do you think Colin's gonna say about this?"

"Fuck Colin," said Aaron.

Seth had drifted over to the front door. He opened it and the room filled with moving air. On a bamboo side table, reef-dive brochures and motel stationery fluttered. Outside in the darkness, palm fronds rustled in the sou-easterly.

"Mick," said Seth, walking back to them.

The gun came out; a totally cut down .22 rifle. It was a bullshit gun, only good for shooting a sleeping bloke.

Mick shook his head in disbelief. Seth went up to him.

"We're gonna all go out to your car now," said Aaron, his undisguised desperation giving Seth a stupid little thrill.

Mick swore in exasperation. Seth murmured in his ear, "Hop outside, stay out of range and be ready to run."

Mick swore again, but turned and left; doing what he was told. He had the grumps now, but he trusted Seth. That's why he'd asked him to come along tonight.

Seth beamed at the jumpy-looking ratbags. With the gun aimed at his head he'd never felt more alive.

"Okay boys, let's go to our car." Still talking, he turned and strode to the door. "It's just up the street and . . ."

"Oi, oi!" shouted Aaron. "Slow down or I'll knock ya!"

Absolutely buzzing, Seth stepped outside and ran down the motel's forecourt. About fifteen metres from the door he turned to see the three stooges come tumbling out.

"Hoi! Slow down or I'll fuckin' shoot," yelled Aaron.

Seth spread his big, muscled arms and laughed.

"Go on then, you shower of shit. Go on – shoot me!"

Aaron snarled, aimed and fired. The sawn-off .22 went bang and Seth heard the bullet flit through a hibiscus bush a good two metres from him, and – pock! – hit a wall.

Seth roared with laughter. Down near the street entrance Mick looked both appalled and amused. Aaron, red-faced with anger, manically worked the bolt. Brass chinged on concrete. Another shot banged out. It also went wide.

"See?" said Seth. "Not so bloody easy is it?"

A door swung open on the floor above. A shirtless man looked down. Behind him was a bare-breasted woman; one of the girls who worked out of the Rainbow. Through the balcony rails Seth saw the man's gun-belt; his dark blue trousers. It was a cop getting his end off.

Seth took off down the driveway. "It's a cop," he said to Mick, and they ran down the forecourt onto the pavement out the front of the Rainbow. Slowing to a brisk walk they headed north up Sheridan Street to where Jeffyman was waiting. Above them, moths whirled in clouds around the street lights. As they came up to the truck, Mick looked at Seth.

"Go on shoot me?" he said. "You're still a mad bastard Seth Kelly. That hasn't changed."

Seth came in from the beachside veranda to get more beers. In the kitchen the girls looked up from their drinks. He was pleased at the impatience in Debbie's eyes. She'd had a few and he'd give her one later. Mick's missus Pam gave him a quick penetrating glance. She was a sharp chick; she knew something had gone down.

Back outside he left Mick and Jeffyman's beers on the table. They were deep in discussion, but the wind rattling the dry, spiky leaves of a stand of pandanus by the veranda made their conversation difficult. The neighbour's house was close and the boys couldn't be too loud coming up with their new plan.

Seth took his beer over to the rail and looked out across the road at the sea. White-caps fluttered in the moonlight.

Yeah, right – a new plan. The old one had put him right in the firing line. As he'd been paid to be. Except he hadn't been paid. No deal meant no money. So now he'd have to play the heavy again while Mick and Jeffyman sold their dope. All fifteen measly pounds of it.

They were two of his best mates, with three dope crops grown between them, but back in town four months now, Seth hadn't seen them around at all. They'd been out bush of course. When they all finally caught up last week, he'd been asked if he'd ride shotgun at the Rainbow. He said no problem – straight-up.

Factoring tonight's payoff into his exhausted budget, he had expected a grand, and the possible loan of a couple more. It had been a shock when he saw the titchy amount they actually had. He'd be lucky to get a few hundred bucks.

Being back home after three years in Sydney was great, but resuming the time-tested ways of making a quid wasn't looking so crash-hot.

Cairns born and bred, Seth had boxed at high-school and brawled out of it. He didn't mind a fight and was good at it, so as well as growing dope he'd used this talent working as a bouncer. Sure, it could get bloody rough at times but he quickly found out that most shifts entailed meeting people, listening to bands and chatting up chicks. Sweet.

He got serious when he moved down to Sydney; getting a licence and signing with the pros – Bob Jones Security.

Now his job got turned up to ten. Mobs of total nutcases in cavernous beer-barns, wild bikie hordes at rock festivals, and rival drug gangs in multi-level night-clubs unleashed rough and tumble on a truly big-city scale.

Aside from the usual kicks, head-butts and punches, he'd been shot at and bitten, knocked-out once, thrown from a second storey fire-escape, and stabbed in the thigh with a broken beer glass.

One night he worked directly for a band. This basically involved keeping sexed-up teens off the boys, driving a hire-car, and looking tough in a club later. Aside from the scores of young chicks pushing their sweaty bodies against him there were no punters to deal with. From then on, he only worked security for bands, happy as hell to be away from the battleground of the floor. He had worked with some of the top bands too – Sherbet, AC/DC, Dragon, and especially – The Tygers.

At this next level of security work, he did well and got paid well. Punctual and diligent, he came to work wearing cool threads, good aftershave and a never-say-die smile.

Being big and good-looking was handy of course, but he soon learnt that insider knowledge was essential. Keeping an informed lookout for Sydney's night-pirates, smugglers and stowaways, while negotiating the latest rips, currents and whirlpools, was a crucial part of the job.

And most importantly, he could politely turn a problem around and hustle it out the door quick-smart. Now and then, there would be some actual biff, but he would calmly prevail with swift, brute force.

The bands liked him. Although he was an employee he

never behaved as less than an equal to anyone and he got respect for that. Mostly silent, he'd let slip a few North Queensland stories; ones that really blew minds. He also got Mick to send their rev-head mate Sabbo down with ten pounds of primo dope when it had got awful short around town. Without much fanfare he gave a fair bit away to the musicians and roadies; the rest he sold to music industry players. They all loved him for that, and it was more kudos to him; another layer of cool. Now he entered the outer orbit of some hip inner circles.

He'd often get just a few hours' sleep in twenty-four. With a pistol licence he'd maintained since he was twenty, he scored a daytime job as an armoured-car guard moving cash-boxes around the metropolis. After eight hours in an itchy uniform packing a .38 Special, he'd grab a shower and a feed, and then do another six hours minding the boys in the band.

Then after all that, he would rock up to the Manzil Room, the Muso's Club, or the bar at the Sebel; walking in with the hottest musicians in the country. Heavy hitters, blokes like Chuggi and Rodgers would nod at him, and drop-dead spunks would check him out. Oh yeah, he'd run amok with those Sydney rock chicks.

Other nights he'd end up smoking and drinking in the hotel suites and homes of great players, listening to their new music before it got on radio or in the charts. He wasn't just hired muscle any more – he was a mate. It was pretty damn cool for a boy from Cairns.

One morning he woke up and just knew – he was burnt-out. The city demanded his full participation and its breakneck pace and constant roar, plus the long hours of work and play, had finally worn him down. He'd saved money like a fiend, and with his bank account full, he'd come back home.

It wasn't for good though. Sydney was great: big-time and grown-up. The reputation he'd forged was a passport back into the scene, and except for that singer, and nobody knew the full story there, he hadn't burnt any bridges.

But now he had the house. Or maybe the house had him. Either way – buying it had left him broke.

It was silent at the table and he turned to see the boys looking at him. He went over and sat down.

"How's Colin putting us onto those idiots?" said Mick.

"Total strangers," said Seth. "You're not surprised, aye?"

"I said two grand a pound. Got a yes straight up."

"I would have smelt a rip-off right there."

"We're all masters of hindsight mate. You'll have to be our right-hand eye for the next deal."

That's not happening, Seth told himself. This is too small time, and these two will need every dollar to get through to the next crop.

Jeffyman fixed him with vivid eyes. He could read your mind this bloke, thought Seth. You'd feel him staring at the back of your head and you'd quickly turn, but he wouldn't be there. Next thing you'd see the spooky bugger smiling at you from a car, or from on top of a rock . . . in front of you.

"I'm not coming next time," said Seth.

"Hey, wait a tick."

"Nah, it's cool Mick."

Jeffyman decided he was angry enough to speak.

"Aye you! You think we're bloody amateurs now? We didn't bloody well plan for that to happen."

"It's nothing to do with you blokes," said Seth.

From inside the house came laughter and that made him smile. There was nothing nicer in the world than the sound of happy chicks. Mick and Jeffyman stared at him. Holding the smile, he used it to ruthlessly force the good cheer back onto his mates' faces again. Yeah, that's better boys.

"OK, suit yourself," said Jeffyman. "We worked it out, but. We're gonna see the fellas we should have seen in the first place. They won't pay stupid money but they *will* pay."

Mick quickly nodded in confirmation. Jeffyman stood up and yawned.

"I'm gonna go crash." He gave Seth's arm a slap. "I'm not forgetting what you did tonight."

"Ah, it's nothing Jeffy."

"Bullshit," said Jeffyman.

Mick and Seth watched him go into the house.

"Is he sleeping in the spare room?" said Seth.

"Nah, he's sleeping with the dope in the truck. Won't let it out of his sight. It's his – I just helped him get it started."

Aye? That was odd. Mick grew dope and was bloody good at it, but if the fifteen pounds was Jeffyman's – then what the hell had he been doing all year? Mick winked at him.

"Don't fret fella. Pam's made up the back bedroom for you and Debbie. I don't know what's wrong with your place though. She hitched-hiked from town to see you."

"I told you before – young chicks turning up at my joint whenever they feel like it? No thanks."

Debbie appeared in the doorway, drink in hand.

"Can us girls come and sit out here with you now? Your big meeting over?"

"Give us another ten, hey Deb? He's all yours after that," said Mick. Debbie pouted, went back in.

Mick got a cigarette going and leaned across the table.

"Early this year I was made an offer – a big one. See, growing crops with mates has been cool, but Jeffyman's always got the family on his tail, Freddie's a pisshead with a big mouth, Gary's become a marine engineer, and Sabbo runs with the dirty Macs now. Plus there's dogs and narks everywhere. I reckoned it was time to move up."

"What offer?" said Seth.

"You remember Lyons? Cluey bloke, yeah? Well he put me on to this fella who'd heard about my expertise in all things green. I signed up to grow for him. I'm growing the first crop now. It's gonna be two tons, Seth. Two tons."

Seth nodded blandly and took a swig of his stubbie. Mick was talking about cultivation on a truly massive scale here. Thousands and thousands of plants on acres of land. This was industrial-sized and the money generated would be stupendous, but keeping the vultures away would require more than a bolt-action rifle and a few old revolvers.

"I've got a good crew," continued Mick. "And the fellas I'm working for have got buyers tee-ed-up down south. No mucking around like tonight. But how's this mate . . ."

Mick paused, giving it some.

"I told them I had a mate with experience, and they want you running security before, during and after the harvest."

Mick threw his hands up in grand gesture. "And – I got you two grand a week. How's your old mate Mick, aye? Two months' work – sixteen big ones. Howzat?"

"Who's this bloke again?"

"Mate, I honestly don't know. I work with two of his men, but after I suggested you come on board they said the boss wanted to meet us both. This coming Tuesday."

Seth finished the beer. "Where?"

"Out west," said Mick. "So, what do ya reckon?"

Seth listened to the pandanus leaves clacking in the dark and smelt the salt on the wind ruffling his hair.

Sixteen thousand dollars. This was more like it.

"Yeah alright. I'll give it a whirl."

Later, after he and Debbie had gone at it like monkeys, she whispered, "Did someone try to kill you tonight?"

He made a soft noise like he hadn't heard her, like he was nearly asleep. She couldn't leave it alone, but.

"Mick was saying something about a gun and . . ."

He sat up, knocking Debbie's hand off his stomach. She was a hot young thing, but nosey, and that's how she rooted too, always peering into his eyes for something more. She was nineteen and everyone's stupid at that age, but to have a chick constantly looking at you for some kind of stamp of approval got boring very damn quick.

Seth brought his hand down hard on Debbie's thigh and grabbed it firmly. It was a rough thing to do, but he wanted her to be clear on this. She sat up, naked and alarmed.

"We sat outside for a reason," he said. "It was a private conversation. And you heard nothing okay? Okay?"

Debbie nodded, her eyes big pools of concern, her lovely mouth spoilt with anxiety. He took his hand off her and soothed her with a big smile. Her expression moved from chastisement to relief, as it should, but he liked that faint inward grin as she lay back down.

This little spunk knew a secret about him now. She knew about the latest layer just added to his legend. Oh yeah, the things these girls told each other about him.

"I hear ya babe," she said, like a chick in an American movie. Oh, dearie me, he thought, a small-town girl trying too hard. He tried not to wince, but failed. Debbie saw that and quickly looked away.

There was a good side to her self-doubt and inexperience though. She'd do all sorts of naughty things in bed for him, trying to impress, and when she did that kind of stuff – well she was hotter than a box of fire-crackers!

Seth lay back into the bed aroma; her perfume, his sweat, the pungent smell of the sex, and allowed her to roll against him. Her face pressed into his chest, and when she began to gently stroke his head, he nearly burst out laughing. She was comforting him!

Go for it sweetheart, he smiled – it's no skin off my back.

Cinderella Street

The stylus slid off the last track and began its repetitive crackle and pop. Seth came into his house and put side one back on again. Standing by the speakers he listened as the urgent throb of Precious started. When Chrissie Hynde's sexy, sinewy voice kicked in, he grinned like a kid with a big bag of boiled lollies. He must have thrashed this album a hundred bloody times since it came out a few months ago, but the horny hit of her voice was still a thrill.

His neighbour was out west working and there was acres of bush and mangrove on the other side of the street, so he bumped it right up. The JBL speakers stayed as crisp as cooler-box carrots and he bumped it up some more. He'd also splurged on a Luxman M4000 power amp and a Thorens turntable. Music was too important to be played on cheap gear.

Some of his mates might say he'd been crazy with the amount of money he'd spent, *"I'm too precious – fuck off,"* he sang in delighted serendipity.

In the little outside laundry, he finished the roach and checked on the tool cupboard he'd painted earlier. Touch dry. While he laid on another coat, he made a plan to get some blue metal around the place to keep down the mud in the coming wet. He finished painting and admired the fire-alarm red cupboard in the sun-warmed breezeblock room. It looked hot.

After cleaning up, he put The Police's new album on, sliced and de-seeded a red pawpaw in his little kitchen and squeezed a fat wedge of lime over it. Grabbing a spoon, he went out to where his back lawn turned into the beach and watched the boats passing as he ate. A few locals in tinnies were buzzing along and, in the distance, a tourist ferry full of day-trippers was heading out to Green Island.

A few hundred metres away, unseen, was the mouth of the Barron, a jungle river that came down over a hundred and sixty kilometres from up in the Tablelands. It was good fishing there and the crocodiles had pretty much been shot out.

To his right, ten kilometres or so across the southern end of Trinity Bay, the green rainforest massif of Cape Grafton and the Murray Prior Range stuck out into the sea.

When the sun set in the west, those hills would turn dark emerald and lush deep purple, with every ridge and tree-line a filigree of gleaming gold, while above, a vast sky of painted pink clouds vibrated with colour. It was a top spot alright.

It had cost most of his savings and was nothing flash: tin-roof, timber and Besser-block, car-port and two bedrooms. The address – Cinderella Street, Machans Beach, might be viewed by many in Cairns as a sun-kissed slum populated by bludgers and pot-smokers, but he didn't give a rat's arse. It was private, close to town and right on the beach.

The down-side was that if a big cyclone roared in off the Coral Sea, the storm-surge would inundate the place. The roof would peel off too. Fortunately, everything of value he owned would fit into the Pig, the carefully customised FJ55 Land Cruiser he'd spent the rest of his savings on.

Since buying the house six weeks ago he'd replaced the corrugated iron roof on the car-port, some rusted sheets on the house, and all the down-pipes and guttering. He'd also cleaned and re-painted everything inside and out, and was gardening too – digging garden beds, making soil, growing herbs and happily standing around with a hose. It was all really nice, but the prospect of getting flush again loomed.

Over the sound of the stereo he heard someone yelling his name. Chucking the pawpaw skin into the bushes, Seth nipped through the garden into the house and turned the volume down. When he opened the front door, Uncle Don was standing there.

"That's a hell of a racket son. Who the heck was that?"

"Don't laugh Uncle Don, but that was The Police."

"You're pulling my leg! What was he singing? Da da da, do do do? Have they run out of words nowadays? No, if us lot had a band it would sound like Elvis or Roy Orbison."

They shook hands and Seth led him into the house. The older man wasn't his uncle, but he'd been calling him that since he was a pup. Uncle Don was a Senior Sergeant in the Queensland Police Force though.

"You want a cuppa?" said Seth.

"Yeh, that sounds great mate. I was just passing through, thought I'd pop in. Been at a two-car smash at North Ellis. One fella had both legs broken, just shattered. Terrible. But no one deceased – so that's something."

Uncle Don plonked down at the orange Formica kitchen table and stifled a groan. He was in his late fifties; a cop for near on thirty years, and Seth had been awfully proud of him as a kid. He still loved the solid old bloke today.

"So, you're back home hey? Mary's been wondering why you haven't come around for tea yet."

"Yeah sorry 'bout that Uncle Don. Been a bit busy with this." Seth gestured at the walls and roof. "I'll give Aunt Mary a ring soon for sure."

"Well, it's a beaut little place son. All you need is some decent music on the hi-fi and you're set. Your dad gave me the address. Paid it off straight-up did you?"

Seth began to vibe this wasn't just a social visit.

"I sure did. The whole time I was in Sydney I worked and saved my money."

"Security guard for the armoured cars, right? How much does that pay? More than us policemen make I reckon."

"I was working nights too, knocking out a heck of a lot of fourteen, fifteen-hour days."

"Your dad told me – rock'n'roll bands and all that. Lots of ladies I'll bet. Big mug like you must have gone down a treat."

Seth put a tea-bag in a cup, flicked on the electric jug and kept his yap shut.

"Yeah, I thought I'd come and have a gander at your new place," said Uncle Don. "So whatcha doing for a crust now?

I can have a word with a bloke I know at Brambles security. He's an ex-copper; good fella. The pay probably won't be as good as Sydney, but it's an honest living."

Now we're getting to it, thought Seth. Over the years, aside from one assault occasioning bodily harm charge, he had never been arrested.

He was pretty sure Dad suspected that he and Alex had grown and sold dope. He'd questioned them a few times, curious about the new trucks, motorbikes and gear. They'd cheerfully lied to him, re-spinning the story about the Yugo barra fisherman giving them heaps of work up on the Cape. Not to mention the gold nuggets they found fossicking. This bunkum also helped to explain their long absences when they were out bush growing crops.

But Uncle Don was a policeman, and in a town as small as Cairns, you could be sure that there was at least one policeman who'd heard something dodgy about you. That was another reason for going to Sydney — he'd got too hot.

"I've been caught up finding the house, buying it and fixing it up and all that," said Seth, pouring the water and adding milk and sugar. "Still a bit to do. I'll be looking for work soon."

Uncle Don stared at him like . . . a cop.

"Yeahhh, working at Brambles could be alright." Seth mused as he stirred the tea. He felt like a bloody teenager.

He took the cuppa over to Uncle Don, who after nodding thanks, absently sipped at it while gazing into space.

Jeez, he's looking frail, thought Seth. Not like the tough fella I remember from three years ago. Uncle Don suddenly looked up, his expression as serious as a bayonet.

Here we go, thought Seth.

"Now listen up mate. Things have been changing around here while you were down in Sydney. From bad to worse I might add. I've seen some jiggery-pokery in my time, but I kept to the straight and narrow. It hasn't always been to my advantage. Still a senior sergeant after all these years."

The policeman hitched his gun belt up on his hips.

"You're a good fella Seth, but I know what you've done – cultivating and selling a prohibited plant. Stupid mate, real stupid. It's a miracle you haven't ended up in Stuart Creek."

Uncle Don paused, expecting denial, but Seth nodded in agreement. This pleased the old bloke and he went on.

"So, here's a warning you want to get your ears around. You've been out of town a while and there's new rules now. We searched a property up the Tablelands last month and found a crop of nine thousand plants. Imagine the value of that? We also seized firearms, including two machine guns. Machine guns, for the love of Harry! Criminals like that are dangerous. They have influence everywhere, and I mean everywhere."

"I joined the force in nineteen fifty-one and you knew everyone you worked with back then. Blokes might get a free feed and a few beers at the pub, but nowadays . . ."

Uncle Don made a strange noise in his throat.

"If this is what the future is bringing then I'm glad I'm retiring this year. Things are now well and truly fucked."

Seth felt a chilly burst of shock. He'd never heard Uncle Don swear before, but what really made him sit up and pay attention was the despair he'd seen in the old policeman's eyes.

Like a big chunk of rainforest flattened by bulldozers, a dependable piece of his youth was cleared in an instant.

"You understand what I'm saying Seth?" said Uncle Don. "You play with the bull – you get the horns."

Well how was this? First Mick's offer, and now a warning from Uncle Don. Here were two sides of a coin he'd flipped a few times and always won on. It wasn't just luck either. When it came to dope, Seth played it for keeps; consistent and careful, on top of every detail, always one step ahead. And that sure as hell wasn't changing.

Seven Schooners

When Uncle Don had gone, Seth went into Cairns to look at fridges, as his rattler at home was getting close to white-goods heaven. Feeling distracted, he couldn't pick one and he left Kennedys empty-handed. Now he felt like a beer.

He got a park outside the Courthouse, crossed the road into Shields Street and checked out the new building on the corner; called Katie's Corner no less. He remembered the Cairn's landmark that had once stood here – The Impy.

Demolished while he'd been in Sydney, the three-storey red-brick Imperial Hotel had never been a favourite of his. Sure, they'd done a reasonable steak in the downstairs back-lounge, and there had been just about twenty-four-hour takeaway grog, illegally sold down the alley around the back, but the smell of the place had always put him off.

With the hot climate, and all that drinking; the corner there perpetually reeked of piss. Sometimes it ran down the outside tiled walls of the place, the putrid animal stink making a mockery of polite society passing by. It was very bloody Cairns actually.

At Lake Street, he crossed, and went into the front-bar at Hides. Wreathed in cigarette smoke, it was full of knocked-off workers and the layabouts who'd been there all day. In a corner were four young travellers, and both girls, all tight shorts and tanned legs, were attracting wolfish winks and grins. Seth ordered a beer and cast his eye over them too.

"Bet they root like rabbits," an old bloke next to him said. "Sound like Frenchies. They'll do anything that lot."

Seth had to agree. European chicks could be a lot easier than the local girls. After a few drinks and a toke on a joint, they'd open up like so many night orchids.

The boys were uneasy, aware of the attention their girls were getting. Yeah, I'd be finishing up here soon, thought Seth. As night fell the jokers would come off their chains. The girl in the denim cut-offs would feel rough calloused hands squeezing her bum, and some sweaty rascal would press against the other one and put his tongue in her ear. Next thing, the boys would be defending their girls' honour by getting their teeth knocked out onto the tiles amongst the spit and butts.

As if on cue, a big growl of sleazy laughter came from a table. Seth turned and recognised a mob of men, though Parrot and Sabbo were the only two he'd call friends.

Parrot – real name Laurie Keats – saw him. "Hey Seth! Mate! Long-time no see."

Poor old Parrot. Despite being the butt of nasty jokes and blatant rip-offs, he'd invariably return for another serve of the rough end of the pineapple from the fellas who'd stuck it up him in the first place. He wasn't a bad bloke, but he was a weak sister, easily forced into doing things.

Also sitting at the table, eyeballing Seth, were two blokes who were specialists at forcing people into doing things.

Gordon MacIntyre – Gordy Mac – and his brother Liam were right bastards. From ripping-off crops to kidnapping, rape, fraud, serious assault, and it was rumoured, murder, these criminal siblings did as they pleased. Fit as Tableland bulls, the Mac brothers sauntered around sunny Cairns in a dark cloud of bad juju. Seth had once admired their mad style: now he couldn't stand them.

Back in the day, he and his brother Alex had hung with them – getting on the grog, selling dope, buying and selling used cars – but as more and more nasty stories began to surface, first him, and then Alex, had backed right off.

Stories like Liam knocking a bloke's eye out with a piece of steel pipe, and Gordy raping a chick in the back of his ute at a party across the Daintree. When he was done, he'd chained her up like a dog while he went and got his mates.

And with evil smiles and muscled shrugs, the Mac boys had no comment about the story that they'd shot Connie de Vries in the face then dumped his body down a tin-mine shaft a few klicks out of Herberton.

Like a bow wave in front of a Gulf trawler at full steam, the brothers' reputation preceded them. Sometimes it was all they needed to get what they wanted.

"Come over and grab a pew mate!" called out Parrot.

Sabbo – Gerry Sabbotini – called out too, looking pleased as Punch to see Seth.

Sabbo was an old mate; they'd grown a crop and shared wild times together, including some life or death stuff. He was a real good bloke, trustworthy and brought up right, but his family of Catholic sugarcane-growers from Innisfail would be horrified to see the company he was keeping nowadays. Seth was pretty surprised himself.

Giving Parrot and Sabbo the thumbs up, he turned back for his beer. Behind him the filthy honey voice of Gordy Mac rose, telling a story about some blokes he had sold a stack of dud building material to.

Seth got his beer, and as he sat down, Gordy Mac's voice deftly grew a bit louder. Liam Mac gave him an unpleasant knowing grin. What a dill, thought Seth; three years down the bloody track and he's still trying to play mind games with me.

The other blokes – Fuckinkev, a crim mate of the Macs, and another barely remembered meathead – ignored him.

"So, these stupid wogs wanted their dough back," said Gordy Mac. "But Liam starts tapping on their windscreen with a bit of pipe – and they pissed off real bloody quick!"

Seth doubted there were any Italians in the story. This felt like a dig at Sabbo's friendship with him, but his mate was listening with a big smile. That was pretty sad.

Gordy Mac kept on talking, deliberately forestalling any catch-up between Seth and his two mates. When he finally paused to swig his beer, Seth said, "So how you all been?"

Sabbo began to speak, but with a flash of menace, Gordy Mac cut him off, jumping right back into his story. Seth's question disappeared into the air like a fart at the urinal.

Seth nonchalantly drank some of his beer. I've seen this my whole life, he thought – the top dogs controlling the conversation; determining what was said. Someone would pipe up and they'd ignore him like he was a chick.

It was a hard-nut hierarchy. The young fellas and new-comers waiting weeks, sometimes months, before they were allowed to get a word in. Even then they might be cut short by cold-eyed stares and amused sneers. You just had to wait your turn . . . and take some shit while you did.

The only real short-cut to being in with the big boys was through acts of violence. In the long run it was also the only way to be taken seriously. You might be good at things that counted, but if you couldn't blue, you'd get no respect.

Getting heaps of fanny was admirable, but unless you were handy with your fists, you'd always be a lady's man, so therefore soft and compromised. Chucking money about was certainly appreciated, but if you couldn't hold your own in a punch-on, you'd be laughed at behind your back as you got the next few rounds. Even being a top fisherman wasn't enough – you had to land big punches as well as big fish.

So Gordy Mac was right out of line here. Every bloke at the table knew Seth was a well-seasoned biff merchant. He was being treated like a junior because Gordy and Liam Mac liked him even less than he liked them.

After Alex finally dropped them, they'd run him down around town, bagging him as a little girl too scared to run with the real thing. Seth got tarred with the same brush and the bad blood had some front-bar wits pretending to take bets on an all-in Macs vs Kellys stoush.

That brawl never eventuated, but it had got heavy for a while. Alex had even looked worried and that was rare.

Gordy Mac's sneak of a voice was getting hoarse now and he wet his throat with the last of his schooner.

"So where you been, Seth?" said an oblivious Parrot.

"Been down in Sydney for a few years," said Seth. Gordy Mac belched and looked around the front bar.

"Sydney? That woulda been alright, aye?" said Parrot.

Gordy Mac turned to Seth with a cold grin.

"I don't know about that," he said. "All that time across the borders' got you looking like a Mexican. You look a bit pale, mate. A bit fuckin' soft."

Now enlightened, Parrot laughed nervously, his eyes on everyone. Liam smirked through his fingers; rubbing the stubble around his mouth. The other two yobs bared feral teeth, their eyes glittering with amusement. Sabbo stared at the table, looking like a cowed dog. Seth gave Gordy Mac an easy smile.

"A few beers with you lot and I reckon I'll be back up to speed," he said.

"Is that what you reckon?" said Gordy Mac. "Well, if you wanna drink with us – you better get a round."

The silent mirth deepened. Seth finished his beer and stood up. "Yeah, no worries. What are you boys drinking?"

"What do you fuckin' think?" said Gordy Mac. "Fourex. None of that Mexican piss."

There were snorts of laughter as Seth went over to the bar. From the tough old barmaid, he ordered six schooners of Fourex, and a schooner of NQ for himself. He waited, relieved to see the European boys and their girls had gone, and when the brimming schooners arrived, he turned back to the boys. They were listening to Gordy.

"Oi! Give us a hand willya?" he called. The table looked over and Sabbo hopped up. Gordy Mac said something to him and he slouched back down in his seat. What the hell? thought Seth.

"Hey give us a hand. I can't carry them all!" he called out again.

The table studiously ignored him; Liam with a tiny fuck-you smile. A bristly-jawed bloke next to Seth said, "Those lazy bastards can't be that thirsty then."

Seth tried not to frown; tried not to get angry. In some pissant power-trip, Gordy Mac wanted him to not only buy the round of beers, but to also ferry them across to the table like he was a coolie boy.

Irritation ran over his skin like ants looking for sweat. He turned back to the seven schooners. Okay cool down, he told himself. It was nothing really; he was bigger than this. It would take a couple of trips but he'd do it and . . . the fuck he would!

He stared at the lovely little beads of condensation on the beers – then picked one up and drank it in several big gulps. It was the NQ lager and it was bloody nice.

He picked up a second schooner and also drank it in one go. Knocking back the third got the barmaid's attention. As he gulped the fourth, she gazed at him with something like love, and then bellowed with laughter. Blokes alerted by this hilarity, turned to watch him pour the fifth schooner down his throat.

The whiskery fella next to him had cottoned on to what Seth was up to and he quickly filled the bar in. The whole place began to buzz.

Hey, check this bloke out. Sticking it up his ungrateful mates. He's gonna drink all of their beers!

The whole bar watched Seth pick up the sixth schooner and when he downed it – a huge cheer rang out. Now fellas were coming from the back lounge, jostling close, everyone beaming cheerfully at this wonderful prank.

Seth licked his lips. The whole time, his back had been to Gordy Mac's table. They'd be paying attention now.

As he reached for the seventh schooner, a chant began. "Scull! Scull! Scull!" roared the delighted bar. He picked up the glass and turned around. Parrot and Sabbo's eyes were lit with glee, the knucklehead side-kicks were frowning, all confused, and – funny as hell – Gordy and Liam Mac were looking like somebody had swapped their liquorice bullets for possum poo. Seth winked at them and drank the last schooner.

The chanting now climaxed in a full-throated roar of joy. Blokes drummed madly on the wooden bar and fell about with laughter. Hands slapped Seth on the back and voices yelled in his ear.

He wiped his mouth, took a grandiose bow, then made for the door. Stepping out into the street, he heard the unshaven fella over the buzz of happy voices.

"Now that's how you separate the men from the boys!"

Just Like That

Back in town the next day, he *still* couldn't find a fridge he liked, so he parked the Pig on Spence Street and went into Tom Cowles. While he waited for a set of spare keys for his house to be cut, he looked at the rifles. Among the cheap and cheerful Savages, a gleaming semi-automatic .308 Winchester caught his eye. It was a nice gun, but what he really needed was some new strides. Not jeans or dress pants, but something solid and straight-looking to wear to a job interview.

With the newly cut keys in his pocket, he drove over to Tom Hull's Man's World where he bought a top pair of tan chino pants, and, on impulse, a light blue cotton shirt with a subtle pattern built into the weave. It would look good going out to dinner in. The thing was, he needed to find a chick he actually wanted to take out to dinner.

The clothes went into the Pig and he went for a wander, his thoughts on buying open footwear - but not thongs.

Cairns was dry and dusty, not yet truly hot; the build-up to the wet season just beginning. Tourists, either southern-winter pale or freshly-cooked red from the sun, wandered the streets. Mad mobs of rainbow lorikeets screeched in the hanging roots of a Moreton Bay fig tree; in its shade, three council workers took their smoko break. A bloke in short sleeves, neatly pressed shorts, white knee socks and shiny shoes, munched on a white-bread sandwich. Two Islander nanas in voluminous floral-print dresses bellowed with laughter around a pram. There was no rush, no scurry and hustle. Nothing particularly urgent was happening and nothing particularly urgent was likely to happen. Everyone was operating on Far North Queensland time.

Near the corner of Shields and Abbott he saw a carved sign at the entrance to Knudsen's Lane. That's right – a craft shop had opened up there, with leather work; maybe even sandals. He strolled down the lane to check it out.

Above the shop's doorway another hand-carved sign said, 'Albatross', the word also mirrored and carved upside down as though reflected in water. Apparently, a group of Kuranda hippies had set this place up. They were a hard-working, capable mob from the hills above Cairns; nothing like the southern bludgers with their filthy matted hair and tropical ulcers, with hands forever out for a feed, a bed or a smoke.

Inside the shop a real social scene was bubbling away with long-haired blokes talking up a storm and a little knot of women engrossed in conversation down the back. By the doorway there was a good little selection of leather goods, including some well-made sandals.

Seth recognised the leathermaker and remembered that he was a musician too. While he tried on sandals, they had a rave about music. The bloke played in a band that was doing alright, recently scoring the support slots for Chuck Berry and Bo Diddley in Cairns. Very damn cool.

He bought a pair of sandals, thanked the leather fella and went back out into the sunshine. As he walked up the lane, a voice called from behind him. "Seth! Is that you Seth?"

Turning, he was stunned. The woman running towards him was Peggy. She came up, batik shoulder bag swinging, looking so damn beautiful, *and* pleased to see him.

"Wow," was all he could say. Unbelievably, they hugged, her hair a soft scented cloud, her body a forgotten marvel. Seth felt the best of days flooding back – the exuberant memory like the rush of a drug.

Peggy released him, looked up, her sweet lips apart, and a proper kiss fluttered in the air between them. More than three years on and the mutual attraction was still very much there.

But she stepped back, her chest moving up and down, and just blew him away with that smile. Wow, he thought.

"Wow indeed," she said. "I was chatting away and I just looked around –and there was Seth Kelly!"

He wanted to hug her again but she got busy retrieving something from the depths of her shoulder bag.

"So, how's tricks?" said Peggy. She had a long green pack of More menthols out, but didn't light one. Seth smiled like a goof and cracked his knuckles.

"Me? Well, I've just got back actually. I spent a few years in Sydney then I bought a place and I've been fixing it up."

"Oh, congratulations Seth! I'd love to see it."

"I can show you if you're not doing anything."

"Lead on, Genie."

Seth's heart somersaulted; joy fizzed in his blood. It was grand hearing that nickname again.

Butterflies were kickboxing in his guts as he drove to his place, Peggy following in a friend's Nissan Skyline. A friend obviously not short of money, and hopefully not a bloke.

He felt light-headed. Around him the bright, cloudless, sky was intense; the jagged green peaks of the McAllister Range acutely defined against the humming blue. He was buzzing, like he'd just had a fight, or come off a motorbike. This was incredible – Peggy was back!

She had first appeared in Cairns three and a half years ago; a slim, elegant and sophisticated chick with a husky, classy way of talking that had got him real perked up. The way she spoke, and the things she spoke of, immediately told him that she was well-educated, worldly and from money. It had been a gigantic turn-on.

Being with Peggy made him feel like an adult, which at the age of twenty-six was kind of stupid. Alex had bagged him out because she was six years older than him, but the age gap had been exciting too.

She looked gorgeous, like a model from Cosmopolitan or an actress in a romantic movie. She didn't need make-up or fancy clothes to look good either. Touched by God when he'd been in a dreamy, horny mood, she had a figure that looked willowy and pixyish . . . until she took her clothes off. He'd almost passed out the first time that happened.

Oh yeah, Peggy had cut a sweet-scented swathe through

sweaty old Cairns. Blokes, and lots of chicks, stared when she passed by. He'd loved that.

The real cool thing about Peggy was that she never made anything of how up-market she was. Right down to earth, like a mate really; she just got on with it – enjoying him.

Though casually confident, she was never overbearing with it. The usual female point-scoring and game playing was absent. Peggy was a grown-up and the world felt like a bigger and more interesting place when he was with her.

Red-hot together in bed, they played it cool out of it. The chemistry was just perfect; their enthrallment intense, and they were wary of spoiling it by talking about the future. They had lived in the now and what a now it had been.

Dazzling aquamarine days out on deserted white sand cays. Full-moon beach parties and wild musical jams. Cool mountain hikes to secret jungle waterfalls. Freshly speared painted crays, sweet mangoes and soursops. Purple heads, Indian hash, and ice-cold champagne. Pink sunset swims, pure golden mornings and lazy sun-drenched afternoons. And the best sex.

It was like every dream he'd ever had about being with a chick had turned out real. There had been lots of girls in his life, a few absolutely amazing, but they all seemed to pale in comparison with Peggy.

He'd never been one for dropping his bundle though. Chicks were good to root and cuddle up with, but all of that only went so far. Plus, there were heaps of them.

Getting sooky over one was laughable; dangerous too. Next thing you'd be married with kids, trapped in a bullshit job and driving a bloody family sedan.

But it hit him like a tackle on the ten-metre line. What he really wanted – no, really needed, was right there behind him driving a Nissan Skyline.

Peggy was different, special; he could love her, live with her. But would she feel the same – after what he'd done?

He slowed and turned into the Machans Beach turn-off. Looking into the rear-view mirror he saw Peggy following him. The butterflies were doing axe-kicks and elbow-strikes now.

He kept a tight lid on all that while he gave her the tour. When they walked to the end of the garden with the white sand and the big ocean view – Peggy clapped her hands in unabashed happiness. Seth glowed with pride. Well here goes, he thought. This moment looked as good as any to get right down to it.

"So, you came up to Cairns to see me?" he said.

"In a roundabout way – but yes."

"Really?"

"Yes really. Cairns being the size it is, I knew it was only a matter of time before I found you."

This was better than he'd hoped. Much better.

"I missed you," he said, moving closer. Peggy took her bag off her shoulder; casually held it in front of her.

"What happened to you Seth? You vanished."

He grinned in dismay. It had got down to it fast. Though Peggy wore half a smile her eyes were full on. Panic closed his throat, but he had to say something. Just not the truth.

"Peggy, I'm sorry. Things got . . . heavy."

"Apparently so. I waited in the suite at The Tradewinds for two days wondering what the hell I'd done. You always had good marijuana to smoke so I figured it had something to do with that. I was worried Seth."

"I'm really sorry Peggy, really sorry. It wasn't anything to do with that. Something else happened."

He gulped, his Adam's apple a choking lump. Inside, he felt the black box of memories buckle and creak.

Peggy's eyes widened at his discomfort. Shame stung his.

"All okay, Seth. Tell me when you want to tell me."

He fixed his eyes on a boat out in the bay. Peggy followed his gaze and they stood there tight-lipped in the sunshine.

"It wasn't someone else," he finally said.

She flashed him a killer smile. "Oh, I knew that. I had you around my finger. I could see the girls of Cairns hating my guts – don't you worry."

He gratefully let her smile bring him back up, thinking how good she was turning his weakness into a bit of fun.

Grinning like a total idiot now, he drank her in – her long fine nose, faintly freckled, and deceptively sleepy-looking eyelids framing her extraordinary green eyes. Please let us get back together, he prayed.

"Did I tell you I was married?" she said.

He felt a ton of ice drop in his stomach.

"I told you I had a daughter?"

Seth, aghast, slowly shook his head. Married? Daughter? She had seemed so footloose and fancy-free.

"I got divorced six months after I got back from Cairns. Graham and I are good friends, but we weren't meant to be together. I think I came up here to find that out."

He cheered silently, the news making him cocky.

"And I helped you find that out?"

"Yeah . . . in a funny way."

"In a funny way?"

She threw him an indecipherable look, and then burst into laughter.

"What? What?"

He was missing something, but her capriciousness was captivating, and his own laughter bubbled up, carefree and liberating. Peggy's eyes flashed with encouragement; the delicious blossom of her mouth spurring him on. It was a moment auspicious with promise, and his little garden now felt like a lush magic carpet that they were about to fly out over the Coral Sea on.

"Show me your house, Genie," said Peggy.

Inside, he explained to her the work he'd been doing and what was yet to come, and maddeningly, she got all serious; listening intently and asking questions like a bloke would. He wanted that sudden joyous laughter again. Maybe she's dealing with butterfly kicks too, he thought.

When they got to his bedroom, a smile touched her lips as she looked at the woven coconut mats on the polished wood floor, his big low bed neatly made with good cotton sheets; a mosquito net knotted above it. He'd been a bit bold, painting the room a warm yellow, but it worked a treat with the green garden and strip of blue sea.

"This is sweet," she said.

"So are you," he said, moving in close.

Peggy's big eyes said yes and he put his arms around her, inhaled her, and nearly swooned. As they kissed, she closed her eyes. He did too, and it was like they were trying to avoid responsibility for what was going to happen next.

Thank you, lovely woman, he thought. I so, so need this. Their embrace was like a beauteous cure, reviving him with sublime pleasure; a feeling that encompassed the sexual, the emotional – maybe the spiritual too. This is the person who does this for me, he thought. I can't let her go.

Time slowed right down and he didn't care if it stopped altogether. He could die right now and it would be fine. But Peggy took her lips from his and gently pulled his hands off her.

"Not now, Seth."

It was like a slap.

"Then when?" He was petulant, a little boy.

"I don't know. Maybe never. But not now."

"You've got a fella?"

"No, I don't actually."

"Then what's the problem?"

Speculation flickered in Peggy's eyes.

"Are you working?" she said.

"Me? Well no, I'm just fixing up the house."

"I need your help. I'll pay you."

Seth felt groggy, like a solid punch had just knocked him around the way he'd come.

"Ah no – you don't have to pay me."

She nodded firmly and he sensed another hit coming.

"What do you want me to do?"

"I might have a cigarette."

They sat outside. Seth filled tumblers from a jug of iced water, while Peggy took a manila folder out of her bag and put it on the table. She lit a cigarette and laid it out for him.

"I had my daughter, Melanie, when I was nineteen. I was studying at East Sydney Tech; textiles and design, but being a mum became my full-time job. Graham went out and . . . well, made a fortune. He's not just a smart guy – he works his boots off. Banking is his forte, and he finally got the big house at Point Piper just like he told his father he would.

"When I met you, Melanie was fourteen and living with Graham. I needed a break from them both and I wanted to think about my life. I was young when I had Melanie and I felt that I . . . hadn't done enough living. Yes, I know it sounds selfish but that's how I was then."

Peggy drew in a lungful of smoke; exhaled. Overhead a pelican sailed along, making for the mouth of the Barron.

"I felt like my life might have been . . . a little wilder. When I arrived in Cairns I'd been travelling up the coast looking for that. I suppose I found it with you.

"When I returned, Graham and I got divorced. I got the house in Rose Bay, and Melanie lived between Graham and me. That seemed to work okay, but when I began setting up my clothing business, things between Melanie and I got really difficult. Stupid arguments over stupid things, so she moved in permanently with Graham."

Peggy sighed. "Oh, Seth – I love her dearly, but she's so stubborn. It doesn't take much for us to knock heads."

Seth nodded, looking at the folder on the table.

"Two weeks ago, we had another spat. A few days later Graham rang me. Melanie had taken off."

"Where to?" said Seth, but he already knew.

"To Cairns."

The ice in the jug tinkled as he poured more water for them both. Peggy watched, rubbing a finger backwards and forwards across her lips.

"You want me to find her," said Seth.

Peggy looked up, her eyes brimming with concern.

"Seth, I'm frightened for her."

"I'll find her, but don't think about paying me."

"No – I want this to be a real job. I want you working on finding Melanie from the very moment you wake up."

"Yeah, yeah – of course," agreed Seth, taken aback at her vehemence and tone of command. Hell, even blokes didn't talk to him like this.

"I'm absolutely serious about that. If you don't take the money, you're not doing it. I'll find someone else."

"Like who?"

"I don't know, but that's how it is."

Peggy's voice had risen and her green eyes burned hot. This was new to him and not much fun.

"Have you contacted the police?" he said.

"We did, but because Melanie has just turned eighteen, and phoned Graham several times since she left, the police say there's nothing they can do. Something bad has got to happen to her first."

"You think something will?"

Peggy crushed her cigarette into an ashtray.

"Graham and I think something might."

"Why? Does she drink, use drugs?"

"It's not that. She has friends, nice kids who probably smoke a joint or two, but it's the man she met in Sydney that is worrying us. He's from up here. Cairns."

Peggy opened the manila folder and put its contents on the table – a few printed flyers, two typewritten pages stapled together with a letterhead on the cover page, and three photographs paper-clipped to a hand-written note.

"Graham paid a Sydney investigator to look into him."

"So, the wild boyfriend from Cairns, hey?"

Peggy didn't even come close to laughing.

"He styles himself as a new-age teacher. He's also at least twenty years older than her."

"Oh – sorry."

"And she's enamoured with him. Spiritually I hope."

He felt a zing of shock, because for a second, Peggy's face was alien to him; her mouth a harsh slit, her eyes blazing murderously as she looked at the face on the flyers.

Seth had met some brutal blokes in his time; grievously cruel bastards, a few of whom he'd had to savagely beat senseless to keep the peace, but to see ruthless menace on a beautiful woman's face was somehow scarier.

Peggy, with her eyes averted, passed him the flyers and he focused in on the face staring happily out from them.

The bloke was white, Anglo-Saxon white, early to mid-forties, with long hippy hair and a beard. He had a pair of alarmingly alert eyes that looked like they'd been cut from another photo and then stuck onto the flyer. The creases etching his face were testimony to some hard living. Maybe he was an ex-alcoholic spreading the word about how good he now felt.

I bet he hasn't given up rooting though, thought Seth. Coming on with Jesus in your trouser pocket was a time-tested lurk for getting fanny. His brother Alex had popped a number of churchie girls like that, using the sacred to get all profane.

Years of manning the door at pubs and clubs had given Seth a knack for reading faces. Sure, it was only a cheaply printed image in his hand, but he knew deep inside, in that place where knock-out punches and real laughter comes from, that this bloke was wrong.

Except for the different venue locations and dates, the text on the flyers was the same; proclaiming that Arnold Jessop, Inner Guide and Teacher of Love, was holding a weekend seminar. Spiritual guidance would be dispensed with a nourishing lunch thrown in – all absolutely free.

"He looks pretty rugged," said Seth. "You ever see him?"

"I went with Melanie to one session. What he was saying wasn't original at all, but he had a kind of rough charisma and real enthusiasm in his eyes. Melanie wasn't too thrilled when I told her I'd heard it all before, and from better people. Another little wedge between us."

"Were there many people there?"

"Surprisingly, yes. However, there was a decent spread of food which everyone tucked into. Most of them looked like homeless people and runaway kids."

"So, the feed was the main attraction?"

"I think so. In the investigator's report, they saw Jessop walking around Kings Cross and Woolloomooloo talking to street people, drug-users, down and outs; handing out his flyers. I suppose a day or two of second-hand spirituality is worth a few good meals to people like that."

"Can I see the report?"

"It's your copy." He took it and she lit another cigarette.

"It's the mention of heroin that disturbs me," she said.

"Aye?" Seth looked up, but she was on her feet walking into the garden. He watched, absolutely amazed she was here, and then forced himself to look at the typed report.

Chester Waterman, private investigator of Surrey Hills, Sydney, had done his best, but there wasn't much to read. Arnold Jessop, put under surveillance during two visits to Sydney had stayed at a good hotel and driven a late model hire-car. He parked it away from the venues he hired, and went on foot while giving out flyers and talking to people. In his interactions with the people on the street nothing untoward was observed, and in the evenings, Jessop ate by himself at a quality restaurant and went back to his hotel alone.

The cover letter advised that Peggy should engage the services of an investigator in Cairns, if there was one, as Chester Waterman did not have the time or man-power to investigate Arnold Jessop's life in the wilderness that was North Queensland. He had managed to find out that the Jessops were an old Cairns family, but that rang no bell with Seth.

The bit about heroin was brief, and surprisingly, it came from Cairns. In contact with someone here he'd known in his previous career as a police officer, Waterman had found out that heroin was being sold at the Jessop family home in Edge Hill. And that was it.

Seth carefully re-read the report until Peggy came back to the table and picked up her water. She finished it, cracking the remaining fragments of ice between her teeth. Her eyes, serious and expectant, bored into him.

"Yeah, that is a bit of a worry," he said. "Could you give this investigator a ring? I'd like to ask him something."

Peggy caught Chester Waterman at his office, and after a brief explanation, handed the phone to Seth.

"G'day Mr Waterman, the name's Kelly. Could you tell me who in Cairns you got your information from?"

"No, Mr. Kelly I cannot. I don't reveal sources, but I can tell you what *I* know." Waterman sounded like an old cop alright.

"That would be very helpful Mr. Waterman."

"Well, there's bugger-all about that fella here in Sydney, but I'm sure you're onto it up there. Birth and property records, newspaper archives, libraries and door-knocking. What us investigators get paid for right?"

"It's the reference to heroin I'm interested in."

"OK, wait a minute while I find the file. I deal with six or seven cases most weeks y'know."

Seth heard a filing cabinet open somewhere in Surrey Hills and smelt Peggy's perfume here. She was by the back door, silhouetted against the green and blue; scarlet canna lilies brushing against her. This is a dream, he thought.

Over two thousand kilometres away, a filing cabinet door banged shut. Waterman's voice came back on the line.

"I don't normally do this, but you're at the arse-end of the earth there, so in sympathy, I'm extending you some professional courtesy. Okay, my source in Cairns deals with . . . informants as it were, in the course of his work, and one of them overheard a conversation in an establishment called the Marlin Bar."

Waterman laughed at the name.

"Like a movie up there isn't it? Anyhow, this informant heard a man say that a house located in the suburb of Edge Hill, and owned by Arnold Jessop was, and I'll quote, 'a house of hammer'– hammer being street slang for heroin. Also, I quote again, "Jessop's putting up the bucks for it." It being the heroin I'd assume. That's it."

"Thank you, Mr. Waterman. Would you have a name for the bloke in the Marlin Bar?"

"We just went through that."

"No, no, not the informant, Mr. Waterman – I mean the bloke that the informant overheard."

"Oh him. Some pissed fisherman. Ah here it is – name of John Pepi, also known as Johnny Pep."

A smile exploded on Seth's face. He knew Johnny Pep alright. He thanked Chester Waterman and hung up.

"How did you go?" said Peggy.

Seth did a little drum roll on his chest.

"Got my first lead," he said, and just like that – he was a private investigator.

"That's great, Seth!" Peggy's eyes glowed. "I knew I had to find you. And that reminds me."

From her bag she pulled out an envelope and gave it to him. Inside was what looked like a grand in fifties.

"That's way too . . ."

"Stop," said Peggy. "I'm very not short of money. Very. Graham and I need to find Melanie fast and this is to make that happen."

"Okay then. So, what happens when I find her?"

"If you think she's in danger, or if she looks drugged or sick then bring her to me."

"What if she doesn't want to come?"

"Oh God, I don't know!" Peggy bit her lip. "I've never *been* in this position before, Seth. Look, I trust you."

"Yeah that's great, but I'm not sure how a big bloke dragging a teenage girl into a car will go down."

Peggy's face went weak with anxiety and indecision. He didn't like that at all.

"Don't worry about it. I'll work it out," said Seth.

Peggy smiled bravely.

"Ring me if she's in danger and I'll come. Graham will fly up here too," she said.

That sounded fine, but he didn't think she realised how quick and all-consuming danger could be. He wasn't going to be running around looking for a phone box if something nasty was going down.

Maybe he should get it in writing – proof he was acting on her behalf. I'll need to work that out, he thought.

Peggy had rallied fast, now looking quite resolute, and she firmly gave him more instructions.

"I don't want Melanie getting involved with the police. She's young and attractive and dresses and acts the way she wants to. In Sydney that's usually fine, but it's backward up here, and the police have an unsavoury reputation."

"You're not wrong there. So, what if I find her and she looks fine?"

"Graham and I will work out what to do next, but can you be discreet? If she feels that you are . . . connected to me, I fear she'll run off again. Be incognito."

"Incognito? Sure, I can be that."

"With this guy – maybe there's something we can use."

"Use?"

"I don't want him around my daughter, or anyone else's daughter for that matter."

"Well, getting caught with heroin will get you put away for a long time in Queensland."

"Exactly. If you can make that happen it will help other mothers. And their daughters. It will be money well spent."

"Make it happen?"

"Seth, I'm not unaware of the reputation you had when we were together."

"Reputation? For what?"

"For being a tough guy."

"Aye?" He was pretty damn sure he'd kept that part of his life away from her.

"Maybe I misheard, but if this man deserves to go to jail then you'll make it happen."

It was a demand, not a question, and again, the tone of command in her voice rankled him.

But why the hell not? He didn't like heroin at all.

In Sydney, he'd smoked it once and just felt numb. The others had injected it and their spewing and nodding-off didn't look like much fun either. He also didn't like the creepy vibes around it; the insider arrogance and thieves' secrecy.

Most of all he hated how it destroyed people. He'd seen gifted musos and shit-hot roadies falling by the wayside – sometimes as corpses. Smack was heavy duty and you only had to walk down Darlinghurst Road any day or night of the week to see its gruesome effects.

And he'd just been given a thousand reasons to agree.

"Sure, I'll find your daughter and dropkick this creepy bastard at the same time."

"Now that's the Seth Kelly I heard about."

Seth dug the look he got; a look he'd got from women over the years. Often the harbinger of a wild root, it was the raw appreciation of a man who made his own rules.

Peggy's admiration dissolved into a smile and, man, it was an absolute heart-skipper. She unclipped the photos from the hand-written page and gave them to Seth.

"This is my girl."

The first two photographs were of Melanie and she was a little knock-out – easily as beautiful as Peggy. There was a wilful look to her eyes and he could just imagine them winding each other up. The third photo was of a two-door car, a crappy looking purple Daihatsu Max.

"Jesus, she didn't drive up in that did she?"

"She did, all the while considerately updating Graham on her progress. Upon arrival last week – nothing more. I flew up three days ago. I'm using Rita's car to look for her."

"Rita?"

"You remember I was staying with friends when we met? Rita and I were at Church of England together. She married Michael and they moved up here some years ago. He's into timber, cattle and property; here in North Queensland and in Papua New Guinea too."

"Sounds bigtime."

"He is. Look, I've also jotted down things about Melanie – her interests, her bank, how much money she has, what she'll be studying at university – stuff that may help you find her. She has a friend who lives at Mission Beach, but I don't have a name or an address. I drove there yesterday but didn't find her."

"You've been thorough."

"She's my kid."

It suddenly struck Seth that if they got together again he'd always be the number two person in her life.

"That's Rita's phone number at the bottom of the page. I'll be there until Wednesday. I have to go back to Sydney to deal with the opening of my shop. I don't think Melanie's timing here is entirely coincidental. The shop number and an after-hours number are written there too."

"Listen Peggy, I promise I'll find your daughter," said Seth and he meant it. This was a test. If he did good, he just might get a second chance with her.

She took his hand; looked at him with grateful eyes.

"It *is* good to see you Seth. Not the best of circumstances I know."

Seth shrugged and smiled, his fingers slowly moving.

Peggy took her hand away. "Look, I'm going to go now – Rita needs her car back."

"I'll follow you to her place."

"What for?"

"So you can come back here. We can have a drink on the beach. I've got some nice Trevally fillets in the freezer."

"I just gave you a thousand dollars," said Peggy. "I'm deadly serious about you finding my daughter."

Seth furiously back-pedalled.

"Yep, yep, gotcha."

But he couldn't help himself.

"We're going to see each other again, aren't we?"

It was like he was begging.

"I need to find my daughter first."

She meant 'you' not 'I', and he nodded in a way that he hoped looked professional.

Everything had been spelt out now, but he felt mightily mixed-up. Just like that, Peggy had come back into his life, filling him with soaring exhilaration – and deep regret.

Running away back then without a word to her had been crazy, but he'd been destroyed and close to collapse. No one, least of all her, was ever going to see him that weak.

Now he'd taken her money and agreed, no – promised to find her daughter. This obligation was absolute; one he'd expend blood fulfilling if he had to.

And not just because he was a bloke who kept his word. No, he'd be taking the whip to himself because of the past – and the future.

The Big Money

It was eight thirty in the morning and he was still in bed, mortally slack, just lying there like a boofhead.

After Peggy had left yesterday, a gang of memories had pushed him around. So, he hopped in the Pig and drove up to the Northern Beaches looking for Peggy's daughter's car. Turning back at Buchan Point, he checked out Stratford, Freshwater and Redlynch, before ending up at Edge Hill where he searched every street for the car, and a letter box with the name Jessop on it.

When a brush turkey suddenly darted out onto the road, he swerved in shock and pulled over. Christ! Was he away with the fairies or what? The whole time driving around – he'd been thinking about Peggy.

Well, he sure as Adam wasn't going to keep doing that, and he jumped out of bed and quickly made it – snapping sheets and thumping pillows. After dashing water over his eyes and face, he did a slow circuit of the house and had a good first sniff at the day.

A little fist of sugar bananas, six Wheat-Bix, some cold Malanda milk and a double squiggle of honey quashed his morning hunger. He put a Mahavishnu Orchestra LP on, and while John McLaughlin played God, watered the front and back gardens, pausing only to flip the record.

Apocalypse over, he went to the beach, did an hour of exercises and had a yarn for a bit with an old bloke fishing at the river mouth. Back home he swept and mopped the house, and then grabbed his wallet. In nothing but shorts, wandered bare-foot up to the corner store for some milk.

Passing tree-shaded wooden cottages and Besser-block bungalows, Seth heard little kids unconsciously singing as they played. Softly in a hidden garden, an acoustic guitar slowly picked out a run of notes. From the depths of a dilapidated fibro shack, a parrot repeatedly squawked, "Get me a beer. Get me a bloody beer."

On the way back along the esplanade he got chatting with a hippy lady gardening in her front yard. Braless, and in a soil-marked short skirt, she looked probably ten or fifteen years older than him. With a cheeky grin and sly eyebrows, she pretended to flirt with him while she worked.

She was sharp and quick, and her inventive piss-take on how the game was played made him laugh. As he tried to keep up, he noticed she kept her knees together when she squatted or bent. It wasn't just a bra she wasn't wearing, he realised. But why the hell not? She was gardening at home, and besides – he wasn't wearing any either.

A lull in the banter came and he watched her delicate feet, toes apart in the soil, moving with deft strength. Beads of sweat glistened in the fine nape hair of her neck and her skirt hung in damp wrinkles from her generous hips. Seth felt a sudden zap of erotic shock.

This woman wasn't just shrewd and entertaining – she looked bloody good too!

Now his shorts had got too short, and he had to go find Peggy's daughter and with a quick, bright goodbye he beat a retreat with something like his tail between his legs. Sure, he liked checking out the ladies, but right now he felt like a proper twit.

Back home, he quickly showered, shaved and dressed, and then gazed at the two hundred and seventy-seven albums stacked carefully in rows against the lounge-room wall. Needing something upbeat and uncomplex, he put Jesus of Cool onto the Thorens' slip mat then gently let the needle find the groove on track two, side one.

Singing, "*I love the sound of breaking glass, especially when I'm lonely,*" he put the jug on and got Peggy's folder. Grabbing a notepad and his sterling silver Parker 75, he set up on the table outside.

As he made a good strong pot of tea he thought about the nuts and bolts of doing this. First of all, he needed to record all expenses. Petrol for the Pig and paying for eyes to be on the lookout for the Daihatsu would eat up dollars. Fuel receipts were no problem, but invoices from the cast of characters he knew wasn't likely. Still, he'd write it all down for . . . he laughed at himself. Peggy didn't care – she just wanted her daughter back.

Outside, with the on-shore breeze agreeably fanning his bare chest, and with a stiff cuppa in his big paw, Seth slowly went through everything in Peggy's notes again.

It was obvious her daughter loved the sea. Junior C-card at age twelve; her advanced open water three years later. She had more than twenty ocean dives logged and was a member of two marine conservation groups.

Her school grades were uniformly excellent, so it was a dead cert she'd get accepted into university next year to study the marine biology courses she was applying for.

That's pretty impressive, he thought. She might be a rich city kid but she's good at something real.

In her bank account was a decent stash of money saved from school holiday jobs and birthday gifts. She was fully independent then and would have no problems paying for petrol or accommodation. Smart kid.

So why was she playing it stupid, dropping out of her expensive private school with two months to go? It meant missing out on her final exams and not graduating, not to mention throwing away the opportunity to get into uni.

It didn't make an ounce of sense. Mooning after a third-rate guru wasn't a good enough reason to blow all that.

Perplexed, he drank tea, trying to think like an eighteen-year-old. The trouble was, at that age he'd been nowhere as together as this girl. His time had been spent sucking down beer and rum, rolling cars, crashing bikes, busting his fists on jaws and skulls and trying to get into the pants of any chick who took his fancy.

Then it smacked him over the noggin like a cue stick in a pool-hall brawl. Peggy's daughter was going back for her exams and graduation – they were still two months away. This jaunt up to Cairns was no more than a show of young independence, and an exciting way to piss off her mum.

The rebel in him could dig it, and if it wasn't for Jessop he would be inclined to just let her do her thing.

Now the thousand bucks felt way too much. Maybe he could give half of it back when he found the girl. That would make him look good, soften Peggy up and . . .

Nah, stop playing with your pencil, he told himself. Right now, this is a job and that's all it is.

A perusal of the phone book revealed no Arnold Jessop, especially not at Edge Hill. He got irritated getting irritated about it. But what did you expect for a thousand bucks, he asked himself – a stroll down Easy Street?

There were a couple of numbers in the name of Jessop: one in North Cairns, the other in Gordonvale, and he wrote them in his notepad for when he knew a bit more. On the same page he wrote down Peggy's Sydney numbers and her friend Rita's too. That made him feel better.

Being a Sunday, he couldn't search any public records, but he could recruit some eyes to help him spot the car and the girl. He could also go and look for the bloke the Sydney investigator had told him about – his mate, Johnny Pep. The marlin season had already started, but Pep just might be ashore.

Finding a square of card, he cut it into ten pieces, wrote his name and phone number on each one and put them, along with two hundred bucks of Peggy's money, into his wallet. He dressed, grabbed his car keys, and as he began to lock up, the phone rang.

"Hey." Jeffyman with pub noise in the background.

"Hey Jeffy. You at the Redlynch?"

"Yeah." Slightly peeved for even being asked.

"OK, see ya soon."

Jeffyman hung up before him. His mate didn't really like telephones – said they put gammin into people's words. And the hand-pieces were full of germs too.

Machans' streets were empty; the Cook Highway much the same, and he drove all the way to the Barron River with the same car ahead and nothing behind.

Across the bridge he turned into Stratford and drove past the pub. It was packed with drinkers and at least a dozen faces watched him cruise by. What a mob of small-town dills, thought Seth. You blokes should see how many cars there are to watch in Sydney.

He gassed up at Diamond's petrol station, where a trio of wild looking fellas, long haired and bare-chested in greasy jeans, were putting fuel into their bush-bashed ute. In a big wire cage bolted to the utility's tray, two brutal-looking pig-dogs sat patient and alert. The animals, and their owners, had some ripper scars.

Heading west along Kamerunga Road to Redlynch, he could see ahead of him, Red Bluff and Glacier Rock; the monolithic gatekeepers of the Barron Gorge. He'd been looking at them since before he could remember. Just before Redlynch Intake road he pulled off the bitumen and parked.

Walking towards the old pub on the corner, he heard the approaching roar of heavy metal. Two Shovelhead Harleys and a Triumph Tiger sailed past, then rumbled to a halt outside the pub. I know that bike, thought Seth. When the helmet came off, he recognised the Tiger rider. He'd have a beer with him after seeing what was on Jeffyman's mind.

The Redlynch Hotel front bar was crowded with blokes: chippies and labourers built like tanks, timber-mill boys, fishermen, farmers and sugar-cane workers all laughing and talking loudly, while chugging pots and schooners of cold beer and puffing on roll-ups and tailor-mades. A good Sunday afternoon session looked to be in progress.

Jeffyman and his mob were down one end of the long timber bar, so Seth smoothly shouldered through the sea of men, lightly touching elbows and arms in fair warning. You wouldn't want to spill a bloke's beer.

At the bar he said g'day and Uncle Owen said g'day back; the other men giving him an appraising glance before going back to their talking. Except for Jeffyman, they were all big brawny blokes who worked labouring on the railway. There were enough muscles, scars and popped knuckles amongst them for anyone to see that these were hard men. Only somebody really drunk or stupid would have bagged them about their skin colour.

Owen was Jeffyman's uncle and he'd been a tent boxer with the big troupes back in the day. He was still known for getting up and having a go when Brophy's rolled into town. Yep, these fellas took no shit from anyone and were a tight insular bunch, understandably, as they'd been getting stick from day one.

Although Seth had got on the grog with Uncle Owen a few times, he had the feeling that if he drank long enough with this mob someone would physically challenge him. Maybe because he was big and fit; a worthy opponent. Or maybe because he was a white fella in a white fella's world and therefore in need of being taken down a peg or two.

Either way – he didn't want to find out.

Seth leaned up next to Jeffyman and ordered a jug.

"We been talking about State of Origin," said Jeffyman. "I reckon it's alright aye. It's made it properly fair now. Like Artie's from here right? He should drop the Eels and come back to Redcliffe."

"Maybe he will now," said Seth.

"I wish. Problem is, the New South Wales clubs have got the bucks. Any young player is gonna go for that. Like that Mal Maninga, how good was he aye? And that fella from Valleys – Wally Lewis? The southern clubs are waving big bickies at those young fellas for sure."

The chilled golden jug arrived and Seth poured the beers.

" 'ere, take this," grunted Jeffyman, his hand knocking covertly against Seth's leg. It was a roll of money; rubber-band tight, and thicker than he'd expected.

"Aww, this is too much mate, I . . ."

"Nah, nah – you put yourself out there the other night at the Rainbow. You earned it."

The intense little man gestured for him to put the money away. Without looking, Seth slid the tube of cash into his pocket.

"So Mick asked you," said Jeffyman.

Seth nodded.

"I told him no," said Jeffyman. "Not that I wouldn't like all that money but . . ."

Seth waited, watching the bubbles in his beer.

"It's just too big," said Jeffyman finally.

"What's too big?" said Seth. Jeffyman looked around at his mob talking and drinking – then leant in closer.

"It's too big out west," he said. "It's not my country, but I know it can swallow a man up and never spit him out. You won't find bones – nothing. The money? I love it but I'm not fooled. When the money gets that big it'll swallow you up too. And those fellas Mick's working for? They're bad news. We're just like ants to them. Think we chasing honey but we really crawling on a stinking body."

"Huh," said Seth. His mate's fear was something new. He refilled their glasses from the jug.

"And especially for a blackfella like me," said Jeffyman. "While you were in Sydney there was this Aboriginal bloke working for the cops – tracking. I'm OK in the bush but this fella had microscopes for eyes. Well, he's up the back of the Daintree working with these cops, looking for a crop, and someone bashes his head in and chucks him in the creek. He's with the police, *with them,* when he gets done."

"Ah shit," said Seth.

"And guess what? The crop they find belongs to an ex-cop. See, the police have been murdering us fellas since you bastards arrived, but those fellas Mick's with . . . well your lily-white skins mean fuck-all to them."

"We're big boys Jeffy. We know what we're doing."

"Maybe, but when the big money shows up no one knows what they're doing. Footy players, smoke growers – they all get brain damage thinking about those big bags of money."

Seth shrugged and drank his beer.

"Anyhow, I'm off to Brisbane for a couple of months on Wednesday," said Jeffyman. "Stay with my cousin Vernon, have a look at this electrician's apprenticeship he's doing. Might do one myself. And meet some Brisbane ladies too."

"Good one Jeffy. Sounds like a hoot."

"Hoot? This North Queensland owl's gonna gobble up some lady mice down there – that's for sure!"

They laughed at that, but Seth felt a bit put out.

"I just got back and you're heading off before we've even had a proper drink or a fish."

"You sounding like someone's missus."

"Ahhh, I just wanna see me mate, that's all"

"Don't be a big sook – the beer and fish won't run out."

They clinked glasses. Then Jeffyman got serious again.

"I meant that before aye. You and Mick watch out."

"Who's sounding like a missus now?"

Jeffyman looked exasperated.

"Hey, don't worry," said Seth. "We'll be on the ball."

"Yeah, really Seth. Those bastards aren't like us."

When Jeffyman's mob left, Seth took a peek and saw that the roll of money was all yellow and orange; maybe a grand. Good onya Jeffy! he thought. You're a real brother.

Seth ordered another jug of NQ and casually observed the blokes around him. Most wore wash-faded shorts and jeans, t-shirts advertising farming gear, grog and cars, with rubber thongs, sandshoes and work boots on their feet.

Next to him, a fisherman polished brown by the sun and smelling of ingrained diesel and old, old fish, blissfully guzzled his beer. Near the door sat an attentive clutch of old boys in white knee socks, polished lace-up shoes and pressed shirts; all wearing their Sunday best hats.

It was a long way from the leather jackets, designer jeans and gold chains of Oxford Street and Kings Cross, but it was real, and it was home.

Seth got the jug, and with two schooner glasses clinking between his fingers, went out the side. The Harley riders had gone but the bloke he knew was sitting at a table.

"Heyyy Knoxie!" he called. The big lean biker smiled in recognition and they exchanged greetings. Seth sat down, and after they'd shaken hands, poured them both beers.

In silence they drank, looking across the road and rail intersection to sun-drenched sugar-cane fields. Up above a Brahminy kite circled in the hard, blue sky, scoping out the rows of cane awaiting harvest; its sniper eyes looking to turn a furtive scurry into a meal.

Back when Seth had the Vincent Black Shadow, he'd go riding with Knoxie, who was a good motorcycle mechanic. They'd chased a couple of the same chicks and got on the grog and choof a few times too. Knoxie was a hard case who liked his drugs, but more importantly, he knew a fair bit about the nefarious shit that went down in Cairns.

Not real close, but always solid, they had a catch-up rave. Knoxie got another jug and when he had poured the beers, Seth handed him the photo of the little purple Daihatsu. Repulsion clouded the biker's face and he threw the picture on the table as though it had been dipped in spew.

"That's the shittiest looking cage I've ever seen!"

"I'm looking for it."

"What for – target practice?"

Seth passed over one of his cards. The biker nodded.

"Yep, I'll give you a ring if I see it. What's the story?"

"Runaway teenage girl."

"Yum."

"Her mum's an old mate of mine."

"Yum yum."

Seth put a fifty-dollar bill on the table. Knoxie cocked his head like a cattle-dog sensing a task.

"Spread it around mate, I need to find her fast."

"This kid in trouble?'

"Not if I can help it."

"Mum gone to the police?"

Seth shook his head.

"Bit of a druggie, is she?"

"Nah, but her mother's not so crash-hot on the cops up here."

"Who the fuck is aye? So, she a goer or what?"

"Put a sock in it."

Knoxie cackled as his greasy wallet swallowed the fifty.

"They're a good, straight family," said Seth. "The father's a big-time suit in Sydney. She's a nice city kid."

"Getcha mate. It's lucky for her, aye? Poor chicks get no one come looking for 'em."

Seth glanced around. Anyone nearby was busy talking. Grabbing the jug, he leaned in close to refill Knoxie's glass.

"Whatcha know about Aunty Jack in Cairns?"

The biker looked surprised.

"Smack? I thought you were into the acid and chouffski mate. You pick up a habit in Sydney?"

"Nah – I hate the stuff. Just want to know what's the story with it up here nowadays."

"Well, I use a bit of speed 'n' acid, smoke reefer an' all, but heroin's not my scene."

Seth drank his beer as Knoxie had a think. Hopefully the fifty-dollar note was invigorating this unhurried process.

"There's a lot more smack around that's for sure," said Knoxie eventually. "Dope got in real short supply a coupla years back and everyone was going nuts paying crazy prices – even for leaf."

Seth knew all about that. The cannabis drought had been felt down south too. Those pounds Mick and Sabbo had got to him in Sydney had been more valuable than gold.

"Maybe the cops were getting lucky busting crops or the growers got slack, but everyone started hanging out big time for a smoke," said Knoxie. "Then all this smack began turning up in Cairns and a fair few people started using it instead. Weird ay? Like it was planned."

"So, there's a few smack dealers around now?"

Knoxie nodded with enthusiasm. It looked like the fifty bucks might be working now.

"Oh yeah, and real creepy bastards too. They got chicks rooting them for gear, and then selling their arses to other blokes. You don't get that with smoking-dope."

"You know anyone?"

"Well, funny thing is, there's blokes who've been selling pot, good amounts too – not some apprentice mechanic in Edmonton or Kuranda hippy flogging off home-grown – and these boys, proper players right, are now selling smack as well. It's like if you're slinging weight then you're selling the white with the green."

"You hear of a smack dealer named Arnold Jessop? Got a place over in Edge Hill."

"Nope. Maybe he's new in town 'cause there's new faces about and some real fuckin' ugly ones too. I do know where there's a couple of blokes who deal in that shit."

"Nah, it's cool – it's this Jessop fella I'm interested in."

"I'll keep an ear out. This got to do with the Sydney girl?"

"Yeah, it might."

"Ahh shit, mate. Smack and young chicks – that never ends well."

The Great Northern

After another jug with Knoxie, Seth went into town. As he drove down the deserted length of Sheridan Street, the northern artery in to Cairns, he felt a sense of dislocation.

He'd driven on this road thousands of times, but after the hustle and crush of Sydney, with the unceasing traffic around Taylor Square where he'd lived, and the sheer mass of humanity packed into flats and apartments, floor above floor above floor – it looked strangely primitive here.

Under poinciana trees, cars slept on grass verges as wide as the road. On either side of Sheridan Street, mainly one-story timber houses sat amid expanses of yellowing lawn. Like the streets, they looked devoid of human life.

It made him chuckle too – his hometown with everyone gone fishing or playing sports, or in the pub or in church, or just snoring on the couch. It was Sleepytown alright.

Closer to town he began to see a few people. An old dear rugged up against the glare tottered along the footpath in wide brimmed hat, long white gloves and huge bug-eyed sunnies. In a bus-shelter some bloke slouched, seemingly asleep or drunk, while a bowl-haircut fella in a torn singlet and tight rugby shorts followed his overhanging belly to the nearest open corner store.

A mob of Murri kids were playing touch footy in Munro Martin Park, the punt sound of a foot on leather audible over the growl of the Pig.

Downtown now, he came across, for heaven's sake, a dog in the middle of the road listlessly scratching its scrawny arse. He gave the mongrel a good touch of the horn and it shambled off.

On Abbott Street Seth parked and went into the front bar at the Great Northern Hotel. In here it was about as far from a Cairns Sunday as you could get.

The Marlin Bar was packed, the air blue with cigarette smoke, the room resounding with the din of excited voices. It was marlin season and some marlin-boat crews and their charters were just back from a day out on the big blue. They were the stars of the bar, suntanned and loaded. Just like the marlin, the money was on; the charters, skippers and deckies all flush, because it cost many, many hundreds of bucks a day to hire a marlin boat to go out past the reef into the deep water where the big bill-fish were.

The clients, rich bastards all, were Australians, Yanks and Europeans, some famous through sports, movies and TV, others known mainly to their peers in the world of big business and industry. They'd been coming to Cairns since the late sixties, each one dreaming of landing a grander black – a black marlin weighing a thousand pounds or more.

The big money being generated by this action, and the rugged glamour of fishing for hard-fighting monsters on the edge of the world, attracted a motley crew to the Marlin Bar. Amongst the ever-thirsty crowd were local fishermen and boaties, marine supplies fellas, travelling businessmen and tourists in the know, all sprinkled through with crims and players with a bit of class, a few chicks on the game and local girls looking for fun, and maybe a bit of education too.

Seth nodded hellos to an assortment of familiar smiles and faces, but down the end of the bar he was pleased to see just who he was looking for.

A heavily sun-tanned and muscled-up bloke in pressed khaki slacks and a faded Hawaiian shirt was raving away to a sweet young chick in a sleeveless sun dress. By their body language Seth could see the man wasn't putting the hard word on her. They'd done the happy deed already and were just digging each other's company. Nice.

They both had drinks, so Seth weaved through the merry throng up to the bar and ordered a double Bacardi and coke with a schooner of ice-cold NQ as a chaser. While he waited, he watched his old mate talking to his girl.

Johnny Pep was a tough North Queensland boy who had the blood of Greek fishermen flowing through his veins. As an eight-year veteran of the marlin boats, he'd worked out of Lizard Island before the resort had been built and sunk many coldies on the Coral Reeftel, the hotel for the boats that had been moored offshore. As an expert deckie, Pep had helped land something like a dozen grander blacks; even one with Jojo Del Guerico. He reckoned he'd fished with Lee Marvin too – but so did everyone.

Seth had a fair bit of history with Pep, mostly good, and when he moved over to the couple, his mate's blue eyes lit up like opal in a red dirt sun. Grinning, they shook hands.

"Seth Kelly! Well my day just gets better! Mate, it feels like I haven't seen you for years."

"That's because it has been years."

"Hey Seth, this is Cassie and this is Seth, babe."

"Hi Seth," said Cassie. Pep was right – she was a babe. His mate had the longest eyelashes he'd seen on a man. They were like Venus fly traps for catching girls this sweet – with his cheeky eyes as bait.

"Do you work on the marlin boats too?" said Cassie.

"No, but Seth came out one season," said Johnny Pep. "Ended up a bit bloody crazy though."

It sure had. He and Pep had been lucky to get out alive.

"Ooooh, what happened?" said Cassie.

"Gosh, it was a while ago now, but I seem to remember a whole mob of tigers off No. 9 Ribbon Reef," said Seth.

Pep's laugh was big and easy, but his eyes flashed with warning. Yeah, it wasn't really a story to tell in public, so Seth winked and let Pep take control of the conversation.

"So, how's this for a joke mate? I was just telling Cassie that the airlines and the Tradewinds have started up this 'Superfish' prize. A hundred and twenty-five thousand bucks for the bloke who lands a two-thousand-pound fish! There isn't a marlin that big. Just looks good in the papers."

"But that's alright," said Cassie.

"What do you mean sweetie? It's bullshit."

"Yeah, but if it's in the papers then people will hear about Cairns and marlin fishing, so then more money and more work for you will come to Cairns. That's why they do it."

"She's right Pep. It's called publicity," said Seth.

"Well, aren't you two the clever clogs. Looks like I'm just a stupid old fisherman," said Pep.

Cassie cheerfully pouted at him and slid her hand up under his shirt over his stomach. As they shared a sloppy smile, Seth got ambushed with thoughts of Peggy. Looking away, he finished his drink.

"Another one mate?" Pep missed nothing.

Seth nodded, and Pep, arm around Cassie, caught the barmaid's eye, made a couple of quick movements of his fingers and ordered another round.

"So, what are you doing getting on the grog Pep? Aren't you out first thing in the morning?" said Seth.

"We had a client drop out – Yank with a sick racehorse. Skipper got the shits, but then – bango! – a charter books in for Wednesday. I got a room upstairs so Cassie and I can spend the next coupla days together. Might check out the bands at the Tudor Room later if you're keen."

The drinks materialised and Cassie happily sucked on the straw in hers. Pep took a pull at his beer and beamed at Seth, looking like the bronzed king of the sea that he was.

"It's good to see ya mate! What's been going on with you man? You took off to Sydney without even a sayonara."

Seth took his cue and laid some rock'n'roll tales on them. Cassie's sweet mouth fell open and Pep yelled in disbelief, his cries of 'no way' and 'true?' turning heads, which was no mean feat in the clamour of this marlin season bar.

"You're one cool bastard," said Pep eventually. Seth got up to get the next round.

"No, let me get them," said Cassie.

"Nah, don't do that babe. I can get them," said Pep.

"I *want* to, and I need to go to the loo too. Those are great stories Seth. I want to hear more."

A big grin split Pep's brown face as he watched her go.

"Oh mate, I think she's the one."

"She's great," said Seth. "Hey listen, I'm working for this woman. She's got a problem you can help me with."

"Aye? It's marlin season, man! I'm gonna be flat tackers til the end of November."

"No, it's not like that. I want to know about the house in Edge Hill where the smack comes from."

His mate looked puzzled and began to smile, but then a violent double-take ripped all humour away.

"What the hell?! I haven't seen you in years and you're asking me that?"

"Sorry mate. Let's kick this over before Cassie gets back."

Pep laughed without mirth.

"It's always something with you isn't it? Starts out fun then goes all bloody weird."

"I got you back on the boat at Ribbon Reefs, didn't I?"

"I'm trying to forget all that. What do you want to know?"

"What I said before."

"All I know it's a shit scene at that house at Edge Hill."

"Like what?"

"Like chicks too young to buy a drink in a bar going there to score heroin."

"How do you know this?"

"This bloke right – Wessels, used to be a sort-of mate – well, he fancies himself a heavy crim. A few months ago, he's off his tits at the Oceanic, big-noting himself, and he tells me he's got a connection for heroin at this big old joint up in Edge Hill."

"A fella called Arnold Jessop?"

"Yeah – that's what Wessels said. Reckon he found that out checking the bills in the mailbox. Said the bloke gives him the gear to sell – on credit. Must want to shift it fast."

"What did he say about young chicks?"

The anger and distress darkening Pep's face looked out of place amongst the crush of exuberant drinkers, and not very encouraging either. It could only mean bad news.

"We'll finish this up quickly Pep – have a few beers."

Pep grimaced; ran a hand through his thick black hair.

"Wessels brings young chicks over to the house to score. Apparently, Jessop digs that, and there's only one way for them to afford to buy those drugs. That's a bad scene man. Real grubby."

Seth felt sick. When Knoxie had told him, he'd pushed it away, thinking, that shit happens in the Cross not Cairns.

"Where's Wessels?"

"I don't talk to him no more."

"Where's he live?"

"I don't know. He drinks at The Crown, the Barrier Reef, most of the pubs. Or used to. He's got a habit now, see."

"What street is Jessop's house on?"

"Mate, I wouldn't have a clue."

Seth could see Cassie coming back.

"Listen Pep, you've helped me stop a young chick from getting sucked into that scene. I'll be going and checking that place at Edge Hill out."

"Yeah? Well, break someone's neck for me. I mean it."

Cassie arrived with the drinks and like magic the old Johnny Pep was back; his laughter and smile infectious, his black sideburns and blue eyes bristling electric. As evening slipped into night, Seth and Pep told truly amazing stories, while the lovely Cassie listened, gasped and laughed; just thrilled to be hanging with two of the coolest blokes on the planet.

A couple of Pep's marlin-boat mates, one with his girl, joined them and the flow of drinks, bullshit and laughter became a flood. When the deckies left, the place was so chockas it took them at least a minute to get to the door.

Now shoulder-to-shoulder, the noise level was immense. Yanks hollered superlatives, and big blokes lobbed belly-laughs over excited yells of assent and mad cries of dissent. Some chick was coming off her chain too, her drunken shrieking somewhere between laughter and screaming.

Then Pep's big blue eyes lit up as a woman's lush chest pressed warmly in on Seth's neck. Perfume enveloped him, two hands slid around his chest and their red painted nails plucked at his nipples. Cassie's eyebrows shot up and Pep hooted in delight as young Debbie leant in and gave Seth a wet, boozy kiss on the mouth.

"Heyyy big boy, what's happening?"

He hopped up, offering his seat, and there was a young chick with Debbie, a slim long-legged cutie who gave him a knowing smile. Ah yeah – the girls loved to talk.

"This is my housemate – Ella."

"Heyyy," said Ella holding out a slender hand. With silly ceremony he shook it, before finding a stool for her.

"Now there's a real gentleman," crowed Pep, pleased as all get out, Cassie giggling along next to him. The girls all hit it off, slim Ella not saying much, and Cassie and Debbie set to stirring him and Pep with outrageous cheekiness.

Man, oh man, they make a very sexy pair, he thought. I wouldn't mind these two fire-crackers lighting my fuse at the same time. He saw Ella looking at him like she knew what he was thinking and he yelled for everyone to raise and clink glasses. Yeah! This was what it was all about – partying with good mates and gorgeous girls.

They chalked up a few more rounds, and Debbie, her arm around him, absently squeezed his bum. That got him real toey, so when Pep suggested going upstairs to blow a joint, Seth left the boisterous group at the stairs and went out to the desk. He got the last double and when the bloke asked him about luggage, Seth shut him up with an extra ten.

In Pep's room, he twirled the door key on his finger and everyone cheered; Debbie the loudest. They blew the joint, drank some of Pep's bourbon, and Seth, fully out of it, sat between Ella and Debbie talking rubbish. He got all mixed-up and stroked Ella's thigh by mistake. She pressed close against him, her small breast warm against his ribs, and he started barring up. He tried to keep it together, but all he could see was that bugger Johnny Pep smirking at him.

Then Debbie said they were leaving and Pep and Seth embraced while Debbie and Cassie slapped and drummed on their arses, screaming like the mad things they were.

In the room the girls got stuck into him. While Debbie unzipped him, Ella pulled his head to hers and started pashing full-on. Debbie undid his belt and helped him get his strides and jocks off. Kneeling, she started using her mouth on him. Ella got down next to her and shoulder to shoulder, they shared him back and forth.

It was great, but Ella, all pale face, black mascara and red lippy, kept staring intently up at him and his head began to spin. He had to lay back on the double bed, and a frenchie was quickly rolled onto his old fella. First Debbie; then Ella hopped on, squatting and pumping; their faces slack with pleasure.

Ella's gaze was unnerving, like she was trying to win or something, and he didn't mind it when she went into the bathroom for a while. Debbie got back on him and went for it, groaning and grinding until, with a berserk wail, she had great big come.

He was too drunk to blow himself, but they had all night. Besides, it was rather cool letting these young chicks use him. Pretty switched-on for a bloke really.

Debbie got up and went to the bathroom, and when Ella climbed back on, her leg slipped on his thigh and she nearly went over. She's drunker than me, thought Seth. Then he was in her and it felt good. Maybe this chick can get me off, he thought. Firmly holding her skinny little arse in his big hands, he went at her gangbusters.

She bounced above him, mouth flopping open, her eyes stunned pinholes. As he frantically chucked himself up her, Seth suddenly realised that no-one had spoken or laughed, or even giggled, since they'd come into the room.

Then Ella turned her head and vomited a yellow stream onto the bed. Hot sour drops sprayed Seth's face and he threw her off, yelling in disgust, "Ferfucksake!"

Jumping up on the bed he tried to keep his balance as he wiped his face. Ella squirmed to the edge of the bed and was sick on the floor too. Seth stared down drunkenly at her chicken bones and her shocking white skin.

Ella gave a dreamy sigh, shivering with pleasure, rolled back over and blissfully smiled up at Seth.

"Uh, I'm sorry," she husked. Long pale hands tipped with purple fingernails slid between her legs and began moving. She attempted a sexy look, but her eyelids were drooping. Jesus, this chick is really off her head, thought Seth.

And not just from drinks and a joint. He jumped onto the floor and lurched over to the bathroom. In happy nude perfection, Debbie was flushing the toilet.

"Oooo, babe! You liking this, hey?" she said.

Ella's big handbag was by the sink. Seth yanked it open. Amongst the perfume, make-up, condom packets, keys and cigarettes, was a pink plastic toothbrush-case; inside it a needle-tipped syringe and a blackened teaspoon.

With a snarl, Seth showed this to Debbie and her mouth fell open in dismay. She spun around and saw Ella, stoned and boneless, flopped out across the bed.

"Oh bullshit!" said Debbie. "Ellaaaaa! You had some!"

"Uhhh, sorry," said Ella contentedly.

Seth snapped the condom off onto the bathroom tiles, strode into the bedroom and pulled his jocks and pants on. Debbie ran up and threw her arms around him.

He shoved her away; she nearly fell.

"No," he yelled.

Debbie began to cry. His head started to pound.

"Seth don't go! Please! I didn't know. It's not my fault."

The smell in the room was sickening. This was bullshit. He didn't get into situations like this. Pulling on his shoes he made for the door. Debbie blocked his way.

He stuffed his shirt in his back pocket, took her by the arms and forcefully pushed her back. With clenched fists to her breasts, she shook her head from side to side, her face screwed up in misery. It was pathetic.

Forcing her to the centre of the room, he let go, his fingers leaving white pressure marks on her soft arms. At the door he fumbled with the latch. Debbie appeared at his side. Snivelling frantically, her cheeks wet with tears, she wailed, "Please Seth, please don't go!"

With one hand, he used his long reach to push against her forehead so she couldn't come closer. Holding her away from him, avoiding those woeful eyes, he turned sideways to get out the door. As he stumbled out into the corridor, Debbie sobbed, "Please Seth, please. I love you."

Saltwater and Blood

In the Lands Office, the young lass at the counter looked lily-fresh from her weekend. Though Seth had shaved and showered, with Panadol and Visine administered, he felt slightly ship-wrecked. But what really left a bad taste in the mouth was the scene in the double at The Great Northern last night. Knoxie was right. Young chicks and smack – it never ends well.

Sitting at a reading table spread with thick registers and record books, Seth considered the gulf between the straight and bent worlds. If the nice chick behind the counter, in her proper dress and hair-do, even knew one tenth of the debauchery he'd indulged in over the years – she'd run out the door and never come back.

He usually felt a hard-earned pride at being a root-rat and never-say-die party monster. It was part of his rep; a good chunk of who he was, but now he felt kind of empty. And queasy. The young chick at the desk looked up and Seth quickly bent his head back to his task.

After nearly three bum-numbing hours he'd found out a bit more than bugger-all about the Jessops. It was like looking for tracks of a creature that had no form. This family didn't appear to have put their name to anything much at all. Where other old Cairns families had left their mark with acts of philanthropy and self-celebration, the Jessops had kept their charity to themselves and left their trumpets unblown.

All he'd found so far was a long-gone ship's chandler and some real estate sales from the late sixties; a few parcels of land along the Cook Highway and some houses on Martyn Street and around Bungalow. One Herbert Jessop had sold the land. Checking the two Jessop telephone numbers in his notepad he saw neither of them were for that name.

It was no sure thing that this bloke was even related to Arnold Jessop, but the same lawyer had handled all the land sales, and his name – Desmond Croaker – sounded familiar. Maybe this lawyer was still around.

Outside, he located a phone box and was pleased to find Croaker's number in the yellow pages. As he dialled, he remembered; Dad had used him once, said he was alright.

An old secretary bird came on the line and he got an appointment for two hours' time. Happy to leave the sitting and reading for a bit, he got in the Pig and went looking for a purple Daihatsu Max.

At that corner of Spence Street and the Esplanade, the eye of Cairns really, he slowed and looked at the big stretch of dirt. Two classic pubs had once stood there – The Pacific, demolished while he was in Sydney, and The Strand, pulled down ten years or so before that.

As a kid he'd gone to the Strand with Dad, Mum and Alex, and the four of them would have a slap-up Saturday lunch with waiters in long white aprons serving them. He and Alex would have double milkshakes, and Dad would tell them about the famous people who had stayed at The Strand. If he didn't know who Somerset Maugham and Joseph Conrad were, he certainly knew who Errol Flynn was.

After lunch they would swim in the ceramic-tiled pool out at the back. This gleaming treat was far superior to the Cairns Sea Baths with its murky salt-water pumped in from the inlet every Monday and skin-ripping barnacles on the bottom and sides.

Yep, the Strand's pool was ace, but best of all, among the splashing kids, there were women in swimsuits; now and then even one in a bikini. With eyes stinging from chlorine, he and Alex would swim like hunting sharks, ever closer to those mysterious forms. Sometimes this force of attraction would produce a collision, totally accidental of course, and he'd just about faint at the sensation; the warmth and weight of breasts, hips and bottoms.

One day a woman, red-faced and fairly screaming with anger, slapped Alex. They got banned from the pool after that, and even though his brother got a rare strapping from Dad, it was worth it. I've felt one now, he smirked.

The Pacific had been the place when he'd got older and started drinking. On his own, and with Alex, he'd had some wild times in that big old building.

It smelt of mad history, of saltwater and blood. Kamal and Johnny Farnham had played there, but the public bar was full of hard fishermen, sailors and sons of the sea. They could look through the windows across the Esplanade to Trinity Inlet and see who was coming and going.

One time, in an upstairs room, Seth had rooted a woman he'd just met downstairs. Lean and fit, she had fair savaged him; biting and sucking like a beast. It was hot, stuffy and sweaty, the pub noise beneath, and suddenly someone was bashing at the door; screaming blue murder! The woman's enraged husband, his ship back early, was trying to smash his way in.

Seth, running with sweat and God knows what else, had thrown his shoes and clothes out the window and climbed stark naked down the side of the building in full view of the cool moonlit Esplanade. Some blokes were outside, alerted by all the upstairs banging and yelling, and they just about pissed themselves laughing at the sight of him.

After that he gave The Pacific a wide berth for a bit. A few months later he heard that the woman, mad as a cut snake for being interrupted, had knocked her spouse senseless, emptied his wallet and gone back down to the lounge bar.

Up on the second-floor veranda he'd drunk with fellas from all around the world – Yanks, Poms, Dutchies, Germans – you name it; quietly selling pot and listening to their traveller's tales. Compared to them, he felt like a real small-town drongo.

But when they quizzed him about fishing and the reef, and heard his tales of Far North Queensland, he saw the excitement in their eyes. They were having the adventure of their lives, and what felt like the furthest corner of the earth to him, was exactly what they were looking for.

Now it was gone, a Cairns institution vanished, leaving behind dust, weeds and memories. Apparently the Kamsler family from the Tradewinds were all set to build a big, flash hotel there – something really modern like in Sydney or Honolulu. Welcome to the bloody future hey, thought Seth. Progress could be a bittersweet thing.

Turning off the Esplanade, he spent a futile half hour looking in the motel car-parks along Sheridan and McLeod streets. Peggy's daughter had close to two thousand dollars in the bank, so an air-conditioned room was not out the question. It was unlikely though. He had her picked as a nature-freak, someone who'd rather sleep on the beach than in a tourist shoe-box. Still, he had to check.

Back in Edge Hill there was no purple Daihatsu Max, no letterbox labelled Jessop, but there was a cheerful postie riding a red Honda CT110. Seth gave him ten bucks and his phone number, showed him the photograph of the car and the happy chappy said he'd keep look out for it on his twice daily postage run.

Over at Bungalow and Portsmith, he looked in the auto repair workshops, as Peggy's daughter's car had likely got a beating coming up two and a half thousand kilometres from Sydney. The last leg, from Brisbane to Cairns on the Bruce Highway, was notoriously bad; a pot-hole pocked, piss-poor pretence of a major national highway.

There was a wrecker's yard's worth of cars being worked on but none fitted the bill. It wasn't a total waste of time amongst the spanner-heads though, as he caught up with a tow-truck driver he knew, flashed the Daihatsu mug-shot, and left him with his phone number and another tenner.

At a servo on Mulgrave Road he filled up the Pig and got set to use payphones; changing ten bucks into twenty cent coins. He also bought a frozen mango Weis Bar which he savoured slowly, standing in the sunshine like a big kid.

Outside the long red brick expanse of the Cairns railway station, Harry Spinks, an old cabbie mate of the family, was waiting in the sun's glare for a fare. Seth showed Harry the photo of the car; gave him a card and twenty bucks, and the old cabbie said he'd tell other taxi drivers too. Nice one, thought Seth. I'm getting some eyes on the streets now.

Walking to the Pig, he had a brain flash. Harry was in his late fifties and he knew a lot about Cairns back in the day. Seth went back to the taxi and leant over on the passenger side door. Harry raised fluffy caterpillar eyebrows at him.

"Harry, you know anything about an old Cairns family called the Jessops?"

"Jessops? Sure. Those bastards made their money off the blood of the blacks. They go on about the slaves in America but the Jessops did all of that right here."

"Is that right?"

"Yep. My granddad's first boss worked for them and he told Grandpa about the disgusting things they got up to. Pioneers? High-class members of Cairns society? Bullshit. They were just a pack of raping, pillaging, murdering . . ."

"Harry." Seth cut him off. A perspiring Islander lady was now looking in the driver's window.

"You free or has the big fella booked you up?" she said, dabbing at her brow with a massive white handkerchief.

"No, no – he's all yours," said Seth. The woman, with a wave of her hankie, got in the back of the taxi.

As Harry drove off, Seth realised the old cabbie would very likely know the address of the Jessop house in Edge Hill. He'd come back later and find that out.

Checking the Rolex Submariner on his wrist, he felt a sharp bite of anguish. The stainless-steel watch had been his present from everybody for his twenty-first birthday. Refocusing on the dial, he was pleased to see it was time to go and see the lawyer.

Another Country

Desmond Croaker's office smelt of cigars, old leather and paper – lots of paper. Piled on a corner table, stacked on a big partners desk, and as pages in the many books on the many shelves – it all looked dusty and forgotten.

In a crumpled suit the lawyer's six foot plus frame was swallowed in fat. Late sixties, with a big red drinkers' nose, Croaker looked like he enjoyed fillet steak, Stilton cheese and oysters a good deal more than Seth himself did. Which was a lot.

"Mr. Kelly, of what help can I be to you?"

"Mr. Croaker, it's actually not a legal matter, it's more a case of obtaining some information."

"Young man, I think not." Croaker shook his great bald head. "Confidentiality is at the foundation of my practice."

Seth put a fifty-dollar bill on the desk. Croaker eyed it like it was lunch.

"All that does Mr Kelly, is to refrain me from asking you to leave."

Encouraged, Seth put another fifty on top of the first.

"Mr. Croaker I'm not looking for anything confidential. It's public knowledge I'm after – nothing I wouldn't find if I spent a lot of time, time I don't have, looking in places like the Lands Office and the courthouse."

Croaker stared at the money. His tummy rumbled.

"Do you know Raymond Kelly, Mr. Croaker? He was a chemist at CSIRO then with CSR."

"Raymond Kelly? Ye-s, I recall I did some work for him. Recommended by a friend who served with him in the war. At Milne Bay I believe."

"He's my father."

"Oh, I see."

"And do you know Senior Sargent Don Skelton? We call him Uncle Don."

"Of course, Don Skelton! Yes, he's a good man too." The lawyer scooped up the money, fed it into a desk drawer, and favoured Seth with a warm smile.

"Well, that puts a vastly different complexion on things. How is your father?"

"He's real good Mr. Croaker."

"Oh, stop mistering me – it's Des." The lawyer produced a bottle of Dewar's and two cut glass tumblers.

"Fancy a nip?"

Seth didn't really, but he nodded, and the lawyer poured them both something more like a bite.

"These are my last two weeks. I'm retiring," said Croaker.

"Uncle Don's retiring this year too."

"Well good for him. Us old dogs have done our dash. I'm moving down south. Had enough of the heat. Going to live near my sister's family on the New England Tableland. Do you know it down there?"

Seth shook his head and sipped some whisky.

"Marvellous country with proper winters – even snow. You can eat good succulent lamb and fresh green peas, pick pears and apples right off the tree. Decent wines from the Hunter too."

"You've been in Cairns awhile?"

"Oh yes. Nearly thirty years. I came up here for the war and, gosh – I thought I was in another country! After I did my articles in Sydney, I moved up here to practice. Lots of opportunities then. Now I can't stand the heat. A month from now I'll be in a big stone house with three fireplaces just out of Armidale. Twelve degrees at night. Lovely."

"Congratulations," said Seth. "An end of an era for you. I bet Mrs. Croaker is excited."

"Oh, there's no Mrs. Croaker. Never was. I'll give you some advice, gratis, son. Don't get married. You'll end up with more money and freedom if you don't."

"I have to agree."

"Good lad. So, what can I help you with?"

"I'm wondering what you can tell me about the Jessops of Edge Hill."

Croaker blinked, finished his drink and reached for the bottle.

"The old Jessops or the new Jessops?" he said.

"Both I suppose."

"I can't tell you much about the new Jessops because a few years ago I was informed by Arnold Jessop that after twenty-five years, my services were no longer needed."

Well, be-bop-a-lula, thought Seth.

"Why was that?" he said.

"Well after Herb died . . ."

"I'm sorry, who?"

"Herbert Jessop – Arnold's father."

"That's just why I'm here Mr. Croaker – I know nothing about them."

"Yes, they were, *are* private people. What is your interest in them?" said the lawyer, now pouring himself another drink. Evading an answer, Seth quickly finished his glass and put it on the table.

"Wouldn't say no."

"Not a top scotch by any means, but good for daytime use," said Croaker. While he poured the whisky, Seth kept it moving.

"You said the Jessops stopped using you after all those years. You must have felt a bit put out."

"Ahh, to a degree. It was Herbert I'd done all my business with – not his son."

"How did Herbert Jessop die?'

"It was a long illness, cirrhosis of the liver and a few other things. A life lived hard is not always a life lived long."

"I'll drink to that," said Seth. He made Croaker clink glasses with him and the lawyer's pale blue eyes twinkled with amusement.

"Did Arnold take over when his father got ill?" said Seth.

"Yes. Power of attorney was passed onto the children and after Herb died, I got a phone call one day and that was it. Surprising really, because Arnold Jessop was very much his father's son"

"They are very wealthy right?"

"I'm not going to discuss figures, but yes, they were a wealthy family."

"Were?"

"They certainly were, but the family's fortunes changed over the years. Still rich of course, those children will never have to work, but the Jessops are just a shadow of what they once were."

Croaker took a good chomp of Dewar's and relaxed back into his chair. Seth put on the big ears and shut up.

"The Jessops were a clever family in the beginning. Old Man Jessop and his nephew came here from Mackay with three ships they owned. They had big sugar plantations in Mackay, but had made their initial capital in China and America. Gold, opium, tea, slaves – no one knows."

"Y'see, back in the early days, if a man had money and the will to action, people were grateful to have him around. The Old Man invested in Cairns, in land and in sugar cane, and because he had his ships, he could import cheap labour to work the cane-fields. At first it was the Chinese, Malays and Singalese. Then his boats went to the islands and got the Kanakas. *Very* cheap labour."

"So, the Jessops were Cairns pioneers?"

"Indeed. They had a ship chandlers, dry goods stores, dray and bullock teams, horse yards and shares in the first mills. They built the big house at Edge Hill and two more of almost equal grandeur. One burnt down early on, and the one at Hambledon got turned into a rooming house."

"What street is the house at Edge Hill on?"

"Everknell Street. Number One. Very run down now."

Seth held back a cheer, nodding instead. Connecting the

dots and getting a result was unexpectedly satisfying. He could grow to like this.

The old lawyer took a ruminative pull on his whisky and continued.

"Old Man Jessop – he was a man alright, equal to any taipan, any boss man, from Port Moresby to Hong Kong. And what a time it was. The eighties into the twenties were the golden years and that family were colonial kings, their estates and plantations were their kingdoms. Y'know, in those places – their word was law."

Croaker paused, softly sighed; looking back across time. His faded eyes were the only blue things in the room.

"Then Old Man Jessop got sick with malaria and died. Two of his three boys perished in the Great War. Through his daughters' marriages, things changed, and the control of many of his businesses devolved into different hands."

Croaker licked his lips. "Is this what you want to hear son? Bloody old history?"

"No, this is great Mr. Croaker – please go on."

"Herb did well with what was left to him. When the war with Japan and Germany came, he got an exemption from military service for providing essential supplies. His older brother Frederic served in intelligence, and when the Japs got kicked out, Freddie set up shop in Hong Kong to fight the next war – communism! That was a rough old time: the emergency in Malaya, Indonesia nearly going under, and Vietnam, where we dropped the ball entirely. Kids today think communism is a fad! You never played around with it, did you?"

"No, Mr. Croaker. I have never been a communist."

"Your Dad would never have forgiven you."

"He fought in the war to make us all safe."

"Yes, thank God. Well, Freddie Jessop fought the good fight too, and being a Jessop, he got into business in Hong Kong and did very well for himself. When times got tough here in North Queensland, as they sometimes do, like a good brother, Freddie would help Herb out."

Seth emptied his glass and made an appreciative noise. Croaker automatically refilled the tumbler as he spoke.

"In nineteen-fifty-two Herbert Jessop took me on as his lawyer. I received a goodly amount of work from him, but in the late sixties and early seventies Herb decided to liquidate and consolidate his assets so he might enjoy the fruits of both he and his ancestors' toil. I can tell you, in confidence, that he liked the horses and a drink, and we spent some very enjoyable times together. And when his wife Evelyn passed away in nineteen-seventy, he was then able to enjoy the company of the fairer sex with much more freedom."

So, he was a gambling piss-pot and a root-rat, thought Seth. With all that money who wouldn't be?

"And his children?"

"Ah yes, the new Jessops. Arnold was the oldest son, the natural heir to the business, close to Herb, and he shared his father's . . . tastes. The other son, Robert, showed no interest in his family. Preferred Uncle Freddie in Hong Kong, and after boarding school in Sydney he went to live there. As far as I know he's still there."

"Is the uncle alive?"

"Apparently he is. Forced to retire after some corruption

rubbish a few years back. Should have been knighted."

"So, Arnold took over the estate then?"

"He must have, because the sisters were a feeble pair. Sandra was a giddy socialite who spent years in Melbourne and London. Never married, no children. She got ill, and I think lives at Edge Hill with Arnold. No one's seen her in years. The other sister met a Yank; an airline pilot. They married and went to America – Arizona I believe. Bloody hot there."

"Do Arnold Jessop and his brother have kids?"

"No. This is how a great family withers and dies. To be frank, I have no fondness for Herb's children."

"Do you think Arnold Jessop still has a lot of money?"

"I knew that this would be about Arnold, but as I said, I know little of him now."

"You've met him though?"

"Yes of course. As a young man he was diligent and hard-working, but when his mother died, he began to change. So did Herb. In those days, women didn't have a great role to play outside of the house, but they were often the rock that the men could anchor themselves to. With all this women's lib stuff today, people forget that. Do you understand what I mean?"

Seth nodded. He knew just what the old lawyer meant.

"With Evelyn gone, things changed at Everknell and it got a bit . . . well, messy."

"Messy?"

"No, no, I've spoken too much as it is."

"You'll be eating lamb and peas in Armidale soon."

Croaker laughed. "You're a pushy bastard son, but as I

said – the horses, drinking, ladies – just fellows having fun. Absolutely nothing compared with what you lot get up to nowadays."

You could be right, thought Seth.

The lawyer launched himself to his feet.

"Well, that was a trip down memory lane. Now I'm off home for a nap."

"Just one more question Mr. Croaker. What does Arnold Jessop do now?"

"Well can you believe it? He inherited well and learnt business acumen from his father. He also proved to be no slouch when it came to enjoying himself, so I have to laugh at the ridiculous irony of it. He is now – a hippy preacher! With long hair, beard, white robes, the lot. And now as pure and clean as the driven snow. Hah! He's probably a bloody communist!"

"Would he be selling drugs? Hard drugs?"

"Mr. Kelly, as I have indicated, my knowledge of him is extremely limited nowadays. Please."

Croaker had the door open and was gesturing for Seth to leave.

"But it's nothing you've ever heard of?" said Seth.

"No. But to be honest – it wouldn't surprise me at all."

Someone at Some Time

With the history of the Jessops and three or four inches of Dewar's buzzing around his brain, Seth drove to Edge Hill. Using his Gregory's directory, he found Everknell Street; the faded street sign unreadable with dried mould.

Up the far end of the street where it turned into Mount Whitfield, big mango, poinciana, fig and black bean trees formed a massive grove. In this cathedral of green Seth glimpsed a rusty red expanse of corrugated iron roof. With growing excitement, he drove right up there to where the road finished and parked by the decaying gutter. Here a row of huge, ancient frangipani trees dropped perfumed pink and white flowers to rot into brown mush on the road.

Nearly obscured by these gnarly old trees, and the chaos of a tropical garden gone wild, was a large house. A cracked and mossy driveway disappeared up around the back of it – and the post-box featured a faintly painted number one.

Seth grinned like a jam jar full of worms coming back from a fishing trip. He'd found Arnold Jessop's place.

Twenty metres away was a shabby old Bedford truck. He reversed, parked behind it, and was just about to jump out when a car turned into Everknell Street. He slid down out of sight and listened to it pass by, hearing a well-tuned V8 engine grumbling nicely. Stretching his neck, he snuck a look. A Holden HX panel van with mag wheels and tinted windows – not a cheap ride – turned into the driveway of the Jessop house and powered up behind it.

After giving it a few minutes listening and watching, he quietly locked up the Pig and went up to a front gate almost concealed amongst the frangipani trees.

Over the timber gateway, cracked with age, a once-proud wooden sign attempted to disclose the property's name. The weather-worn letters crawled black with rot and it took Seth a moment to make out what was carved there.

Just like the street it said Everknell. It was one of those meaningless names that would have meant something to someone at some time.

Through the gaps in a lichen-encrusted brick and rusted wrought-iron fence, Seth peered into the shambles of what would have once been extensive and carefully landscaped gardens. Beyond these botanical ruins was the house.

It was more than a house, a mansion really: with high-peaked roofs, long runs of big sash-windows, and even a one-story octagonal-shaped tower. Everything was in fine proportion; the windows, roof-lines, doors and veranda columns all balancing out the building's stately bulk. The details – cast-iron lacework, decorative brick-work and jig-sawed wood gable infills – were clearly pre-federation and of unusual beauty and design.

Wow, it's really special, thought Seth. I never knew this old joint was here, tucked in against the rainforest slope. It was at least ninety years old, probably even older, and definitely one of the first grand houses to be built in Cairns. This was old money alright.

In that first wave of white settlement, craftsmanship had been the only real artform. The builders of this house had been real artists, but the recent generations of Jessops had shown little regard for the architectural glories that they had wrought. Like Desmond Croaker had said – the place was now a dump and it was a real pity.

The trees close to the house hadn't been pruned in years and they hemmed the building in with long branches and moist shadows. The gutters were stuffed with leaves, the down-pipes split and riddled with rust; one hanging out at an angle. Constellations of lichens and ingrained tropical mould like dark sweat stained the lower parts of timber walls and the brick-work foundations.

Metallic flickers of green and black caught Seth's eye; a trio of Cairns Birdwing butterflies cruising past a massive row of traveller's palms. These fluttering jewels passed a runaway stand of painted bamboo and a multitude of red and pink torch ginger flowers; each lush bloom looking as if it had been carved from wax. It was a feral Eden in there.

He refocused on the other side of the overrun gardens and examined the ground floor of the mansion. A wide set of low maroon-coloured concrete steps lead up onto a long wooden veranda that dripped with wrought-iron arches; their poles engulfed in a mass of flowering creepers. Five doorways opened on to the big veranda, and through their

French windows Seth could faintly see some rectangles of light; open doorways leading on to a large and well-lit interior space.

On a wall he recognised a brass symbol called an Om. He also knew it represented the cosmic sound. Along with a weather-beaten Buddha reposing by the front steps, it was reasonable evidence that this was indeed the lair of a guru.

Feeling like he was pushing it now, he went back to the Pig and climbed in the back. Moving around the usual gear there he settled in to watch the house with binoculars.

After an hour he realised he'd need something to have a slash into while on this private detective lark. He found an almost empty Golden Fleece oil bottle and gingerly held it between his legs as it filled.

It took another hour for him to realise that sitting around watching nothing happen was going to drive him insane. A sullen little hangover from the Dewar's didn't help.

When a figure dressed in white clothes appeared on the second-floor veranda, Seth eagerly got the binoculars up. He saw a beard, longish hair, a lined face and jazzed eyes. An open shirt revealed a strand of beads. It was Arnold Jessop alright. Curious as, Seth watched him.

With his hands resting on the rail Jessop stared out into space for twenty minutes; motionless except for the faint movement of his chest. Maybe he's not only selling gear, but using it too, thought Seth.

Then Jessop smiled beatifically and gracefully swept his arms around, bringing his hands together as if in prayer. Without pause he turned like a trained dancer and glided into the house. Maybe he was just high on God after all.

After that bit of excitement, Seth waited and waited and waited. Shit and damnation, he thought. Looking through those ledgers and records this morning had been as boring as bingo, but this house watching was going to kill him.

Darkness slowly arrived. A light went on in the depths of the house and then – nothing happened. After another brain-scraping hour he chucked it in, just making it to the food store for some groceries.

Back at Cinderella Street he emptied the foul mess in the Golden Fleece bottle into the bush across the road, before putting away his shopping.

Grabbing a cold beer, he sat down and rang the number of Peggy's friend, Rita. She sounded well-educated and that was sexy, and although cheerful and polite, the underlying tone of concern in her voice meant she knew why he was ringing.

Peggy sounded expectant, eager for news, and he was grateful he had more than something to report.

"OK, I've found Jessop's house. I've started watching it and will continue to do so. I spoke to my mate and it might well be that Jessop is involved with heroin."

"Oh, that's not good," said Peggy.

My oath it isn't, he thought, but that's all I'm saying now.

"So, making sure she doesn't step foot in Jessop's place is my number one priority. I've also got some people now looking for her car. We'll spot her real soon."

"Oh my, you're doing well."

"It's a start. I'll contact you every twenty-four hours for an update."

"Yes please, every twenty-four hours."

He waited. She misunderstood his silence.

"I've been looking for Melanie too, Seth, driving around Cairns, but I have to fly to Sydney tomorrow. It might be a few days until I get back. Probably next Sunday."

"It's all fine Peggy. You have to do what you have to do. We might even find her tomorrow, hey?"

"I hope so Seth, I really do."

He was in the shower, thinking about what to make for tea, when the telephone rang. Dripping wet, he ran into the lounge. This might be one of his spotters with a sighting of the Daihatsu. It wasn't, and the voice on the line pissed him right off.

"It's Debbie. I'm really sorry about last night."

She had his phone number. Soft-hearted Pam must have got it off Mick for her.

"Seth, I had no idea that Ella was going to do that."

"Look I'm busy and I'm expecting a call."

"Please Seth don't be like this . . ."

"Like what?"

"I thought you'd like it, y'know . . . with both of us."

"Debbie, I think we might have done our dash," he said.

"What? Why?"

"Mate, you're . . . you're just so young."

"You like that when we fuck."

"It's not just that . . ."

"What am I supposed to do then? Separate myself from my body? I'm a stupid know-nothing girl from Cairns, but you knew that from the get-go. Nothing's changed!"

For God's sake, thought Seth.

"Debbie, I really am busy. Let's just back off for now and see what happens."

"You've got someone else."

"No. I've got this job on. I told you."

"Well, when will you see me?"

"I'm not putting a time on this."

"I feel like I've been waiting all my life."

Seth felt that strike a resonance inside him.

"I gotta go."

He slammed the phone receiver down, making the bell ding, and frowned at the water on the floor.

When he'd been younger it had been hard finding chicks who'd get stuck into you as quickly as the ones today did. Getting girls back then meant putting in lots of work. Lots of talking, talking and talking, the endless nattering about nothing. It meant dealing with their dumb families, idiot girlfriends and the relentless small-town tongues.

When you finally got a bit, and then said ta-ta, out would charge the irate brothers, dads and uncles, all with a sense of family honour bigger than bloody Ben Hur. Things could get rough and it would be time to go bush.

Thinking about Debbie, Seth sighed. Getting into girls undies may have got easier, but getting out of them again was still looking like the same old hassle.

Leafgold Weir Road

The next day Mick knocked on his door and they headed out west to meet the boss man. They had a proper yarn on the way, first talking about Mick's pride and joy – the Yammie YZ 250 rocking away in the back of his Toyota Land Cruiser. Even with the trail-bike's forks compressed with tie-downs, it was a tight fit.

It was five years old, but the Jap two-stroke was still the duck's nuts to Mick. Seth had got a measly fifteen-minute ride when he'd first got it. After that, no-one else but Mick was allowed to sit on it, let alone turn the ignition key.

"Yeah, she's been at the mechanic's," Mick explained. "Got new shockies and swingarm; fully tuned too. Had to drive a Husky WR up there for the last few weeks. Not bad, but nothing like my baby. Whatcha think of the respray?"

The dirt-bike was an army green.

"Every bastard keeps that factory yellow," said Mick. "But I wanted something nice and quiet for my girl. Cool aye?"

Seth nodded and smiled, pleased to be hanging out with his mate. They talked some more about bikes and cars and boats, but not about who they were going to see. Peggy and her daughter didn't get a mention either.

The fact was, if these boys wanted him running a team of

crop sitters, they'd have to wait their turn. What Peggy was paying him was peanuts compared to what he could make toting a gun in the scrub, but he sure as hell wasn't going to let her down.

It was a two and a half-hour drive, first ascending the Kuranda range, going up and over the narrow belt of dense coastal rainforest. The lush green petered out on the road to Mareeba and the further west they went — the drier it got. Soon it was scrubby hills, crows and dust.

At Dimbulah they pulled off the tarmac opposite the Junction Hotel. Mick killed the engine and it ticked and sighed in the silence. Right next to them ran the hot steel of railway tracks; beyond it the old wooden railway station shimmered in the morning heat.

Across the road the pub looked quiet, but when the sun started dropping in the west, the famously long bar inside would be packed three blokes deep with tobacco pickers, growers and farmers. There were a few dinged-up utes and a mud caked trail-bike out the front, but it was the khaki Land Cruiser with the twin spotlights on the bull-bar that drew their attention.

Its passenger window slid down; a man looked out, his sunglasses glinting as he nodded at them. Mick nodded back, the window slid up and the Landcruiser pulled away, heading west along the Bourke Development Road.

"We're off to see the Wizard, the wonderful wizard of Oz," sung Mick as he started the engine.

A few klicks out of town the khaki Land Cruiser turned onto a dusty unsealed road; an ochre-encrusted sign said Leafgold Weir Road. Mick and Seth wound up the windows as thick, fine bull-dust billowed from the vehicle ahead.

Sweat tickled Seth's neck and scalp. This was unknown country. He knew the Walsh River, but not on this side.

Presently the Land Cruiser turned into a rutted clay and sand driveway and they followed it to where a little wooden homestead sat high on tin-topped timber poles. Its peaked corrugated-iron roof was orange with rust. The walls were grey, their weather-faded planks faintly spotted with the white dandruff of a long-ago paint job. Behind the building Seth glimpsed a cream-coloured car.

When both vehicles turned off their motors it was very quiet. Mick rubbed his hands together.

"Alrighty," he said. "Let me do the talking."

They got out and so did the bloke in the sunnies. Tall, well-built and balding, he gestured for them to follow him to the house. The driver was leaning over into the back seat of the Land Cruiser.

"You know these fellas?" said Seth.

"Sort of. The one driving is out at the crop. Smiles a lot but doesn't say boo. The other bloke's a bit new."

They walked up to the house. The tall fella had got to the top of the timber staircase and he turned and looked down at them. He'd taken off the sunglasses and his lizard-cold eyes observed them. Seth felt his shirt sticking to his back. He reached behind, flapped it; vainly seeking cool air.

He trooped up the staircase behind Mick, their footfall making the worn, grey timber steps rattle in their hand-chiselled slots. Halfway up, Mick looked back over his shoulder to the vehicles and softly said, "Shit."

Seth turned. Real close to the house, he saw the driver,

a little fella holding a sawn-off shotgun loosely against his leg. The gun's humpback receiver meant it was a Browning Auto 5. With a fast finger and the magazine plugs pulled, it could fire five 12-gauge shells in a just few seconds.

The little driver flashed them a happy-as-Larry smile, stopped at the bottom of the stairs and waited. Up on the veranda came the sound of a throat being cleared.

Seth tried to catch Mick's eye, but his mate hurried up the stairs. He followed and they both got a quick pat down. The tall bloke smelt of nothing; no sweat, no aftershave, no tobacco. Seth looked him in the eye. The stare he got back was totally blank. No aggro, no fear, no communication. It was like looking at a photograph.

It was a touch cooler above the heated ground, with a little breeze that had the smell of water on it. From the look of the tree line and the sounds of birds, Seth guessed the Walsh River wasn't far away.

The homestead was ancient, uninhabited, but it didn't look abandoned. A successful miner had built it for the wife and kids back when there was still gold, tin and wolfram to be found. Now it was a place adrift in time.

Up the end of the veranda were a couple of old kitchen chairs and the lizard-eyed man nodded towards them. Seth followed Mick across silvered grey floorboards, listening to the sound of the driver coming up the stairs behind them.

Now Seth smelt a man's cologne, something unusual and expensive. He also smelt mentholated cigarette smoke. The chairs were next to a lattice-work screen that divided the veranda at its corner. The screen was scaled with flaking white paint but it ran solidly from floor to ceiling. Wisps of cigarette smoke drifted through the diamond-shaped gaps in the latticework.

Seth could just make out the figure of a man, sitting on a chair, just around the corner.

"Take a seat," said the lizard man.

They sat down on the chairs. Mick pulled out his Drum and Zippo. Lizard man stepped into an open doorway right next to them. In easy listening range, he wasn't standing on the veranda anymore. At the stairs the driver, cradling the Auto 5, was lighting a cigarette. From there he could fire the gun down the veranda – and hit only Mick and Seth.

"Michael Lovett," said the man behind the screen.

"Yeah?" Mick spilt some tobacco on the floor.

"Is that right? I call you Michael?"

The man's accent was a slurry of North Queensland and European; his words slow and considered, the voice a little hoarse.

"Sure. Or call me Mick. Most people know me as that."

"Mick." There was a short silence before the man spoke again. "It's a good Aussie name hey?"

Mick laughed. "That's me – a good Aussie."

"And what kind of name is Seth?"

Mick nodded at Seth as though giving him his cue; then lit his rollie. The lizard man stared from the doorway and down the end of the veranda the driver was watching too.

"It's the name my father gave me," said Seth.

"You a local boy, right?"

"Yep."

"You shoot, you got a licence – an' no police record."

Mick shook his head. It wasn't me, said his eyes.

"I'm sorry mate – what do I call you?" said Seth.

"Richard."

"You seem to know a bit about me."

"Oh yeah. If we gonna do some business together then I have to know about you."

"Seth is one hundred percent, Mr. Richard," said Mick. "We go way back."

The floorboards creaked in the doorway. Seth closed his eyes; listened to the birds down on the Walsh.

"You want to make some money Seth?" said the man and his chair scraped on the floor.

Opening his eyes, Seth saw the man's profile through the lattice screen now. Short-haired and thick-necked, with a strong nose, he wore sunglasses in the veranda gloom.

"How much money?" said Seth.

"More than you've ever dreamed of."

Mick grunted.

"Not just tens of thousands, but hundreds of thousands," the man continued. "If we get along – maybe a million."

Seth said nothing.

In the silence Mick smoked furiously. From the doorway the lizard man's eyes now watched with interest and that felt kind of odd. Then he understood. It would be this fella that he'd be taking his orders from. He'd never see the man behind the screen again.

Turning back, he nearly jumped right out of the chair. Less than a foot away, the man's face was pressed against the latticework, looking right at him. The smell of perfume was strong.

"Mick and Seth, hey?" He pulled his face back.

"See, North Queensland is a very good place. We're lucky to live here. And you boys have a chance to get even luckier . . . with me. It's a changing too; the big moneys' coming. There's gonna be an international airport soon, but in the fuckin' mangroves - not up here on the Tableland like it should be."

The man sighed.

"An international airport is great," said Mick. "Tourists want to party. Acapulco's got Acapulco Gold and Maui's got wowie."

The man sighed again.

"It's all a changing now," he said. "I see a lot of change in the last ten years. You boys know it. You got friends who are rubbish. Hippies. No respect. The girls – no underwear, no bra. And terrible, loud music."

Seth blinked.

"I don't wanna see kids barefoot, on the dole, with girls pregnant an' no father around," said the man. "We lucky this Queensland government is a good one."

"As long as we all make money," said Seth. "Who cares what music we listen to."

The man chuckled. "We'll make a money alright, don't you worry 'bout that."

Mick grinned like a bloody chimpanzee.

"You boys got short hair," said the man. "I like that."

"It's a hot climate," said Seth.

Another chuckle came from behind the screen.

"So, Mick here has a very good talent – to grow," said the man. "An' you also have a talent. You good with people and you know what to do when they don't listen. Right?"

In the silence the tin roof popped and ticked, expanding from all that sunshine. Mick frowned at Seth, gesturing with his head for him to speak.

"So, you gonna work for me?" said the man.

"Look, I've got to think about this," said Seth and Mick moaned painfully. More creaks came from the doorway.

"What? You come out here and you not sure? I heard you was keen," said the man. "What the fuck is this?"

"I'm sorry Richard, but I need some time to decide. I've received a job offer in Sydney as well," said Seth.

Mick glared at him. Jeffyman murmured in his head.

"Are you frightened?" said the man. "Like a little girl?"

Seth looked out at the yellow and gray fuzz of dried lawn and listened to Mick's heavy breathing. He bloody smokes too much, he thought. If he gets emphysema, Pam will kill him.

The man behind the screen sighed.

"OK, take a couple of days to decide, but be very sure you understand this one thing," he said. "We don't talk about this to anyone OK? I'll hold Mick here responsible for this."

"You don't have to worry about Seth," said Mick. "This bloke's solid gold when it comes to that."

"An' it's the same for you," replied the man. "If he's not working for me you don't talk to him about anything. You boys might be mates but in business there are no mates."

"I understand. Thank you for your time," said Seth. He carefully stood up. Down the end of the veranda the driver changed his stance.

"Look I'm gonna go take a leak," said Seth. "I'll meet you at the truck Mick."

Mick nodded curtly but didn't look at him.

Seth ignored the reptile eyes in the doorway and walked down the veranda. The driver stepped away from the stairs, the shotgun held in both hands; his forefinger flat across the trigger guard. Seth nodded at him and the little man smiled amiably back.

Out in the garden he emptied his bladder onto the hot ground, his thoughts on his water canteen in the car. He finished up, turned and looked back at the house. Mick was talking to the lizard man. The driver was at the veranda rail looking out at Seth, his smile luminescent in the shadow.

A few miles from Dimbulah, Mick broke the silence.

"Fuck you!" he yelled. "How many blokes our age even get a sniff at this sort of dough? You blew all yours on your house, which is great, but what are you going to do about money? And don't give me that bull about a job in Sydney."

Seth pursed his lips tightly. He felt like punching Mick, hard, but he'd most likely lose control of the vehicle and roll them into the irrigation channel that ran next to the road. He took off his sunglasses and looked at his fool of a mate.

"It's bad enough having to shit in the scrub and eat out of tins for weeks on end, but with these fellas, and all that dope, I can tell I'm going to end up having to shoot blokes."

"Nahhh – it won't be like that," said Mick. "There's some serious guns there; sometimes six or seven fellas too. We start firing and it will sound like a bloody army. Any rip-off merchants will run for it."

"Unless there's ten blokes with guns doing the rip-off."

"You're sounding like an old woman."

"You know who these people are, yeah?" said Seth, and he had to unclench his fist.

"Uhhh – professionals?" said Mick in a stupid voice.

Somehow Seth's fist had curled up again and it slammed into Mick's shoulder. The truck swerved and dust exploded through the windows as they veered across the road. Mick fought the wheel, gained control and pulled over.

"Jesus Seth! What the fuck!" He turned off the engine and rubbed his shoulder.

Seth grabbed his water bottle, jumped out and let the dust blow away around him. He took a drink and stared out at the hot arid landscape. Brown termite mounds as big as people stared back.

"It's really simple Seth," said Mick from the truck. "These blokes are as professional as. They provide the set-up and when we harvest, they collect it and take it away. And mate, they gave me seeds from Amsterdam. How's that for . . ."

"Stop," said Seth. "Didn't you hear what he said?"

"Yeah, yeah."

"So stop telling me stuff then."

"Does that mean you're not coming in on this then?

"Bloody oath, I'm not."

"Hundreds of thousands of dollars. You heard him."

"You know where Mareeba is?"

"Uh yeah. We're about to drive through it."

"And you know where Griffith is?"

"Mate — I know who they are," said Mick.

"Who are they?"

"For fuck's sake!"

"Who are they?"

"The fucking Mafia OK! Jesus Seth, I am done with the bush leagues. This is a chance to set myself up for the rest of my life."

"You are dealing with big shit here."

"Two or three seasons – I'm done."

"Shit sticks, Mick. You reckon they'll let a green thumb like you just wander off? After what you've seen and done? There'll always be an eye looking at you."

Mick got out and looked across the bonnet at Seth.

"Pam's from Western Australia, right? Albany. So, when I'm cashed-up good we're going to quietly split and get a place by the ocean there. I'll buy the best boat and just fish and make babies with Pam. She's got a big family and her brothers are tough bastards. They look out for each other and they'll look out for me and her. No one's gonna touch us out there."

A few hundred metres away the wind conjured up a willy willy, and the little whirlwind of dust snaked across the ground for a few moments, and then fell apart as though its controlling strings had been cut.

Mick wiped sweat from his eyes and pulled out his baccy. Seth took another hit of water; listened to the Zippo snap and Mick's grateful inhalation.

"What did you have to punch me for?" said Mick.

"I just don't want to see you get hurt."

That fully cracked Mick up, his shout of laughter blowing away the tension between them. Under the killer blue sky, Seth laughed too, the two of them hooting like crazy men.

Like a Spent Brass Round

It had kept him real sharp – the game of turning a quid growing and selling dope. The scary buzz of it was fun, and for the longest time it had fuelled his sense of himself as a rebel, an outlaw living beyond the crushing ordinariness of straight old Cairns. It had also cemented his reputation.

The growing was a secret only a few close mates knew, but always having a bit of good smoke meant that chicks fluttered around like butterflies and young fellas looked up to him. It was a top position to be in, turning earth, water and seeds into plants that grew naturally – then turning those big stinky bushes into lots of tax-free cash. Having dope *and* money made you doubly cool.

It wasn't that much work really. Nothing like crewing on a trawler three months straight in the Gulf, sleep-deprived, and stinging from cuts that never healed. Or busting your arse on a farm, or laying railroad track in the blistering sun. That made it sweeter, and although he basically respected any bloke who worked hard for his pay – he'd always felt a little bit smarter, a little bit cooler than them.

The big difference, and the real hard work of it, was the constant low hum of paranoia. If you were plugged into pot it never went away.

The uneasy flutter at sighting a strange car in your street for the second time. The jump in the guts at seeing cops. Odd noises outside had to be investigated; new friends had to be evaluated. Even your old mates sometimes made you wonder.

The repetition of suspicion ground down the mad thrill that had been half the fun. You grew to live with it, but it wasn't good. What had started as a happy fever was now a disease. The paranoia was perfectly legit though; the cops had undercover blokes looking like hippies or fishermen – or like you, and they got smarter and smarter at working out plays to trap you.

And there were the rip-off merchants and crop-raiders who'd sit down for a beer disguised as a friend of a friend, or God forbid – as a friend. Trust became a currency as valuable as money. Seth had been lucky, and vigilant too, but he'd seen long-time friendships between good mates degenerate into swindles, bashings; maybe even murder.

It was just like what Jeffyman had said — all that money made people lose their heads.

While living in Sydney he'd thankfully forgotten about that paranoia, but what he'd seen in Uncle Don's eyes, heard in Jeffyman's voice, and now just felt at Leafgold Weir Road had put the wind up him. This was a level of bad vibes not worth the small fortune he'd turned his back on.

Mick dropped him home, and a cool shower washed it all away – the sweat, the dust, the sixteen grand. While a pot of tea brewed up, he ate some Vegemite on toast and five mandarins; tearing open their bright orange skins to suck down the sweet pulp. He got on the outside of a nice cuppa, and then with little enthusiasm, went over to Edge Hill.

Parking behind the old Bedford again, he lay hidden in the back of the Pig and watched Jessop's house, fidgeting in the heat as no-one came or went. A dog appeared and shat on its neighbours' yard and who'd have ever thought that was worth watching? Two tiny jewels; blue and white Sacred Kingfishers, perched on the overhead power line for a while. He envied them when they darted off.

Trying not to think about Peggy, or what Mick had got himself into, Seth imagined himself made out of marine stainless steel; impervious to the rust of emotion.

Eventually the afternoon turned to dusk; the street all deep shadows, the birds making roosting calls. Finally over it, Seth slid over the seats and started the Pig.

Driving back down to Greenslopes Road he pondered one more spin around Cairns looking for the Daihatsu Max before going home and ringing up Peggy to report nothing. After that he'd eat dinner, play some records and wait for someone to ring with news of that purple shitbox.

Another big night, he thought, and at that moment the orange Holden HX panel van from Jessop's house passed him going into town.

Well how about that? Definitely one of the advantages of living in a small town. He easily tailed the panel van all the way onto Marlin Parade where it pulled up next to Tawny's.

Set on Trinity Inlet, just north of the jetty, Tawny's was a great seafood restaurant that stayed open until two am. Either one of those things was a winner in Seth's book and he'd left a few dollars in there over the years.

As he drove over to the far side of the foreshore car park, a fella got out of the panel van and sauntered into Tawny's. He looked fairly young and was dressed smart-casual. He also carried a briefcase.

Seth parked and sat waiting as night swallowed the day. Minutes passed, a hundred and twenty of them, while his belly grumbled and whined at the thought of what was being served at the tables inside Tawny's. Visions of garlic prawns and bugs, crispy slabs of fish and ice-cold Crownies taunted him.

He used his binoculars to take a look at the few diners who came and went, looking for . . . someone or something dodgy? He felt pretty sure he'd know when he saw it.

For a change, the wind had dropped and the water was nice and smooth. There was some boat traffic – aluminium tinnies coming in from the boats and yachts moored in the inlet, and Seth idly watched them through his binoculars.

Now a little wooden tender, with its outboard growling at the regulation five knots, came alongside a pontoon that stuck out into the water next to Tawny's.

The Holden HX driver came out of the restaurant and strode quickly down onto the pontoon. With the grace of a trained athlete he jumped down onto the small tender, scarcely moving it in the water; then sat down with his back to the shore.

Seth barely caught the face of the bloke at the tiller as the dingy moved off into darkness, chugging out into the inlet.

Slipping out of the Pig, he casually went to the water's edge, staying away from any lights, and had a shufti. With the binoculars he caught the dinghy's wake and followed its shimmering glints of light to where it stopped alongside a yacht. Voices, too far away to make sense, skipped across the flat inlet. The Holden HX driver, with two other blokes in tow, passed through the lit-up wheelhouse of the yacht and went below.

It was a night or two before the full moon and there was enough light to make out the yacht as it slowly turned on its mooring. It was a catamaran, probably eighteen metres long and perfect for oceangoing. It looked very capable of sailing up the Great Barrier Reef, out through the Torres Strait and . . . onto South-East Asia.

The penny dropped like a spent brass round. Heavens to fucking Betsy, there's heroin on that yacht!

His mind raced. Uncle Don. Ring him – try the station first then his home. How quickly would the cops get here? Damn, if only Arnold Jessop were on that yacht too!

Dobbing someone in to the cops totally went against the grain with him, but this was different – this was Peggy. And her daughter.

By the jetty was a phone box and he hurried over. Inside a big, suntanned fella was talking loudly about marine fuel bills and torn spinnakers. As he waited for Mr. Shouty to finish, Seth's rush of thoughts slowed right down.

Calling the cops was a serious move that required serious evidence. Evidence he didn't exactly have. Sure, he would bullshit Uncle Don and the police if it produced a result, but right now he wasn't so sure it would. And what if his hunch turned out to be all froth and no beer? Uncle Don would be absolutely ropeable.

Defeated by reason, he sighed and took a deep breath, inhaling that jetty smell of salty wood, fish guts and diesel. Bugger it! He needed more than a feeling. Jaw tight with frustration, he walked back towards the Pig

An outboard motor started up in the inlet. Seth quickly slipped into his truck and used the binoculars. A bow-wave flickered in the moonlight. Presently the same tender came into the foreshore lights. Now he got his first good squizz at the Holden driver as he hopped easily onto the jetty and walked to his vehicle.

Clean-shaven, well-groomed and of medium height and build, the bloke was probably in his early twenties. He also looked quick and agile to the point of being physically dangerous. And he still had the briefcase.

Seth was glad he hadn't called the cops. The briefcase and its contents were going back to Everknell Street – he'd take bets on it – and that meant Arnold Jessop would be in the picture if a bust went down.

The young bloke drove off with Seth discreetly following him. On nearly empty streets, he fell back. At Greenslopes Road he let the Holden HX vanish ahead, only speeding up to turn a corner up the top of Mullins Street to catch sight of the Holden's tail-lights turning into Everknell Street.

Certain now the briefcase had gone to Jessop's, he went home and rang up Peggy. It was getting on and he wasn't surprised that the Sydney shop number rang out. He rang the second number and it also rang out. So, she was out.

Seth sighed. Good for her. But he wasn't going to stay up waiting for Peggy to get home. Nah, he'd have another go in the morning – give her his report then.

And when he did, he wasn't going to mention what he'd seen tonight – the hard, young bloke with the briefcase. It would worry her. It sure as hell worried him.

Briefcase Boy

Up good and early, Seth cruised Cairns looking for the purple Daihatsu before stopping at a bustling trucker's cafe for the big breakfast – and savoury mince. Done eating, he tore out a page from his notepad, wrote up a description of Peggy's daughter's car and added his phone number and a twenty-dollar reward. Prompted by a two-buck tip, the cafe owner sellotaped it on the glass front-door for the truckies to see. He drove further into town until he found a phone-box. He rang Peggy and it went cool and professional; done and dusted in a minute. It looked like he was getting the hang of it now.

Resisting the urge to go and get a mango Weis bar, he considered driving south to Mission Beach and having a look around. Peggy's daughter might be at her mate's place there. It would be a four-hour round trip, which was easy enough, but thoughts of that briefcase and what it might contain nagged him into driving over to Edge Hill instead.

Parked behind the old Bedford truck, he acutely felt the absence of a plan of action. The idea of sitting and watching held as much appeal as a six-inch nail being hammered into his head. Without much thought, he got out, quietly closed the door and strolled up to the driveway.

Maybe he should just go in and put a scare into Arnold Jessop. Not mention Peggy's daughter, but let him know that seeking the Holy Spirit was preferable to chasing the dragon. He paused. It wouldn't just be Jessop in the house. There'd be guard-dogs too; tough, young human ones.

Ah bugger it. He was doing stuff-all just standing there so he went up the driveway a few metres, thinking he might get a closer look at the beautiful house.

He didn't get too far. A door opened and someone came trotting out. It was Briefcase Boy – the young fella from last night.

"Hello there! This is private property." He had a toffee sort of a voice. Seth smiled and gave him a little wave.

For a second the young bloke frowned, but when he came across to the driveway a smile had blossomed on his face.

He looked casually slick: his longish hair nicely cut and styled, a good silk shirt open to the waist and a gold bangle on his wrist. He wasn't real tall, five six maybe, but he was a handsome bastard; his baby-smooth face making him look like a teenager. Seth instantly disliked him.

The young fella also sized him up, eyes brimming with wild-card humour, and Seth was reminded of musicians he'd known in Sydney, flying high and happy-crazy on the first flush of money and success.

"G'day mate, I'm looking for a friend," said Seth.

"And you haven't found him so you can . . ."

Briefcase Boy's fingers made a walking motion.

". . . toodle-oo the fuck out of here."

"Wait up mate, I haven't told you who . . ."

The young bloke turned his head and whistled two notes.

"Is that to tell your mate to come out and look tough?" said Seth. A fella appeared up the top of the drive, looking tough.

"Yeah, I speak whistle," said Seth.

"You're not a policeman, are you?" mused Briefcase Boy. Without looking back, he raised a hand in signal and his mate crossed his arms and stood watching.

"No. I'm just looking for a friend who I believe has been here," said Seth.

He reached into his pocket and Briefcase Boy tensed, his bare feet moving into a fighting stance.

"Whoa – it's cool." Seth slowly took out his wallet and pulled out a fifty.

"I'm happy to give you a little something for your help."

Briefcase Boy smiled in distaste; shook his head.

"What are you then – a private eye?" he said. "I wouldn't have thought Cairns had any of them."

That sounded pretty damn cool, thought Seth.

"Yeah, I'm a private eye."

"OK, Mr. Private Eye. I'm not interested in you or your friend or your money. I want you off this property. Now."

The last word was a hard directive, almost shouted. Seth felt rage scorch him. You better watch your fucking mouth, he thought. Using that tone with someone older and bigger than you is just asking for a knuckle sandwich.

But getting pissed-off wasn't going to help find Peggy's daughter. Or ascertain if this flash young prick really did have heroin in his briefcase.

"You work for Arnold Jessop, right?" said Seth.

For an instant, recognition flared in Briefcase Boy's eyes. Then he good-naturedly pulled out his wallet.

"Listen chum, what say I pay *you* to leave?"

The wallet was fat with white and orange currency.

"Gosh, I wouldn't have thought there were that many junkies in Cairns," said Seth. "Business must be good."

Another flash of admission lit up the little bastard's eyes. Gotcha, thought Seth. You know exactly what I'm on about. The young pup's eyes refroze and he put his wallet away.

"I'm going to leave you here," he said. "I'll have a look again in five minutes, and if you're still here – I'll call the police. OK?"

It wasn't easy but Seth kept a lazy smile going. The little shit winked at him and turned. As he walked off, he said, "Be careful, there's lots of low branches around here. Might put that private eye out."

Keenly aware of being watched, Seth nipped back to the Pig, where he needed to unclench his fist to get his keys out. His white knuckles gripped the steering wheel, as nice and quick, he backed a fair way down the street before driving off. It was a big relief that no-one came out and sighted the Pig. He was spending enough money as it was without the added expense of a hire car.

At the food store in Edge Hill he rifled through the chest freezer, before finally locating a mango Weis bar. Throwing a dollar note on the counter, he hurried outside and started wolfing it in angry mouthfuls. The ice-block tasted fine, but it didn't cool down the steam coming out of his ears.

Taking shit wasn't something he willingly did, and that little bastard had just heaped a bucketful over him. While working security with the bands he'd come across a few pricks that he'd been sorely tempted to give a backhander to. Of course, he couldn't, and besides, he always had a soft spot for the talent.

Briefcase Boy certainly reminded him of any number of smart-arse Sydney boys, but was too well-spoken and well-dressed to be any of the drongos that Knoxie had told him about. He was junior enough not to be able to hide the fact that he sold smack for Jessop though. A hardened old crim with concrete eyes would have given nothing away. This cocky little squirt had let him take a peek at his hand.

His sleek looks and nice wheels meant that he was high up in Jessop's gang; probably a partner. He'd be taking all the risk while the hoodoo guru provided the bucks.

Seth crushed the ice-cream wrapper into a tight little ball and hurled it into a bin. Damn it. With that arsehole kid as his front, Arnold Jessop would walk away scot-bloody-free if a bust went down.

Digger Street

Over a couple of pots at The Redlynch he thought it over; finally arriving at his favourite answer – go for it.

Briefcase Boy's reaction to his crack about junkies was the vindication he needed. There was heroin at that house – he knew it. Calling down a bust might turn out to be just a spoiling action, but it would apply pressure and hopefully scare Jessop out of town for a while. Until the school year was over would be just fine.

Down the street in the privacy of a public phone box he rang Uncle Don. His wife Mary gave him the bad news. The old cop was down in Brisbane for the week – a school mate had died, and he'd be visiting rellies in Ipswich too. He'd be back Monday. Seth thanked her and sincerely promised to come visit soon. Now he deliberated the next call.

Over the years he'd got to know the names of some of the local detectives, but were they still around? He found the Cairns copshop number in the phone directory, dropped another twenty cents into the metallic green telephone and dialled. A duty officer answered and Seth asked for either of two ranking coppers he remembered. After a short wait a voice came on.

"Detective McKenroth here, what can I do for you?"

"I have a tip."

"OK, who am I speaking to?"

"It's an anonymous tip."

"OK, what is it?" The detective almost yawned.

"There's a quantity of heroin at a house in Edge Hill."

"Right. How did you come across this information?"

"I saw a fella with a briefcase full of it drive there. He got it from a yacht in Trinity Inlet."

"You saw that also?"

"I sure did."

"What's your connection with this man?"

"Detective, it's at the house right now. You blokes want to get over there before it gets moved."

"Yes, but what's your connection with this man?"

"There is no bloody connection! I'm a concerned citizen, alright? Listen, there's another bloke at that house who's involved too."

"You got a name and address?" The detective sounded like he was nodding off.

"Jeez mate, you don't sound very excited about this."

"I'd be excited if you came and spoke directly to me."

"I'm not going to do that."

"If this information proves correct then I may be able to secure payment for you, and also for any information you may provide in the future."

"I'm not ringing up to be a dog. I just want these bastards done. It's the house at the end of Everknell Street in Edge Hill. Number One Everknell Street and the bloke's name is Arnold Jessop."

"Jessop? How do you spell that?"

As Seth spelt it out, he became uneasy. The phone box felt like a glass cage.

"Jess-op. Ever-knell," breathed the detective through his nose. "Got that. Can you hold the line?"

No way, thought Seth, these bastards could trace calls.

"Listen mate – go to that address now. What you'll find there will get you a promotion."

He hung up and got the hell out of Dodge.

Back home he felt foolish at his paranoia, and angry at the cop's disinterest. His tip-off was probably going to be filed and forgotten, or just chucked in the bin. Over the next week or so he'd check the Cairns Post, and listen to the radio for news of a big heroin bust, but the positivity he'd felt before was fading fast.

After a pointless nap on the couch where he woke up as pissed-off as when he lay down, he put on Jeff Beck Group and irritably drank a beer. It wasn't until Sugar Cane, and another stubby of NQ, that he felt a little less uptight.

When the phone rang, what he heard made him feel even better.

"G'day mate, I seen that car you're looking for."

It was the old cabbie, Harry Spinks.

"Harry, you little beauty! Where and when?"

"Well, no big surprise there. It's on Digger Street. Passed it about fifteen minutes ago."

Fairly buzzing, Seth drove to Digger Street in fourteen minutes flat. Sure enough, the purple Daihatsu Max was parked outside an old Queenslander house. He recognised the place – his old growing mate Gary Sparks used to live in it. He parked up the street, and then slowly walked back and had a sticky-beak.

Afternoon shadows and the shade of a venerable mango tree covered the ramshackle timber house in cool gloom. Loud music blared out of the open front door and windows; Disraeli Gears – an oldie but a goodie. A discarded home-brew kit lay under the high-set house, along with dozens of long-neck bottles covered in dust. Someone had a thirst – but not that bad. By the failed brewery was a row of jerry cans chained to a house pole, all patiently awaiting a Cape York adventure, or a long run out west.

Seth went up the shaky flight of wooden front stairs and paused at the open doorway, smelling an ancient ingrained mix of incense, coconut oil and dope smoke. He knocked loudly on the door and waited while Ginger Baker gave it some – and then some more.

"Hello? Anyone home?" he yelled.

A bloke; fairly fit, with his hair pulled back in a pony tail appeared. He came loping down the hallway, his wary eyes pretty much saying, 'there's a stash in the house.'

"G'day," shouted Seth, nodding appreciatively. "Cream aye? Wish I'd been around to catch 'em live."

The bloke offered up a pretend smile that deepened the worry-wrinkles on his forehead.

"Yeah, yeah, what do you want?"

"I'm a mate of Gary Sparks. He used to live here."

"Yeah, yeah, I know Gary."

"I'm looking for Melanie."

"Who?"

"The young chick who's driving the purple Daihatsu."

"Melanie?"

"Yeah, Melanie. She's just come up from Sydney."

"OK," said the bloke, visibly relaxing. "Come on in."

The timber-floored living room featured a line of multi-coloured, stained-glass windows, all open to the street. On the walls were posters of sixties and seventies music stars. Indonesian sarongs covered beanbags and a New Guinea mask stared from above a dusty TV. While the bloke turned the music down, Seth quickly cast his eyes around, looking into the open bedrooms and down the hall to the toilet and kitchen. There didn't appear to anyone else in the house.

"Hey, sorry to muck you about," said the bloke. "Can't be too careful aye? So, what's your name brother?"

"Seth."

The bloke stared, his mental gears whirring.

"I'm not that pretty," said Seth and the bloke laughed.

"Nah, nah. I've heard of you," he said.

"All good I hope."

"Yeah, yeah. I'm Babinda Ross."

"You're from Babinda?"

"I'm the monkey's nuts there," declared Babinda Ross. "You want a smoke Seth? I got some good heads."

"Nahimright mate. Just looking for Melanie."

"She's not here aye. Gone with Electric Trev to look at a Kombi van. These southern kids – they all need a Kombi to get around in up here."

"Any idea when they'll be back?"

"Mate, I couldn't rightly tell you. Tonight, I'd say. They rocked up here lunchtime. Sarah brought her."

"Sarah?"

"Yeah, she lives here. She's been down at Mission Beach where she met Melanie at a mate of hers'. She used to go out with Gary; knows Electric Trev too."

"Ah yeah, that Sarah." Seth didn't have a clue who she or Electric Trev were, but if the chick was an ex-girlfriend of Gary Sparks it might make things easier.

"So is Melanie staying here?" he asked.

"Yeah, maybe. She wants to do meditation with some guru bloke and go up to Kuranda – all that hippy stuff. They'll be back later. Have a seat man. Sure you don't want a smoke?"

"It's all good mate, I'll pop back later. Oh yeah, what's Trev driving these days?"

"A white Falcon, a bit old but lots of power. Hey, listen mate," said Babinda Ross. "I'm into selling a bit of pot. You wouldn't be able to get me a few pounds wouldja? Some of that good stuff you've got."

"Mate, I'm not in the business any more. It's all gonna be a story for the grand-kids now – when it's all legal."

Babinda Ross laughed. "I wish! Yeah, yeah, no worries, just thought it was worth an ask."

"Always worth an ask. And, oh yeah – I wanna surprise Melanie. I'm a family friend, so don't mention me hey?"

"Yeah, yeah," said Babinda Ross. "My lips are sealed."

Seth nipped off down the stairs and ambled up the street. As he walked up to the Pig he casually glanced back to see if Babinda Ross was checking out his car. He wasn't, so Seth got in and sat waiting for a white Falcon or Kombi to come down the street. After two hours the yawns started, but he perked up when a Kombi van appeared. Its driver was a skinny bloke and Seth slouched back in his seat. He felt hungry again. Listening to his stomach grumble was a loser's game, so he went off for a feed.

It was an in-and-out mission at Hides Hotel back lounge. While it grew dark, he got a fat rump steak, baked potato, garden salad and two Bundy and cokes on board. It took forty minutes all up.

Out in the street, starlings swarmed, shrieking in their hundreds as they massed in trees. Cable came out of the front bar, calling out to Seth over the din. After three years away he couldn't just cut and run on the old pirate, so he had a beer with him, just one, and heard all about Cable's new boat; getting the verbal tour, inch by inch, bolt by bloody bolt.

"Not that keen on the radio though," grumbled Cable. "Next thing you'll have to report where you're going, what you're doing, what you're catching, where you caught it and who yer flippin' rooting too!"

Finally, Seth got a leathery handshake and a toothless love-ya-son smile from the old fisherman. He had a grin on his own mug going back to the Pig. Yep, you had to love those old blokes.

Back at Digger Street, no white Falcon or Kombi van had turned up. He parked up the street and looked back. The house had just one light on; glowing from somewhere deep inside, but the music was pumping, and louder than before. Seth smiled. It wasn't even seven o'clock. Very Digger St.

He locked up the Pig and wandered over. Iron Butterfly's In-a-Gadda-da-Vida, obviously another heavy nugget from Babinda Ross's youth, thundered from the open windows of the living room. He must be stoned off his head in the dark, thought Seth, just laying right back and feeling that monster riff.

He stood in the driveway, tossing up whether to go in or not. Talking to Babinda Ross didn't grab him so he began to turn away; then stopped. Inside the house, shadows now jumped and jerked across the living-room roof and walls – the quick shadows of people in motion. It didn't look like dancing.

Darting out of the street light in close to the house, Seth heard over the hard rock pulse, several hefty thumps on the wooden floor above. Moving carefully, avoiding a car tyre, a low mango tree branch and a stack of louvre glass, he went around to the back stairs and looked up. The door was open and a man's shout sounded over the heavy music. Seth ghosted up the stairs, his step light; careful not to send vibrations through the high-set wooden house.

Up the top a cat sat glumly next to its empty bowl. Seth stepped over it and looked through the door. A glow of light came from beyond the living room. The timber floor shook underfoot as something bounced off it. A nasty voice yelled a command. Someone was copping a hiding in there. Odds on it was Babinda Ross.

Seth opened and closed his fists, wondering how much pain they might give or take in the next minute.

He could just walk away, but it wasn't a dead-set thing Peggy's daughter wasn't in the house. Nah, he couldn't take the risk. Something brushed his leg. It was the cat fishing for a feed. He bent down, stroked its back a few times, and then went through the dark kitchen into the house.

In the living room, the only light was spilling in from a lamp in a bedroom. Seth could see over by a big couch, two men punching and kicking someone on the floor. The poor bastard looked like Babinda Ross alright.

Luckily the light wasn't behind Seth and he ran across the room; catching the two bash merchants by surprise. The guitar solo in In-A-Gadda-Da-Vida was in full flight as Seth hammered both fists into the kidneys of the closest thug. The astonished man jerked upright and Seth put three seriously hard punches into his head. The bloke spun like a fainting ballerina, fell into a wide-open window and flopped over the sill.

The other prick pulled something from his belt – a pistol. Adrenalin exploded through Seth. He leapt sideways and bang! – gun-muzzle sparks lit up the room. For an instant John Lennon stared accusingly from a poster on the wall. The gunshot was loud enough but Seth felt no impact.

His jump landed him on the big old couch. Surprisingly for Digger Street, it was still fairly bouncy and he used its rebound to spring forward. The prick with the gun swung his arm around and like a ton of bricks, Seth crashed onto him, managing to pound in a good solid head-butt before they both tumbled to the floor.

Jumping up, he saw the gunman laying still and quickly punched his head into floor to make sure. The guitar solo came to an end, and the song's slinky riff cruised back in.

Yeah, this is one cool track, thought Seth.

He quickly turned, ready for the other bastard again, but he was motionless, stuck in the open window with his arse-crack showing. Charming, thought Seth, resisting the urge to go over and tip him down five metres onto the ground below. Instead he went to the stereo, and as the drum solo started, carefully took the needle off the record.

"About fuckin' time!" someone yelled from next-door.

Seth went from room to room looking under beds and behind doors; most thankful to find nobody else in the house. Back in the living room he saw that the bash boys hadn't moved. He'd knocked them cold.

Babinda Ross was groaning and Seth went over to him.

"Who . . . who are you?" said Babinda Ross.

"The Phantom." Seth felt his knuckles. Nothing hurt too much.

"Aye? The Phantom?"

"You right?" said Seth. "You want me to call an ambo?"

"Nah, nah, don't do that." Babinda Ross slowly sat up and looked around.

"What happened Ross? Who are these bastards?"

"Who are you? Who am I talking to?"

"It's Seth, the bloke from this arvo."

"Ahhh right – Seth Kelly. Mate, you sure turned up at the right moment." Babinda Ross felt his chest and ribs, and then looked around the room. "Where are they?"

"There and there," Seth pointed. "So how come these bastards were giving you such a flogging?"

"Well, I started buying pounds of dope off them but now they tell me I have to sell smack too. I said no fuckin' way, and they went to town on me. I gotta get out of here now."

"Back to Babinda?"

"I reckon."

"Where's Melanie?"

"Who?"

"The chick from Sydney. The purple Daihatsu."

"Yeah, yeah," said Babinda Ross as he checked his teeth. "She bought the Kombi aye. She and Sarah are going to the full moon party at Wangetti, but they're getting a feed first. Oh yeah, they'll be checking if her guru mate is home at Edge Hill first."

"When did they go?"

"Ah . . . ah, not long after it got dark."

While he was eating at Hides.

"They say when they'll be back?"

"I don't reckon they're coming back tonight. Oh fuck, I've gotta get out of here. I gotta ring me mate."

"What's the Kombi look like?" said Seth.

Babinda Ross slowly rubbed his face and got up.

"Ross! What colour is the Kombi?"

"Mate, I'm spinning out here. Give us a sec."

Seth gave the dazed man an encouraging pat on the back, and went to check out the comatose knuckleheads. He located the gun, pocketed it, looked in the gunman's wallet and found a New South Wales driver's licence. Just like Knoxie had said; here were Sydney boys come up to push heroin in the Queensland sunshine.

He riffled through the wallet, ignoring the money in it, but saw nothing else of interest. Over at the window he checked out the other grub, looking for, but not seeing, the shape of a gun in his Levi jeans. The bloke was right on the edge though and Seth felt very tempted to push him out.

"It's a lime-green, single windscreen, pop-top fitted out for camping. Just under a hundred thousand on the clock, newish tyres and good brakes," said Babinda Ross.

With a faint sigh Seth turned away from the window and watched the battered pot-dealer limp across the room to the telephone. Babinda Ross picked up the receiver, stuck his finger in the rotary dial and looked at Seth with a gap-toothed smile.

"She did real good, aye. It started out at sixteen hundred, but she got the bloke down to twelve fifty. Electric Trev said she didn't muck around."

He sounded like a proud uncle. Then his voice took on a tone of real concern.

"She doesn't smoke dope, but."

Wangetti Beach

Outside the house, Seth watched Babinda Ross, toting a bagful of essentials, ease himself into a hastily summoned mate's Bongo van. Inside the house, nothing stirred; the two Sydney crims still out for the count. Best to let sleeping mongrels lie, thought Seth.

Back in the Pig he took a gander at the gun he'd nearly been shot with – a .22 calibre Smith and Wesson Model 34 revolver; outdated and distinctly unloved. He put it in the stash under the dash and started the engine. Now to find Peggy's daughter.

Over at Everknell Street there were no lights on in the mansion and no Kombi van parked out the front. A quick reconnaissance up the drive and around the back revealed a single sportscar parked next to a couple of darkened buildings. Everyone was out.

To Wangetti Beach then, and as he drove through Edge Hill making for the highway north, he considered how close he'd come to total disaster. Half an hour earlier and Peggy's daughter would have been there when those two maggots turned up, and blokes like that – toting guns and bashing fellas – wouldn't think twice about hurting, or even raping a chick in order to put a scare into someone. And he'd been stuffing his face with steak and baked potato.

The steering wheel felt hard and he consciously relaxed his grip; releasing the tension in his hands. Don't freak out, he told himself, nothing happened and nothing will. Just bloody well find her.

There was a trickle of traffic on the Cook Highway and as he approached the turn-off to Machans Beach he did a mental stock-take of the Pig in case he needed something from his place. Sleeping swag, flash light, spare battery, twenty-litres of water, mozzie-coils, insect repellent, spare clothes, hiking boots, cooking gear, some tinned food and a bottle of rum. More than set, he kept travelling north.

Up ahead at Smithfield he saw a long sweep of fire in the darkness; sugarcane being burnt before harvesting. On the side of the road a bright yellow and black burn-off warning sign came into view. He slowed down, every other vehicle doing the same, and in convoy they moved into a smoky haze. Two coppers appeared; their patrol car and two cane-farm utes parked next to the road beside them. Then he saw the burn crew silhouetted against leaping flames; one fella moving along setting the cane brakes alight, his drip-torch dispensing liquid fire.

Another hundred metres and the fire was much closer to the road — the smell and heat coming into the Pig. Seth wound the windows up as a crackling roar filled the air. The smoke grew thicker, visibility now down to three metres. The line of traffic slowed to a crawl. Two little creatures, probably climbing rats, scuttled across the road into the shadows where fire-light flickered on the wall of unburnt cane. Glowing red cinders and twists of white ash fluttered down onto the Pig's windscreen.

The fire was beside the road now. Thousands of stalks of burning sugarcane, outlined in the blackest black against the blaze, trembled and shook in the rocketing heat. Clouds of thick white smoke, lit up by flames, billowed up into the night. Above this sunshine-bright inferno, sparks spun and whirled into the darkness like runaway stars. The windows and chrome of the cars ahead flowed with bright molten light.

The sea of flames began to recede and the fog of smoke lessened. The column of vehicles picked up speed again. Seth impatiently pressed down on the accelerator pedal, but the brake-lights from the car ahead came on, slowing him to a halt. He made a noise of frustration and waited as the car turned off the Cook Highway onto an unsealed farm road. As he eagerly moved into the space ahead, the smoke cleared, and right there in his headlights was the back of a lime-green Volkswagen Kombi van.

Seth felt a surge of elation. For the first time since he'd taken Peggy's money, he felt like he was getting a chance to earn it. Grinning from ear-to-ear, he happily settled in behind the Kombi, his anxiety now turned to exhilaration.

The plump orb of the full moon was rising perfect in the clear night sky, and at Buchan Point, the view opened right up. The glittering, black-velvet ocean stretched away to a glowing horizon, and for a spellbinding moment Seth felt like he was floating out in space; the Coral Sea massive and serene below, and above – a big, big sky, incandescent with stars. Yeah, he loved it up here.

Down in the tunnel of trees on Ellis Beach, moonlight danced and flickered along the road as it found gaps in the overhanging branches. Seth could smell tamarind now, the crushed fruit pods littering the road, and close by, the thick tannin tang of the creek-fed back lagoon.

Up ahead the Kombi made good speed, Peggy's daughter not afraid to give it some, and the camper van's brake lights lit up rarely. Soon he was slowing down behind the Kombi, and then following as it crossed over the highway and pulled in at the southern end of Wangetti Beach.

In amongst trees were some cars; all front wheel drives as the deep sandy tracks to the beach were notorious for getting totally bogged in. The Pig would make it no worries at all, but he pulled in across from the Kombi and killed the engine.

A car stereo was pumping and Seth recognised the fat, funky grooves of War. Groovers stood around the vehicles smoking and necking bottles, and some decent-smelling dope smoke was wafting up into the bright moonlight.

Seth watched two chicks get out of the Kombi and open the side door. He got out and slowly walked towards them. The girls were laughing as they got their swags out.

"Hey, how's it going?" he said. "Nice night for a party."

The driver turned quickly, her face a pale shape in the shadows. This must be Peggy's daughter, thought Seth. He came to a halt in a big patch of moonlight so that they could see him clearly. The other woman slid the Kombi door back with a bang, turned and put her hands on her hips. This had to be Sarah – Gary Sparks' ex.

"Hey, is that you Sarah?" he said, wondering if he'd ever met her before.

"Who's that?"

"It's Seth Kelly. Gary's old mate."

"Seth Kelly! No way! That's too cool!"

Scampering over, she hugged him; putting her boobs and belly into it. With her arm around him she turned to the Kombi, her face in moonlight. Seth now recognised her as a hard-partying chick from some years back.

"Hey Melanie check this out!" said Sarah. "One of our local legends has rocked up. I told you this was going to be a cool party."

As Melanie came over, Sarah looked up at Seth with I'm-so-ready-to-root-your-socks-off eyes.

"Haven't seen you in ages mate," she purred.

Seth released himself, went forward and stuck out his hand, stooping down because Melanie was a little short-arse. They shook and her grip was firm and dry.

"Hi Seth," said Melanie. In the moonlight her face was as confident as her handshake. She smelt nice too – perfume, something expensive, with a tang of girl-sweat.

"Hey listen, I've got a four-wheel drive. I can give you girls a ride down to the beach if you like," he said.

They readily agreed and he helped them put their gear into the Pig. Sarah quickly bagged the front seat, and as they bumped slowly down the rutted track, she ear-bashed him with a shit-stream of gossip and conjecture, with Gary Sparks coming in for a serve as a treacherous root-rat.

On a couple of big dips Sarah's hand grabbed Seth's thigh as though she needed to steady herself.

When she paused for air, he tried to find Melanie's eyes in the rear-view mirror.

"So, Melanie, where do you hail from?"

"I've just come up from Sydney," she said.

"Oh, OK. Having a holiday?"

"Yeah, kind of. I've taken some time before university starts and I want to do some study."

"Time off school?"

"Yeah. I'm getting into meditation-based learning and there's a good teacher here in Cairns."

"Except she hasn't got his phone number and he's never home," said Sarah.

"Well, good for you," said Seth. "You're doing what you want to do. And your folks are cool with that?"

"My folks? What have they got to do with it?"

The volume of her voice didn't change but the tone did, clearly indicating that she required a credible answer. Seth was silent, changing gears as he negotiated a wash-out in the track.

"Oh, I thought, you know, taking time off before end of term, they might be dark about that," he finally said. "My folks were always onto me to get a degree."

"And did you?" said Melanie and Sarah laughed.

"Seth's got a degree in life, darling," she said. "He's been in rock'n'roll in Sydney."

"What instrument do you play Seth?" said Melanie.

"A big one I've been told," said Sarah.

"Jeez, you're a cheeky bitch," said Seth.

Sarah cackled.

"You're in a band?" said Melanie.

"No, not me," said Seth. "I help bands at shows."

"With the stage and sound?"

"With security."

"Do you have to get physical with people?"

"Unfortunately, sometimes yes."

"Is that why you're a local legend?"

He laughed easily, but he'd have to watch himself – she was sharp.

"Seth is the nicest bad guy around," proclaimed Sarah. "He's always got good dope, stops any trouble, and knows all about the bush and the reef too."

"Wow," said Melanie. "You sound like a cross between Batman, Tarzan and Captain Goodvibes. I'm very lucky to have met you."

"For fuck's sake," said Seth, happy when they laughed.

Under the beach almonds and whistling pines at the end of the track was a group of four-wheel drive vehicles. Seth parked then helped carry the girls' bedding down a short sandy path onto a long crescent of beach. No-body lived around here. The only houses were right down the far end; nearly four kilometres away.

Forty or fifty people were gathered around a proper fire made of driftwood logs; the large white trunks would burn all night. Swags and open-air camps were set up amongst the low sand dunes. There were Eski's full of ice and drinks, and people stood around on the sand, or sat on logs and woven pandanus mats; everyone talking and laughing.

Two guitarists and a voice were putting in their two Bobs worth – Dylan and Marley, and thankfully they were not too flat. There was a roughly even mix of boys and girls, ages ranging from late teens to mid-thirties, and a few cool older bods too. Seth could hear some overseas accents, and in the firelight, he made out a couple of his old muckers standing by a jumbo-sized Eski.

Marty and Rockwell Pete were good fellas. A few years younger than him, they grew and sold nice dope to hippies, international travellers and the domestic groovers up from down south. He went over, happy to shake Sarah. And he needed a bit of distance from Melanie right now.

Greeting the boys and their new friends – two bare-chested, sarong-clad, French lads – he gratefully accepted a beer from Marty, and checked out faces around the fire.

He recognised Stasia, an ex-girlfriend of his, and some local hippy chicks – Lanie: blonde, busty and big on bongs, little Evie Moonbeam, sweet-as, but not super bright, and Angie . . . Angela, Angel? Anyhow, you wouldn't know from her fluffy armpits and kohl-rimmed eyes that her father was a senior pilot for ANA and her family staunch bible-bashers.

One of the guitar players, Reggie, was a Murri bloke from Ravenshoe. Rake-thin, with a devilish smile and a goatee and moustache, he drew fascinated European girls to him like plump moths to a flame. Seth also saw Buggy, a cool ex-Adelaide bloke who had a Mini Moke and motorbike hire business, his Pommy lady Clare by his side.

As ever, his bouncer's eye methodically took in every face and vibe, and over by the fire talking bullshit to some girls was a skinny scrounger he'd seen around over the years, a bloke with a rep for nicking things, or climbing aboard drunken chicks — he couldn't remember which. This shifty prick looked like the only person who might be trouble here tonight, but Seth could take him easy.

He grabbed another beer and Rockwell Pete produced a four-paper joint. They all smoked it and talked, the young French blokes, totally ripped on the dope, nodding along. Eventually one of them, his eyes bloodshot and wide with wonder, told them that he was very, very happy to be here.

"Just don't tell too many people mate," said Marty.

"Really? More people is cool man. It's a big beach," said the French boy.

"Nah, I mean Far North Queensland, mate. There's just the right amount of you lot here now. We all make a few dollars but I don't want to come to this beach in twenty years' time and see hotels and bloody high rises."

"You'd think differently if you'd bought land here," said Rockwell Pete. "Be worth a fortune down the track."

"Yeah?" said Marty. "Reckon we should buy property?"

"Start a business first," said Seth. "It's the legal cash-flow you feed the green profit into. You start buying land on a tree-loppers wage and the tax office is gonna get right up your coit."

"Coit?" said the French lad.

"Yeah, it fuckin' hurts," said Marty.

"Hurts?"

"Oooo yeah."

"What . . . what do you guys do?"

"Whatever we can get away with," said Marty.

Silver Fairy Floss

While Seth drank more beers with the boys, he covertly watched Melanie. She wasn't shy, easily talking to people, but she was good at listening too. Eventually she connected with Stasia and that wasn't so surprising.

Presiding over a beach bar making Bloody Marys, with a fat joint between her crimson lips, Stasia looked as sexy and gorgeous as ever. Big-haired and full-bodied, her bare arms jingling with bangles and her fingers glinting with rings – Stasia was a sex-bomb, and a highly explosive one at that. Sharp as a tack, very funny, and truly devil-may-care, she had a dissolute sangfroid that either scared the shit out of blokes or turned their brains into supplicating mush.

Part earth mother, part witch, and at times utter pirate, Stasia was a magnet for all the cool young chicks. She was wise and she knew about things – about drugs and herbal medicine; about women's stuff. She knew how the dirty old world worked and how men were. Like a tough big sister or a hoodlum auntie, she dispensed savvy advice and inspired strength. Amongst those young women, and many older ones too, she was fiercely loved and deeply respected. Seth had lasted four months with her – something of a record he was later told.

Now Stasia's face lit up at young Melanie and soon they were engrossed in talk and laughter. Seth watched from the corner of his eye feeling a strange mix of lust and awe, and when Stasia's eyes looked around, seeking him out in the shadows – he knew Melanie was asking about him.

He quickly hid in a discussion with Marty that developed into a post-mortem of an ex-mate who'd dobbed in a crop to the cops. When he next snuck a look, Melanie was sitting with the mob by the bonfire, her curves sweetly outlined by flames behind her cotton dress.

Spying again, he saw how she deftly moved in and out of conversations, sometimes sparking delighted laughter. At one point she confidently and eloquently held forth with everyone listening; all eyes intent on her. One young bare-chested fella lay on the sand at her feet looking up like a boofy dog. And why not? Peggy's daughter was a real gem.

Sarah was doing good too, sitting thigh-to-thigh with a bearded Alby Mangels look-alike, stroking his thigh and nuzzling his ear. By the look of it, a wildlife safari with an appearance from the swag python later was on the cards.

A tall chick in a tight floral skirt began to dance, her feet slipping through the cool sand, her bum uncontained by panties. In stoned, appreciative silence, Rockwell Pete and the French boys watched her.

"Here," said Marty and he put a tiny piece of cardboard in Seth's hand.

"Strong?"

"Yeah, a bit. But it's real clean. I mean, how do I look?"

Marty looked alright and there was nobody on the beach that Seth couldn't handle, so he washed the acid down with a swig of cold beer. Haven't done this in years, he thought. It was time to have some fun again.

After talking some more with the boys, he went and sat in the sand next to Melanie. In the firelight he could see her clearly. She was lovely, her resemblance to Peggy as sexy as it was distracting. Talking to a young couple about whale migration, her small hands were animated, her thoughts and words precise. The couple were getting into her rave and he got drawn in too. Then she noticed he was beside her. Smoothly finishing up, she turned to him.

"Hi Seth, this is such a great party. Really cool people in a really cool place."

"It's how we do it up north," he said. "You'll never want to leave."

Melanie laughed. "You may be right."

"So that's your Kombi van hey? I was driving behind you on the way here. You drive good."

"It was a bit scary in the dark, especially on a winding road I don't know, with the sea and high cliffs on one side."

"You did bloody well."

"Thank you." She sounded pleased but not grateful. "So, Seth – do you know anyone who fixes up Kombi vans?"

"Is there a problem with it?"

"No. I just want it looking good for when I sell it."

Smart move, he thought. Make a little profit and pay for your trip.

"There's a fella in Kuranda," he said.

"Oh cool – that's a place I want to go."

"Well, just before you get to town there's VW Empire and the emperor there is Nils. Born in a Kombi I reckon, with the biggest collection of parts anywhere on the planet. He's a bush mechanic so he's cheap."

"Wow, that sounds perfect. How do I find him?"

"It's not that easy. I'll take you there in the morning if you like."

"Don't you have to go to work?"

"We don't work up here if we can help it."

Melanie laughed but she was thinking too.

"I'd so appreciate it Seth. I don't know a lot about cars so your advice would be really helpful."

"Sure. Can't say I know much about Kombis though."

He got up, wary of overplaying it.

"Hey listen, I'm gonna get a drink. You want one?"

"No, I'm fine."

"What about a smoke? North Queensland green?"

"No thanks – it's wonderful enough here already."

This girl's alright, he thought as he walked back to his vehicle for the rum. She's got a head on her shoulders.

He got the bottle, and back with the boys, he watched as a young bloke in tiny swimmers tried chatting up Melanie. He was unconsciously rubbing his chest and nipples as he talked. Melanie's face, polite and interested, looked subtly tinged with amusement.

She said something to the teenage Tarzan that left him looking tragic, but still smiling. After patting him kindly on the arm, she went back over to Stasia and deftly resumed their conversation from before. She's a smooth operator, thought Seth.

The party started getting loose with screams of laughter rising through the still night air. A reasonable rendition of

'Listen to The Music' got an exuberant mob of near-naked girls and boys dancing. Joints were in constant circulation, and a few times Seth found himself passing one to someone who was passing one to him. A big log got pushed deeper into the fire and faces turned upwards to watch the orange sparks join the stars.

People were fully charged-up, drunk and stoned, but the beautiful night brought out a gentle silliness in everybody.

If you fell over – the soft sand would catch you. If you forgot what you were saying, everyone would just happily laugh. There was no pressure to be clever or cool.

Needing a slash, Seth wandered into a sea of silvery sand dunes away from the party and had a nice long whizz. After the joints, beers and rumbos he was feeling pretty good. His guts did a naughty roll and a thrill zinged through his old fella as he imagined holding little Melanie in his arms, her legs around him while he slowly – woah!

A sudden vivisection; crystal-clear, razor-sharp – sliced right through his fantasy, and the hard truth it exposed left him standing there pissing in abject mortification.

Shame punched him deep in his chest. He felt sick. What in the hell was he thinking? This was Peggy's daughter! Where was the basic respect, the common decency – the honour and care? Had he always been such a filthy, rotten bastard? A razor-blade of disgust scraped inside. Yes, he had.

He shouted out incoherently; staggered, nearly falling to the sand. He wasn't a real man – he was a cunt-struck grub.

Revulsion boiled sour in his gut; self-loathing flooded his head. Do something, he thought – *do* something.

Focusing hard, he fumbled his zipper closed and he went to the Pig. In the back he found the airtight tin box. Inside it was the toy he'd made to entertain his niece Sophie with. When he'd first got back from Sydney, they'd all camped at Brampton Beach, with her mum and his dad too, and at night, him playing with the toy had gone down a treat.

It was a ball of rags wired together and he re-soaked it in petrol from the jerry can. Feeling a little better now, that awful shame almost gone, he walked back to the party. Someone lent him a lighter and he set the ball alight. He kicked it in the air and with more kicks kept it aloft.

Young fellas ran in whooping with delight and began punting the burning ball around. It was a mesmerising comet flying bright and orange above the luminous beach. Seth did a few trick kicks, and a header that got some cheers and yells of alarm, and then left it with the young blokes. He located the bottle of rum standing in the sand and had a decent swig.

Around him, Wangetti Beach was a wide, long sweep of sand, but it felt somehow intimate too. Here they were clustered together on a small part of the beach, surrounded by jungle-covered mountains and a sparkling ocean, with a star-spangled ceiling above. It was huge, it was wild, and he could not have felt more at home.

A saucer-eyed chick materialised by his side; a curly haired possum in a short cotton skirt and a tie-dye top. He passed her the bottle and as she drank, her eyes watching him, there was a flash of pure oneness between them. He knew that she knew that he knew that she knew that this moment had always been happening; that it was an infinite déjà vu, a holy instant beyond any beginning or end. She passed the bottle back then gasped, feeling the strength of the overproof spirits. They both laughed. Then fell silent. There was really nothing to be said.

Glowing like a young goddess under the full moon, this woman already understood everything he might have said to her and he could feel the perfect absence of explanation or talk in her too. This was communication that precluded conversation and made speech obsolete. But her eyes lit up and Seth's heart beat faster as a thought began to move her lips. They smiling at each other madly, almost giggling at her determination to hack words, in all their coarseness, out of the ocean of immeasurable feeling they were in. Her lips opened; the thought formed in her eyes – then slipped out of her mind like a raindrop off a leaf.

Her mouth was gorgeous, strong and fine, and that was enough really, because even as the words came out, he knew just what they'd be.

"It's nice acid aye?"

They hugged in agreement and she danced off.

Seth felt the LSD put the big tingle on him. He walked off down the long, long beach, his feet squeaking on the sand sounding like an invisible companion walking next to him.

The moon was overhead now, dead centre in a dome of a million stars. A few clouds hung like wisps of silver fairy floss above the horizon.

There was no wind, and all down the beach the same small wave repeatedly slapped and hissed on the sand. Seth felt like he was walking in an immense painting, his lone figure right down the bottom of the canvas.

Now a silent hum filled him with immeasurable comfort and a century or more passed while consummate peace vibrated wonderfully inside him. Relief overwhelmed his mind; creating a bliss he'd given up on.

Perfect comprehension now poured through his mind and heart and soul. A total understanding filled the space around him, breaking down the barriers between him and his surroundings, reducing everything to one boundless atom. He *was* here; just one wave in the ocean, just one grain of sand on the beach. And he need do nothing.

Then it got freaky. Hot tears fell from his eyes; tears that felt oily, dense and poisonous. Scabs and chunks of hard, toxic shit – encrustations of sorrow and regret – cracked off and dropped to the beach like dried sewer mud. It felt so real he looked down, but there was nothing around him but silver sand shimmering in the lunar glare.

It took a minute, maybe a millennium, before he knew he'd be OK – that he'd always been OK.

He wiped his eyes, breathed in the sweet salt air and the universe filled his lungs. I'm here, I'm alive and doing the best I can, he thought. That's enough.

An enormous wave had broken. Now it was returning to the sea leaving him completely soothed and utterly calm. He'd known a perfect soul-deep quietude and its profound memory would always be there for him like medicine. And who knows? – maybe he'd feel it again someday.

A great shiver ran through him. Looking back down the beach he saw the fire twinkling red and yellow, heard faint laughter and guitars. He smiled deeply, feeling bloody cosy on this long remote beach, because a beautiful mob was just over there having a good time.

It took another century to walk back to the party, but the stars overhead were closer now, alive and sympathetic. As he got nearer to the fire and dancing shadows, he realised that Marty must have spread the acid around.

A small group of people, their faces occasionally lit by the flare of cigarette lighters, were sitting in a close, dark mass on the glowing white sand; the stop-start rhythms of their trippy conversations punctuated by explosions of group hilarity. None of it made sense but it looked like great fun. A couple lay on the sand together, speechlessly looking up at heaven, and near the shoreline a bloke was sprinting up and down for no obvious reason.

Back at the party, he looked about for Melanie and saw her unrolling her bedroll. He happily floated over to her, full of compassion and care.

"Hey, Sophie how are . . ." He instantly recognised his mistake. Melanie wasn't his niece, but it felt like it.

"So how ya doing? You OK?" he said.

"Yes, I'm great thanks," said Melanie. "I'm going to lay down, look at the stars, probably fall asleep soon. It's so beautiful."

He nodded, very pleased with everything until he saw the unease creeping into her eyes. He realised then that he was standing there grinning at her like a big galoot.

"OK! Cool! Enjoy the stars. Sleep well," he said.

"Thanks," said Melanie watching him closely.

Jesus, he must look like he was off his scone, which he was, so that was alright really, and he smiled, gave her the thumbs up and went to join the last of the party.

Marty's acid had burnt up a lot of energy and those still talking didn't sound very coherent. Some people were staring blissfully into the fire; others lay around in swags murmuring to each other, and a few bods had flaked out right where they'd been sitting. Seth joined a pie-eyed Marty and Rockwell Pete and they had a disjointed and pleasant conversation about something for a while.

Aside from a group of drinkers burbling away by the fire and the giggling mob holding full telepathic court down the beach, most people had crashed out now. Giving the boys the nod, Seth went and got his swag and brought it onto the beach. He unrolled it under a beach almond where he could see Melanie. She was fast asleep, curled up like a cat; one small foot sticking out into the moonlight.

Seth drank half a canteen of water, lay down and stared up into the sky, just buzzing away. The smell of sea salt and burning driftwood was just grand. It was an aroma for the ages, a part of Seth's life since he could crawl. He felt so content, so at home, just floating here among the stars.

He awoke with a camel's thirst and gratefully sucked on his canteen until he noticed that Melanie's swag was gone.

He scanned the beach. People were still sleeping. Others, looking cheerfully dazed, shared joints and drank beers. Stasia was still making Bloody Marys, and a handful of boys and girls were swimming naked in the calm flat ocean.

He jumped up, his head a jumble. Then to his massive relief he saw Melanie appear at the mouth of the track. She'd taken her bedding back to her Kombi.

When she came up, glowing and well-rested, he saw that

her eyes were violet, not the off-blue of the photographs. He hoped he didn't stink of grog and look like rubbish.

"I'm going to say goodbye to Sarah. She's going back to Mission Beach with Davey," said Melanie.

"Davey?"

"Yeah, that's his car there."

Melanie pointed to a real beast by the tree line; a Land Cruiser with power winch, river crossing snorkel and a roof rack loaded with no-bullshit camping gear.

Seth now remembered the Alby Mangles doppelganger. That's good, he thought. Sarah wasn't going back to the house at Digger Street just yet, and when she did, it might be with a capable bloke by her side.

"And I want Stasia's phone number," said Melanie, and with the hint of taking the piss, held up a pad and a pen.

"Oh yeah, good idea. There's not much she doesn't know about the scene up here."

"She told me a few things about you."

"Yeah? All good I hope."

"You hope," said Melanie.

"But enough for you to still go to Kuranda with me?"

"Ye-s . . . just enough."

He pulled a hurt face and was pleased when it made her laugh.

VW Empire

With Melanie following, Seth drove back along the Cook Highway with the sparse morning traffic. She was on the ball, easily negotiating a few stray cows wandering on the road at Clifton Beach and she stayed on his tail when he turned off at Smithfield and drove up the winding two-lane range road. They passed through thick rainforest crowding in on the steep hillslopes, and at the top, over four hundred metres above the coast, Seth pulled over at the Henry Ross Lookout. As the Kombi van pulled in and parked in front of him, he wrote down its licence plate number.

Despite some haze from last night's cane burn-off, the view out to the Coral Sea was enormous, making Melanie ooh and ahh like he hoped it would.

"Yeah, there's lots of cool things to see up here," he said. "You'll need to take breaks from your studies to check it all out. Will they take up a lot of your time?"

"Oh, it's pretty informal."

"Sounds like my kind of study. So, where's it happen?"

"There's a house in Cairns."

"You just rock up whenever you want?"

"Not that informal. I think it will be fairly intensive."

"You'll be staying there?"

"You ask a lot of questions."

"Well I've actually been thinking about getting into what you're doing – meditation and all that."

Melanie gave him a look of deep curiosity.

"We're all searching," he said.

Those violet eyes homed in. He didn't know where to go with it, and in a blatant cop-out, he looked away; nodding reflectively as though he was pondering the mysteries of the bloody universe. In the jungle behind them a sulphur crested cockatoo squawked with derision.

"What are you looking for?" She really wanted to know.

Seth tried to think of something, but not more bullshit, and he flashed on his extraordinary epiphany last night – the dark poisonous crust falling off him, the incredible sense of release.

"Peace," he said. This time he looked her in the eye.

Melanie looked back, right *into* him; not only absorbing his unplanned honesty but also understanding it. He was rocked to the core. Without knowing any of the facts of his answer, she had got his truth – pain, grief and all.

His mind recoiled in dismay. This young chick had his number and he didn't like it at all. Fumbling for a snappy comeback, something to put her right back in her place, he saw emotion flood her eyes; a sadness and regret at what she really wanted to do, but couldn't. With perfect clarity he understood.

If Melanie had felt herself a bit older and closer to him, like Stasia perhaps – she would have hugged him out of compassion for what she'd just seen in him. And that was her truth – with all its regret and frustration at maturity yet to come. She quickly turned to look out at the blue void.

Seth felt her sadness. This was screwed up alright. He wanted to thank her for caring. He wanted her to know he understood her sorrow; that he cared about her too. But he couldn't do it. He couldn't speak. Or reach out and hug her.

So they stood there looking at the view like a couple of tourists and after a while she turned to him. Her face was wonderfully open and clear of regret now; a regeneration Seth instantly felt in himself. Thank you, he thought.

"I think you'll find peace," she said, and bless her, she sounded pretty damn confident.

"Yeah – I reckon," he said, feeling oddly comforted.

They shared a little smile and it felt conspiratorial, like something subtle but undeniably real had just happened to them. Seth had heard a lot of hippy-trippy spiritual guff in his time, but he had seen, and even felt enough to know that beautiful shit did happen sometimes. And when it did, it was best not to talk or think about it too much.

It seemed that Melanie knew about that too and in a comfortable silence they enjoyed the vista a little longer, before going back to their vehicles and continuing on up the range road.

Just before Kuranda they turned onto Black Mountain Road and Seth kept his eyes out for VW Empire. It had been a few years since he'd last been there. A kilometre up the dirt road he recognised the entrance. They turned off in a cloud of dust, went down a short track and came to a halt in a big clearing in the rainforest.

Creeper-smothered trees and tangled webs of lawyer-cane vine had constructed high, green walls around the open space. Dozens and dozens of dead Kombi vans sat on flat tires and rusted wheels in various states of decay. Big parts – doors, wheels and bumpers – lurked under lengths of rusting roofing tin and disintegrating canvas tarpaulins. Leaves, twigs and plant-dust coated everything. Five good-looking Kombis were parked in and around an open tin shed whose sides were filled in with a greasy mess of tools, van engines and work benches.

Next to the workshop was an odd dwelling made from two Kombi van bodies joined together by a corrugated-iron roof. Atop a lop-sided wood frame was an open-air kitchen: the stained stainless-steel sink, rusted gas-rings, dented pots and chipped plates all speckled with vegetate debris.

From out of the workshop emerged the shaggy haired, heavily-bearded emperor of VW Empire. Dressed in black lederhosen, battered boots and a once white dress shirt, Nils was a picture of feral freakdom. Sheened in grease, he reeked of motor oil and vintage sweat. His fingernails were black, his hands permanently tattooed with motor oil, and he frowned distractedly in welcome.

Seth's explanations didn't shift the frown, but they all stood and stared hard at Melanie's Kombi until Nils grunted with something like approval then mumbled his verdict. He had no bloody time right now to look at the engine; they would have to come back in a few days.

Looking for parts was OK though, so they made a list of things, like a cracked side-mirror and a missing window-winder handle, that they could replace themselves.

With a crude string of grunted words and gestures, Nils impatiently explained that spare-parts were stored in the unmoving herd of Kombi van bodies scattered around the clearing. The irritated mechanic shrugged in exasperation and retreated into his work shed when Seth showed him their list.

This meant they had to check inside every busted old van to locate a particular spare part. The first one was full of steering wheels, the next contained windscreen wipers. Lizards and spiders did a runner every time they opened up a decaying hulk, and Seth told Melanie to be on the alert for snakes.

As they searched Seth got back to work.

"You gonna be staying in the van?"

"Yes, it's fully set up. I just have to empty the toilet tank from time to time."

"And you're on your own?"

"What's wrong with that?"

"You want to be careful. It's like the wild west up here at times. There's some real desperates about."

"I can tell who they are."

"Is that right? But you've followed a bloke you just met at a beach party all the way up into the rain forest."

"I asked Stasia about you."

"So you did. What did she have to say about me then?"

"She said you were OK."

"Yeah, we're old mates from way back."

"She said you break girls' hearts and men's bones."

"Nice. That didn't scare you?"

"Maybe if it was the other way around."

Seth laughed. The kid was funny.

"Breaking hearts and bones hey?" he said. "Sounds like something for my gravestone."

"You'll come up with something better I'm sure."

"As long it's not too strenuous."

"Strenuous usually results in better."

"Yeah that's right – you're good at school hey?"

"Amazing. You seem to know lots about someone you've just met. It's just like picking who's the bad man and who's not, right?"

Seth acknowledged the point with a bow of the head.

"No, you're smart mate. You talked so well about whales migrating last night, and wanting to study marine biology at uni means you've got a brain in your head."

Melanie opened another Kombi door and looked in. He waited for a reply but none came. Maybe she doesn't like compliments, he thought.

He suddenly caught sight of an animal right near them. You beauty, he thought, she's going to love this.

"Hey Melanie, look up there!"

Draped along a big tree limb was a multi-coloured snake.

"Wow! Is that a python?" said Melanie.

"Sure is. An amethystine."

She was rapt, and Seth was rapt with that. This was like showing his little niece something cool.

"Yeah it's a small one," he explained. "They can grow up to twenty-five um . . . eight metres long."

While they admired it, he told her a couple of true-life python tales that made her gasp and her eyes widen in awe. He loved that. Then they got back to looking for parts.

"I'm going to ask the mechanic when he can look at my engine," said Melanie. "If he can't do it this coming week, I'll find someone else."

Straight up, Seth thought of Gunther's in Cairns. Not as cheap as Nils of course. But he said nothing. Not yet.

"I'll be back in a minute," said Melanie and she headed off through the van infested clearing.

Seth opened the door of the next Kombi shell. It was stacked with gearshifts, but at the back was a rogue box of window winder handles. He banged a couple of gearshifts around to scare any beasties away and got inside the van. Leaning over, he wrestled the box of handles closer and began to sort through them, looking for the best specimen.

A Kombi started up, probably Nils testing an engine, but when the sound went down the drive towards the road he knew it was Melanie.

Jumping from the van he hotfooted it to the driveway, but Melanie's Kombi was gone. Dust was now rising above the trees a hundred metres up the road.

Nils was laughing. "Pretty girl but you too old!"

Seth ran to the Pig. The keys were gone. Damn it, she'd taken them! He heard Nils calling out. The mechanic was pointing to a patch of oily ground.

"She trow 'em dere!"

Seth rushed over and after a mad minute found his keys. Nils was still hooting with laughter as he roared out of VW Empire.

He pushed the Pig hard, speeding down Black Mountain Road, knowing he had a choice when he got to the turnoff.

Melanie was either heading back down the range to the coast or she was crossing the Barron River into Kuranda and maybe even further on to Mareeba and the Tablelands. At the intersection he chose the coast and drove crazy fast, overtaking cars, knowing his more powerful vehicle would catch her before she got to the Cook Highway.

Near the bottom of the mountain he knew he'd made the wrong choice. Throwing up stones, he turned around on a gravelly pull-over and rocketed back up the range. His only chance now was if she were going to the Tablelands. If she was, he'd catch her somewhere this side of Mareeba.

But if she'd turned off in Kuranda, or anywhere else on the Kennedy Highway, it would become a cat-and-mouse game of checking every dirt road and overgrown track, a game the cat was bound to lose.

He drove nearly all the way to Mareeba before pulling over. He swore loudly then went back to Kuranda, where like a headless chook he cruised every street and unsealed road, even going down the sandy trails that lead to the swimming spots on the Barron River.

Bumping back up to Myola Road on the deep ruts of the track from Big Sands, he belatedly accepted the truth. He'd bloody well lost her.

Now low on fuel, he went back into Kuranda. While he filled up at the servo a young hitchhiker came up to him.

"Hey brother – you going to the Tablelands?"

"Nah, sorry mate."

"Oh man! I've been here for hours."

"You see a green Kombi go past? Lime-green?"

"Yeah, I seen it."

The young fella pointed across the Kennedy Highway to an overgrown driveway that vanished into trees.

"It drove in there for a bit. Then went back Cairns way."

"How long ago?"

"About an hour ago. A real sweetheart was driving."

Seth paid for the fuel and found some relief in a mango Weis bar. While he ate, leaning against the ticking hot Pig, he fruitlessly went over what he'd said to spook Melanie into running. Some private eye he was.

As he finished the ice-block he felt a grudging respect. The girl had made all the right choices evading him. In fact, she'd done everything he would have done.

Rascal Guru

Seth hated feeling dirty and hungry, so as punishment for his slack performance he didn't go home for a shower and a feed. Instead, he went to Everknell Street.

As he drove there, he listened to 4CA news, but there was no big drug-bust story. He bought a Cairns Post from the newsagent at the Edge Hill shops. The only crime story that caught his eye was a blatant rip-off at The House of Ten Thousand Shells. A 'hippy type' had calmly strolled off with three seashells worth a grand total of seventeen hundred bucks. Seventeen hundred bucks! He was in the wrong bloody business.

In a phone box outside the shops, he got his notepad out, found Peggy's number in Sydney then put a handful of twenty cent pieces to work.

"Hey Peggy, it's Seth. I saw Melanie."

"Really? How was she? Did you talk to her?"

"Yes, I did. She looked fine and healthy, so don't worry about that. She hasn't caught up with Jessop yet."

"That's wonderful news Seth. So where is she now?"

"Yeah . . . well, she gave me the slip. She bought a Kombi van and I went with her to get some spare parts and have it looked at. But somehow she cottoned on to what I was doing and took off."

Down the faint hiss of the line came suspicion.

"Oh really," said Peggy and the guarded tone of her voice resuscitated his shame from last night. She knew just how attractive her daughter was.

Continuing with his report, he quickly sketched out the party at Wangetti and how Melanie didn't drink or smoke. He left out the unprofessional bits, like dropping acid, but when he began describing what happened at VW Empire, he realised his mistake.

"Ahhh right – now I know."

"What? What is it?" said Peggy.

"I know how she figured it out. I mentioned her marine biology course at uni. You had it in your notes but she never told me about it."

"What did she say about that?"

"Nothing. I was looking for a part for her van and she took my car keys from the ignition, threw them away and drove off."

"Oh, Melanie," said Peggy.

"She was too smart for me."

Peggy laughed and so did he. It felt better between them now and he gave her a pep-talk. It worked, and when he hung up he felt worthy again, his shame gone. Believe and be, he told himself. Just believe and be.

Over at Everknell Street he spent two hours watching nothing happen and that felt like enough punishment for now. It was probably too late for the mail run in Edge Hill, but tomorrow he'd catch up with the postie and give him a new, lime-green assignment.

He drove into town, hooked up two mackerel burgers, and ate them by the cab-rank outside the railway station. Drinkers across the road at the Railway Hotel, some blind-drunk, were out the front yelling and carrying on. Someone lay insensible on the ground, their trousers dark and wet at the crotch. Cop an eyeful of that, tourists, thought Seth.

Eventually Harry Spinks pulled up. Seth went over and gave him two twenties.

"That's for finding the Daihatsu and this is for the lime-green Kombi camper I'm looking for now."

"Mate! If this keeps up, I might chuck in driving cabs." The old cabbie grinned like a plump grey-haired cat. Seth wrote down the Kombi's licence number for him, and gave him two more twenties.

"What's this for? A white Mercedes? A blue Toyota?"

"Spread it around the other cabbies please. The young woman driving the Kombi could be in serious trouble."

Spinks gave him a compassionate grimace.

"That doesn't sound too good. I'll get on the radio now."

Seth went to Portsmith, found the tow-truck driver and put him onto the Kombi. In Bungalow he stopped at a tin-roofed, metal-frame workshop that was full of motorbikes.

Inside the sweltering hot shed Knoxie was working on a beaut BSA Spitfire, and he greeted Seth with a sweaty grin. Putting down a socket wrench, he went and got two cans of Solo from a rusting fridge. The drinks were light on fizz so they slammed them down fast.

"Scratch the purple Daihatsu – it's a lime-green Kombi now." Seth wrote the licence number down for his mate.

"A Kombi? That's better, but only just."

"So Knoxie, you got a mate with wheels and no work on? I'll give 'em twenty-five a day to look for this Kombi."

"Sure, I'll ask around, but hey – here's something I heard around the ridges. Those Sydney bastards pushing smack we talked about? Well, someone's bashed a couple of them at Gary Sparks' old place. Fuckin' great I reckon."

Yeah, that was me, Seth almost said. He trusted Knoxie, no worries at all there, but it was best to keep a low profile right now. Like with minding the bands – it wasn't just him on the firing line.

The sun had dipped behind the Lamb Range in the west and everything was in shadow. It was finally time to have that shower. Driving home along Sheridan Street, Seth saw a man hitchhiking north; a bearded bloke dressed in white with longish hair. It was Arnold bloody Jessop. Ignoring a sensible voice in his ear, Seth pulled over.

He had to laugh. Jessop could afford a car or a taxi, and there were local buses too, but here he was hitch-hiking; a rich man playing poor, a bullshit Jesus walking the streets hoping to get a ride with someone vulnerable and stupid enough to get hooked on his new-age crap. Sort of like the way smack dealers operated.

Seth leaned across and opened the door.

"Hop in mate," he said and Arnold Jessop did.

Up close and personal, he cut a fine figure; his beard and long hair barber-trimmed, his clothes well-made. He smelt of good cologne, the beads around his neck looked antique and valuable, and the chunky bangle on his wrist was solid gold. Yep, this bastard scrubbed up well.

Jessop smiled in greeting and it was an intense thing, radiating outwards like a Catherine wheel on Guy Fawkes night. His teeth were perfect, but his eyes were something else. Penetratingly blue, they pulsed with excitement and joy; celebrating the wonderous glory of the world. Most of all – they were irresistibly inclusive. These eyes said with absolute clarity that you were *in*, that you were *down* with this man – right from the get-go.

Seth checked the traffic and pulled out. He'd seen fellas with this kind of charisma before. Musicians, dealers and criminals who could inspire, direct, and ultimately control people. Alex had been a master at it.

Maybe picking up Jessop wasn't such a good idea, and like a psychic ferret, the guru latched right onto that.

"No, no, it was good and kind of you to stop. Many are fearful but your heart is open."

"All good mate. Where ya off to?"

"Edge Hill, but the Collins Avenue turn off is fine."

"I'm going to Brinsmead," Seth lied. "I'll drop you where you like."

"Thank you so much. Are you a boxer?"

"Aye? My nose is straight, isn't it?"

"Maybe you are as skilled as you are noble looking."

"Listen mate, you're getting a lift – that's all."

"No, please don't take offence. I'm not that way inclined at all. I only notice you are in good shape."

Seth glanced at Arnold Jessop. There was no shame or apology, confusion or fear in his shining eyes. This bloke was dead-set sure of himself. Seth resolved to keep his eyes on the road. Jessop was right onto that too.

"Don't be fearful. I meant no rudeness. I see you are not only strong in body but awake as well."

"Bloody hope so – otherwise we'd be in the ditch."

Jessop ignored that and went on.

"You see the world clearly my friend, as clearly as any of us can. You see me, like I see you."

I should tell him I see he's full of shit, thought Seth, but he knew it wouldn't work. Jessop would ignore the insult and keep talking; the sheer is-ness of his attitude having its own volition. Short of shouting 'shut up' or kicking him out of the car, there was no way Jessop would stop with his humbuggery.

"I see it in your face," said Jessop. "You've been living in shadows and so have I. All of us, every brother, every sister, shares the same love, but unfortunately – the same fear and sadness too. And so, we all seek the light."

His voice, educated but blunt, had a natural rhythm that tugged at Seth's attention.

"There's only ever been light, but we are conditioned to recognise light by the shadows around it. One doesn't exist without the other, right? Good and evil, yin and yang. That is *not* true. Foolishly, we keep to the shadows in order to see the light. Stupidly, we keep that light *above* us, as something to strive for, to *go* to. But the light is always here, always *in* us. We don't need shadows to see it at all."

Jessop's words filled the truck's cabin like incense smoke in a hippy tepee. Seth stared at the road ahead.

"If you live your life in the shadows you will come to see their colours and it is *all* colours. A spectrum of shadows, endless and mesmerising, so vivid and absorbing. But the colour of shadows is the colour of delusion. The colour of shadows is illusion, made in any form you wish to create. It is the perfect lie, because not only is the answer false – the question is too."

Seth concentrated, but the traffic flickered and wobbled. Odd dark shapes snaked through guinea-grass alongside the road and palm trees clawed at the deep blue sky. Like a worm burrowing into his brain, Jessop's voice went on.

"The colour of shadows is the ultimate manifestation of fear because, as you know – pure light has no colour at all."

Seth was being overpowered. He had to do something.

"You like rock'n'roll?" he asked.

The unrelenting love in Jessop's intense eyes flickered then returned in a flash. But the pure blue was now subtly stained with judgement.

"Rock and roll? No, I can't say I do. It's rather primitive don't you think?" he said.

"Fuckin' oath," said Seth, turning the Clarion car stereo up full and thumbing the cassette home.

Van Halen's take on 'You Really Got Me Now' exploded through the truck's cab; the riff like a lava-spitting monster emerging from a volcano.

Jessop jerked in shock, tried to speak over the music, but Seth ignored him. When Eddie's guitar solo kicked in, the rascal guru indicated he wanted to get out.

Seth pulled over near the Collins Avenue turn-off and as he got out, Jessop gestured for Seth to turn the music down so he could say something. His piercing eyes began to arc up in anticipation of speaking, but Seth winked and waved good bye. It was bloody childish really, but man it was fun.

Back home he finally got his shower, revelling in the hot soapy bliss. While he knocked up and ate dinner – five fat pork bangers from Walsh's with steamed buttered carrots and mashed spuds spiked a deep green with a handful of parsley, chives and basil from the garden – he listened to The Who's pyrotechnics in Leeds, unfailingly amazed at the sheer level of sound those boys put out.

At news time he flicked the stereo over to 4CA but it was just more shit about the upcoming federal election. The cops raiding Everknell Street? Yeah sure. It was time to forget about that.

After he'd eaten, he washed up, made a pot of tea, and listened to another live album – the Allmans raising the roof at Fillmore East. Over the rock'n'roll rapture, coming from band and fans alike, his ears listened for the sound of the phone.

How many calls have I missed? An answering machine would be the go, he thought. Like the one in The Tyger's record company office. It wouldn't be cheap though. Better still – a phone right in his car, but only the presidents of countries and big corporations could afford one of them. What would they cost – twenty, thirty grand?

Yeah right, money. Seth grabbed his notepad and totted up what he'd spent. He still had Jeffyman's money, which he'd keep for bills, but more than a third of Peggy's money was gone.

Keeping track of dough was always smart, but this had never been just a job. He'd met Melanie now and the idea of Jessop prying in her head, let alone her pants, made his blood boil. This was as serious as it got. This was family.

When the last notes of Whipping Post had faded from the L150s, he took the needle off the record, sat in silence and thought about Arnold Jessop and his young muscle. He had to neutralise them; cut their balls off. But how?

Then a cheeky idea darted into his head like a streaker at the cricket. What if he stole the briefcase?

He laughed out loud. What a ripper! That would fling the shit amongst the pigeons! Jessop might very well think Briefcase Boy had ripped him off.

Yes, it was a great plan. The hanging about and watching was just too bloody passive for him. This was action; this was actually doing something.

In the morning he'd sneak in through the bush that came down onto the back of the Jessop property, nip in, and nick the briefcase.

As a bonus, Jessop, though rich, would definitely feel a dent in his wallet losing those drugs. But most of all, Seth wanted to freak that little bastard, Briefcase Boy, right the fuck out.

Four Inch Python

Seth woke buzzing with excitement, and this happy state of affairs prevailed throughout breakfast and a watering of the front and back gardens. While repeatedly whistling the chorus to Waterloo Sunset, he assembled a break-in kit: a small prybar, Phillips-head and slotted screwdrivers, and a pair of thin leather gloves. This all went into a small duffle bag which he stashed in the back of the Pig. Dressing in old, green army pants and a khaki t-shirt, he dug out a pair of Blundstones and put them by the front door.

Mad keen to leave, he made another cuppa instead. The streets in Edge Hill would be active right now with workers and school-kids leaving home. He planned to park the Pig in the next street over to Everknell. A strange vehicle parking, with its driver then going into the bush, was not a good look. Best to wait for the morning traffic to settle.

He put on an album that Laidlaw, his strange mate from Sydney, had sent him. It was a Japanese guitar wiz named Masayoshi Takanaka. This fella played impeccably, with a super-tight band and it was very sweet, sometimes a bit too sweet. After that, he took it sideways with another Laidlaw selection – Zappa's Zoot Allures. Suitably refreshed by its bizarre brilliance, he pulled on his boots and headed off.

He'd come just a few hundred metres from the Machans turn-off when a red Corolla station wagon on the other side of the Cook Highway slowed right down while sounding its horn. Seth saw two women in the car. One looked familiar, and as they passed by, he heard her yelling out his name. Pulling off the highway, he got out and watched the Corolla stop by the roadside and wait for the traffic to clear.

There was sugarcane all around, the unharvested fields stretching towards Kamerunga. It was hot already and Seth could smell something dead in the rainwater ditch between the road and the cane.

The station wagon did a U-turn and pulled in behind his car. The passenger got out. It was Mick's missus, Pam.

She didn't look too happy and he immediately flashed on young Debbie. Bloody hell, he thought uneasily, don't tell me she's done something stupid because of me.

Pam walked up, tight-lipped, her hands shoved into the back pockets of her jeans.

"Hey Pam, what's up? You alright?"

She shook her head. Behind her, the woman in the car was staring at them, her face pinched and grim. Seth's bad feeling got worse.

"What's happened?"

"I got a call from Mick. He told me to get out."

"Get out?" said Seth. "Out of the house?"

"Out of Cairns. Out of Queensland."

Fear clipped her words.

"Something bad has happened to him Seth. I could tell by his voice and he hung up on me too."

Seth moved forward, putting out a comforting arm. Pam stepped back.

"What did he say?"

"He told me to grab what I needed and get out. He said do it now – go back to Western Australia. He was scared. I've known that man for nearly six years now and I've never heard him sound like that."

"Did he say why?"

"No. I think he was interrupted. He hung up on me."

Seth pushed his fingers through his hair, squeezing his skull. Around them the dead animal stink was strong.

"You knew what he was doing, yeah?" he said.

Pam nodded. "I'm going to catch the Sunlander down to Brisbane then I'm flying out to Perth. Mick made me swear that I'd go, but what about him?"

Seth nodded slowly, his mind racing.

"Can you find him? Find out what's happened?"

"Jesus, Pam, I don't know where to look."

Pam pulled one hand out of her pocket. In it was a piece of paper and she gave it to Seth.

It was a hand-drawn map showing a valley out west, close to the Mitchell River, with distances, landmarks and the grower's camp marked in Mick's untidy scrawl. At the bottom was a non-Queensland phone number in blue biro.

He looked back up. Pam's face was set in stone but her eyes were screaming.

"Yeah, no worries Pam," he said. "I'll go get him."

"That's my phone number in W.A." She pointed at the map. "I'll be there by the weekend."

Seth nodded.

"Listen Seth, no matter what's happened to him, even if he's . . . I need to know."

"I promise Pam."

She took a deep shivery breath and hurried back to the Corolla. As it pulled out and passed him, Seth leant out and patted her arm. He could tell by her face that a hundred metres down the road she'd be crying her eyes out.

It hadn't taken him more than a few seconds to work out what to do. He had to go and find his mate. Now.

He wouldn't take the Pig up there – he didn't want no bastard recognising it later, so he took it back home and got a taxi into Cairns. At the car hire joint, dressed in the straightest old clothes he could find, wearing sunnies and a floppy hat, he presented the fake driver's licence he'd confiscated off a bloke in Sydney to the nice lady in the office. This piece of card with someone's signature on it did the trick.

There was a Suzuki Jimny for him, nothing like the Pig of course, but the hire-car company logo on the side would allow him to make out he was a lost tourist if he had to. Maybe Gunnar from Sweden out spotting wildlife. He was big and blonde, and if he spoke gutturally and mangled his words then who the hell would know any different?

He drove the little 4WD back to his place and loaded it up with a full twenty-litre water container, a ten by twelve canvas tarp and some old camouflage netting.

He made sandwiches, grabbed some bananas and filled up the three water canteens he owned. These provisions went into his pack, along with binoculars, a first aid kit, a folding knife and a blanket. Over his t-shirt he put on a sleeveless army shirt with big pockets. He got sunglasses and a floppy bush hat, and swapped the Blundstones for his good hiking boots.

Yep, he was a wildlife-freak now, out searching for the perentie, the two-metre-long lizard sometimes spotted in the dry country out west. He'd never seen one himself but Gunnar just might.

A compass and Mick's map went into a pocket in the army shirt. A hundred bucks went into his wallet, and he put the rest of the money, along with the keys to the Pig, into the waterproof stash in his back garden.

He made a short phone-call then locked up. He got in the hire-car. Breathing nice and slowly, he considered what awaited him out west. Blokes with firearms basically. He had the gun he'd kept from Digger Street with him and he examined it. What he saw didn't look real flash.

First up, the Smith & Wesson's six-inch barrel was too long for his pockets. It had also been banged-around. The T-shaped front sight was mashed on one side and when he sighted down the gun's length, he saw the cylinder was out of whack. It was probably dangerous. And it was a .22. He'd be better off throwing rocks.

He started the Jimny's little engine and headed off. The Mitchell River was a good six hours drive away. He'd get there mid-afternoon, but he was going to Kuranda first. He needed some firepower. He needed to see Les.

There must be a lot of smart fellas on the planet, but Seth hadn't figured on meeting too many of them in Far North Queensland. It was a wild and rough place, often the end of the line for people not born and bred there. So, beyond the trials and tribulations of the natural world, and the need for simple pleasures, most locals were unquestioning of their place in the cosmos – and of just about everything else.

It was a real privilege then, to be friends with Les, a man whose huge intelligence was only matched by his capacity to manipulate the physical world. With patience, bone-dry humour and an ever-critical eye intent on perfection, this amazing bloke had taught Seth a whole lot over the years.

Like how to shoot a gun. They'd spent countless hours at the gun club at Edmonton, out in the bush and on remote beaches, cycling rounds through a big selection of pistols and long guns. The older man had inculcated in him a respect and love for firearms.

When Seth first met him, Les had been serving in the Army, with several long deployments to the war in South East Asia. It would have undoubtedly been heavy-duty, but Les rarely, if ever, spoke of what he'd seen and experienced there. When he finally got his discharge, he'd moved to Kuranda, and he and Seth had become better friends.

Les also loved working on machines, cars and electrical gear. When he wasn't doing something with his hands, he'd exercise his gray matter reading manuals and schematics, historical books, scientific journals and magazines; often with an album from his extensive collection of classical music spinning on the Marantz turntable.

For a crust he took rich blokes hunting up on Cape York, and in an unofficial capacity Les helped out the authorities and many others with anything to do with firearms and ballistics. The considerable contents of his cranium were in demand, and it seemed that a whole network of blokes – policemen, coroners, nashos and regular army boys, gun enthusiasts and hunters – all called upon Les' help from time to time. Right now, Seth was one of those blokes.

Stuck behind a Whitecars coach going up the range, he finally passed it up the top. At Kuranda he saw a gaggle of hippies by the servo divvying up a pouch of tobacco. Just out of town he turned right onto Myola Road and drove to Fairyland. He turned off onto Les's long driveway and the forest closed in. After a minute or so of bouncing down the unsealed track he came out into a wide clearing, parked by the big corrugated iron workshop, and got the revolver out of the stash under the dash.

Before he went over to the house, he had a sticky-beak in the shed. A Peugeot 504 pick-up was being worked on and from the look of the shavings on a work bench, Les had been doing something with wood – maybe crafting a rifle stock. From a rafter by the edge of the open shed hung the furry tear-drop of a sunbird's nest. Watching closely, Seth saw the little chicks' beaks poking out. Too bloody cute.

In the one-level house, orchestral music poured from the heavy Tannoy Buckinghams mounted in each corner of the living room. The welcome smell of brewing coffee filled the air. Les was at the table outside reading a battered looking book. As Seth came over, he looked up over the top of his granny glasses and softly smiled.

He was slightly built but fit and brown. As usual, he was in nothing but a pair of faded khaki shorts. On the skin by his collar-bone were two shiny white indentations; bullet scars from the war.

They shook hands, went inside and Les turned the music down. In the kitchen, something spicy bubbled gently in a cast-iron pot.

"I'm making some kusundi," Les explained. "Goes with eggs, cheese – most meats. How's your father?"

"He's good," lied Seth. "I reckon we'll go for a fish soon. Get some bream, maybe a barra."

It had been weeks since he'd last spoken to his father and he'd visited him just three times since he'd got back. He was a coward for not going more often, but Dad's decline had depressed him. And the family home held too many memories. He'd have to forget a lot of them before he'd feel comfortable about spending time there again.

Les gave the kusundi a stir, poured two mugs of coffee, and they sat down at the black bean wood table in the living room. It was covered in small tools and manuals, piles of shooting magazines, bottles of Ballistol and oily scraps of rag. Seth put the revolver on the table.

"I found this the other day," he said.

Poker-faced, Les examined it, opening and closing the cylinder a few times before giving his verdict.

"An unloved child whose foolish parents have watched too many movies. See, the crane is damaged, sprung from snapping the cylinder open and closed with one hand. You wouldn't want to use it in its present condition."

"Any good to you?"

"I never send away an orphan."

"So, Les – could you lend me a gun?"

Les sipped his coffee and looked down at the revolver on the table. Outside in the trees, fig-eaters called raucously.

"What do you want?" he said without looking up.

Seth had already bullshitted Les about his father, so he decided to stick reasonably close to the truth.

"A handgun. Something scary sounding."

"Scary?"

"Yeah, it's a deterrent."

Les now regarded him with soft brown eyes.

"What are you doing for work?" he said.

Like the war in South East Asia, growing dope crops was not something they talked about, but he was pretty sure his old friend knew what he'd been up to over the years.

"It's to help out a mate," said Seth. "I've got to front a few idiots. It's basically for show and a loud bang maybe."

Les scratched his chin as though trying to dislodge the faint frown now on his face. Seth was prepared to tell him more, but only if he had to.

"OK," said Les. "How does a four-inch Python sound?"

"Scary," said Seth.

"Some new shooting magazines there," said Les. "Have a gander at the Benelli. Now that's a high-precision tool."

Les went outside. He had at least a dozen firearms locked tight in gun-safes in the house, but he also had unlicensed ones in waterproof secrecy somewhere on the property.

Seth spent fifteen minutes looking at magazines before Les came back. He wordlessly put a Colt Python revolver on the table, and then went up the hallway to his loading room.

Well, this was the business, thought Seth, picking up the gun. It felt good and solid in the hand; the trigger-pull just perfect. The only drawback was the shiny nickel finish that would glitter in the sun.

Les returned with a speed loader and a plastic box of .357 magnum bullets. Seth looked at the ammo. It was hollow point – knock-down combat rounds.

"Hell's bells Les, I'm not looking for trouble."

"It's when you're not that you have to be prepared for it."

It sounded like a dusty old army maxim, but beneath his mild exterior, Les was an ice-cold man. Seth had seen just how ice-cold, one hot, humid day in thick rainforest up on the slopes of Black Mountain. A couple of blokes with blood on their minds had decided to hunt Les and him as though they were feral pigs. Big mistake.

"Now Seth," said Les. "I don't know the provenance of this wheel gun. While you have it, every shot it's ever made will belong to you."

Seth understood. Though he had no criminal record and his pistol license was up to date, this unregistered gun, if found on him and tested ballistically, would make him the prime suspect for any crime it had been used in.

"Gotcha Les," said Seth.

"Good. Once you've put the frighteners into whoever it is that needs it, you can return it to me."

"Sure thing Les. I should've just got a replica gun hey?"

"No." Les's eyes were hard as steel. "You're in a hire-car and that tells me completely otherwise."

The Mitchell

Seth pulled off the seemingly endless road and looked at Mick's map again. Yep, it was time to walk in. He drove into the scrub for a few hundred metres, heading for a dip in the ground where he stopped and turned off the engine.

He listened to the dry, desiccated landscape. Aside from the occasional rising insect hum there was silence. Not too many birds out here. Bad country for a feed.

Using a compass and topographical map he planned his route, and then filled the speed-loader with bullets. He put it and the box of ammo in a shirt pocket. For now, the Colt Python stayed in his pack. The air was stinking hot out here and he drank mugs of water from the 20-litre drum. He covered the Jimny with the tarp to kill any reflections, and over that went the camo netting. It wasn't perfect, but if anyone on the road wasn't actively searching for him, the little 4WD should remain unseen.

Seth put on his floppy green hat, shrugged on his pack and started walking to the ridge line a kilometre away. Up there he'd follow it west and hopefully it wouldn't be long before he came to the head of the valley shown on Mick's map. Halfway down this valley was the growers' camp.

It took him thirty minutes with the dusty scree slipping underfoot to get to the ridgetop. Using the binoculars, he checked the road below him all the way to the horizon, seeing no distant dust clouds or reflective glints.

Out west were endless rows of sun-baked hills; a devil's playground of harsh gullies and rocks so sharp they tore good boots to shreds. This was country to knock you; an open-air graveyard for miners and prospectors back in the day.

He had a first drink from his canteen. Carrying just three litres all up, he'd need to detour to the Mitchell River for more at some stage.

Back into it, he walked just below the backbone of the ridge, gliding around rocky outcrops and the furry grey trunks of stringybark eucalyptus. He passed small stands of hardy plants that were hundreds of years old – grass trees – their stubby black trunks topped with a ball of green and silver leaves from which projected a flower-stalk spear.

Striding along, his eyes flickered over the ground, alert for serpentine shapes. Taipans were entirely possible out here, but these rocky ridges were perfect terrain for death adders. They didn't always use their venom, but a flurry of wet strikes from one of those chunky bastards could leave him dying in the dust.

An hour later the head of the valley marked on Mick's map began taking shape below him and he tramped along its southern ridge for ninety minutes. Now he began stopping every twenty minutes to scan the valley below. On the third time he saw a flicker of light maybe a kilometre away. This glint appeared at irregular intervals, like the intermittent breeze on his face. Yep, it was a body of water seen through distant moving leaves – the Mitchell River.

When he next stopped to look, it was in the deep blue-black shadow of basalt boulders. He had to be careful now to not stand out against the skyline for any watcher down below to see. Avoiding sudden movements, he slowly swept the valley floor with the binoculars, looking for the green pattern of maturing marijuana plants, and for any man-made colours.

Using a mental grid, he finally spotted faintly defined double lines, incrementally lighter on the dusty ground. Scanning the surrounding area, he made out, bit by bit, the path of a track worn by the tires of recent vehicles. Busted. Lucky for them he wasn't the cops.

It was time for the Python to come out, for as sure as pigs were made of bacon, there was somewhere up ahead – the unwelcoming party.

The gun, first checked, went into his tunic pocket. He ate a banana and one sandwich, finished the first canteen and swapped it for a full one. After a good look and listen, he drifted quietly down through the stringybarks to the valley floor, his eyes searching for tripwires attached to bells or tins full of stones.

Every two minutes he stopped to look and listen, totally alert for the slightest anomaly. Half an hour later he heard a faint voice and sunk down on his haunches. Using the binoculars to scan ahead he saw nothing but dirt and scrub. He slowly moved forward, aware of every leaf and twig underfoot; stopped and looked again. Rising from a fold in the land was a shit-load of marijuana plants.

Grunting appreciatively at the sight, he moved in closer. The plants were of decent height, each one already bearing good-sized heads. Crouching down, he snuck along parallel to the plants. After ten minutes, with no end in sight, the full scale of the crop sunk in. This was tons of dope. This was acres of money. People would kill for this.

Returning to the ridge took some time; the sense of a scoped rifle aiming at his back strong. Extra careful now, he resumed the pattern of walking, stopping to use the binoculars on the landscape below, and then moving on.

The valley had opened out, its far side shimmering in the afternoon heat. On his third scan he spotted something. A straight green edge – a sliver of tent roof. Then the brown side of a fruit box. He'd found the camp.

Creeping up to a big dark pool of shadow under a jutting outcrop, he sat down in its cover and had a good look.

Under a stand of ghost gums and acacia, half hidden in a gully, were several ex-army tents, Mick's J45 Toyota and the khaki coloured Land Cruiser from the other day. The vehicle's outlines were broken up by camouflage netting. It all helped as the cops had a couple of surveillance planes and sometimes called in Army choppers.

Seth eased off his pack, slowly sat down and had a good drink of water. The camp was empty; the boys out in the heat, guarding and tending to all that money.

Time passed. Then a little red-headed finch appeared, curious at the human presence. Seth winked at it and the bird flew off, leaving him alone to wait for the sun to fall.

The heat was finally losing its punch when voices came from below. Seth kept the binoculars to his eyes. Bit by bit, men arrived at the camp. He knew one – Lionel Gorrie, a Tableland farmer's son turned marijuana grower, and he recognised Smiley, the driver from Leafgold Weir Road. He didn't have his sawn-off Browning with him but Seth knew it couldn't be far. But where the hell was Mick?

Now he heard a trailbike. It sounded like a nicely tuned Yamaha 250, and sure enough, Mick's green bike came into the camp trailing a plume of dust. Relief washed over him, but when the rider pulled off his helmet, Seth stared in shock. It wasn't Mick.

Some other bastard was riding his bike.

An icy coldness spread through his guts, numbing him. Nah, nah, nah – don't think that, he told himself. You don't know anything yet. Clearing his mind took real effort, but he managed to do it. Then he sat and watched. Night fell. The crop-sitters cooked up a feed on gas burners, ate and washed up. A few fellas shared a bottle of rum, smoking and talking. The rest crashed out.

In the darkness Seth felt the fear coming back. Breathing heavily, he pushed back hard, keeping an iron fist down on his panic. Do something, he thought, *do* something.

He took a couple of sandwiches from the pack and ate them slowly, just digging the simple pleasure of the food in his mouth. I've been eating Malanda cheese since I was a kid, he reflected. I love this stuff.

After a few rationed gulps of water from the canteen he made a cushion with his blanket, laid back against a rock and closed his eyes.

At first his mind stayed blank and that was good, but sleep didn't come. Now he fought the urge to sneak down into the camp and grab someone. He'd gag them and drag them out into the scrub and make them talk; tell him where the hell Mick was. It was a stupid idea, but he let it run around and around inside his head until sleep came.

When he awoke, the eastern sky was touched with light. He put the blanket back in his pack, ate his last sandwich and drank some water. Dawn now lit the landscape. In this first, fragile light Seth watched the camp.

As the sun rose, yawning, scratching men emerged from tents and swags, some going for a slash, others hacking and spitting before their first cigarette. Presently the sound of early morning small-talk, the clink of mugs and spoons, and the smell of coffee drifted up to the ridge.

Finally, Seth lowered the binoculars and forced himself to face the music. Mick wasn't down there. Two images flashed hard and strong in his mind — that little bloke Smiley with his Auto 5 shotgun, and Mick's body, covered in flies at the bottom of a lonely gully.

Overwhelming realisation held him down while despair stuck the knife in. He felt a horrible tearing inside. Mick had been knocked off – he knew it in his bones. Turning on his arse in the dirt, he numbly looked back up the valley he'd come down. So that was it. He'd just go home now, ring Pam in a couple of days and tell her Mick was dead.

The fuck he would! He'd go down there and shoot Smiley dead. An eye for an eye and all that shit. He'd get payback or die trying. Rage sent a welcome blast of energy up his spine into his head. His heart pounded with fury. This was what he needed.

But the Auto 5 trumped the Python, and the other blokes undoubtedly had guns too. OK, he could go back to Les, get a scoped rifle and then wait in ambush on the road. But there'd be other blokes travelling in the Land Cruiser who'd be maimed or killed when a dead Smiley rolled the truck, or ran it off the road.

Seth groaned. It was all bullshit anyway. He'd dished out many floggings; breaking bones and knocking blokes out, but, as far as he knew, he'd never killed a man. Mick was his mate, one of the best, but he didn't have the guts to kill for him. He couldn't do it.

Full of self-loathing, he sprung up and rubbed his face, trying to push the rotten truth out of his skull. Looking around at the soft yellow light hitting the trees, he felt utter desolation howling inside. He wanted to scream out loud. Death had come again – stealing Mick this time. Stupid, salty water stung his eyes, and ashamed of it, he quickly wiped his face.

Now he heard men's urgent yells. One then two trail bikes exploded into life in the camp below. The rising sun had thrown the ridge line, and his movements, into stark relief. Like a right proper bunny — he'd been spotted.

Whipping up the binoculars he saw down in the camp a man looking through binoculars right back at him. The trail bikes were gone, leaving clouds of dust, and he could hear one coming up the valley floor, the other racing on the track out; aiming to catch him if he came down the other side of the ridge. Binoculars man and a fella with a rifle ran to the Land Cruiser. They were going to blockade the road where the hire-car was hidden.

Fighting back a giddy surge of panic, Seth stuffed the binoculars into his pack, swung it over his shoulders and started running. Dodging the manic fear rearing up inside, he grabbed at ice-cold self-control, got it and held onto it. The fear, anger and regret vanished as he distilled his every thought and emotion into the hi-octane survival fuel of *be here now*.

He'd been a bloody fool, that's for sure, but for the time being he needed to have a crack at staying alive.

Focused now, he ran below the crest of the ridge to hide his moving silhouette. Hearing the sputtering whine of the two-stroke motor on the valley floor, he flashed that there would be two blokes on the bike; one a shooter who would get dropped off ahead to bush-wack him.

With boots thudding on the dirt and sweat springing up between his shoulder blades, Seth kept up a manic pace for a good fifteen minutes. But running off-balance along the slope was getting too hard, so he ran up to the ridgeline; chancing becoming a better target in order to gain more speed.

Running the ridge was better, but at intervals, boulders and scarps slowed him down. Under a rock crag he paused to catch his breath. Out to the west the view was enormous. The soft, early-morning sunlight made those deadly hills shimmer golden like a fairy-tale landscape.

Over his pounding heart, Seth listened. On the road side of the ridge the noise of a trail bike was receding. It had dropped someone off; probably going back for another. They were coming from both sides of the ridge now. He took the Python out, checked it, and began running again.

Soon the ridge became very rocky, forcing him to drop down and travel parallel to it. The ground was rough here; an obstacle course of rubble, and jumping from rock to rock, he suddenly saw the fat coil of a death adder by his foot. Adrenaline spiked through his scalp, but the snake was snoozing. He ran on and a flat, heavy gunshot rang out.

It sounded like a decent sized calibre rifle, but no bullet impacted or ricocheted near him. Seth took heart at that. Either the shooter wasn't much chop or the rifle had no telescopic sights. Taking cover, he located his attacker.

A red-faced bloke, his hair sticking up with sweat, was aiming a battle rifle up the slope and, thank Christ, it had no scope, just iron sights. But holy shit, it looked like an ArmaLite AR 18, a gun capable of full-automatic fire. With a twenty, maybe thirty round, curved box magazine, it was a bloody serious weapon to be on the wrong end of.

Needing something between him and the automatic rifle, Seth crawled through the mess of boulders, up to the ridge-top and down a few metres on the other side. In the cover of a big boulder, he leapt up and began to run again.

At his first stride the basalt by his head exploded in white dust and stinging shards. A deafening bell went off in his head, ringing and ringing, but thank Christ – his eyes were clear. Four or five metres down the slope in a white short-sleeved shirt and aviator sunglasses, was Smiley. The little bastard was aiming his Browning automatic shotgun right at him.

Smoke was curling from its muzzle and Seth flung himself sideways. A sledgehammer blow smashed his left shoulder, the bell rang again and he went backwards across an arse-high boulder. With the Python held tight against his chest and his other arm protecting his head, he fell across several ledges of rock, bounced a few times, hit the ground heavily and rolled onto his back.

Amongst boulders on the valley side of the ridge now, he scrabbled with his boots, trying to get behind any cover he could. His shoulder felt wet and tingled like a bastard.

A moving shadow fell across the rocks in front of him. Two-handed, he swung up the Python. Through a gap he saw a leg appear and he fired a bullet into it. The shot made his ears ring even louder than the shotgun had. He pulled himself up and scrambled around the boulders.

Smiley was on the ground, his trouser leg pulsing red. He saw Seth, swung the Auto 5 around. Seth put a hollow point bullet through the left lens of his sunglasses.

Chips of stinging basalt flew. A white circle with a deep smoking centre appeared in the boulder by Seth's head. Through the unholy ringing he heard the faint sound of a gunshot. ArmaLite man had nearly blown his brains out.

Taking cover behind the boulder, Seth peeked around it, and after a few seconds saw the shooter fifty metres away – crouched behind the spiky pom-pom of a grass tree.

He took careful aim, braced his hands, and emptied the jerking pistol. The percussive gunshots just about burst his eardrums. Black chunks of grass-tree trunk flew. Yellow dust spouted. ArmaLite man rolled for his life.

Seth opened the pistol's cylinder, worked the ejector rod and shook free the empty brass. Pulling the speed loader from his pocket, he slid the six bullets into the chambers, released them and snapped the cylinder back into place.

But he needed the Auto 5. Keeping his head down, Seth looked over at Smiley. A stream of dark blood oozed from his misshapen head, the viscous red pushing grains of dirt and tiny bits of leaf along. Seth checked out the ground around the body and swore. He couldn't see the shotgun.

Now ArmaLite man went full-auto, putting a long burst right into Seth's boulder shelter. Rock fragments pattered and stung; dust flew. Damn, it was too dangerous to look for the shotgun.

His ears were ringing painfully, his left shoulder hurt. Touching it, he inspected his hand and saw water streaked with blood. He took a look. Yeah, he'd been hit, but it didn't look so bad.

The pack felt weightless and he slid it off – then grunted in disbelief. Only the straps and the bottom of it remained. The pack, stuffed with his blanket, first-aid kit and two canteens had taken nearly all of the blast. His sideways move had saved his life. *Am I a tin-arsed bastard or what?*

Seth heard a voice over the ringing in his ears. ArmaLite man was calling out. Other blokes would be here soon. Seth crawled and wriggled over to the other side of the ridge, jumped up, and started running like buggery.

Bad Odds

Nearly two hours later he was still running, but a lot slower. Out of the valley of the growers' camp now he was moving along the ridge he'd first come in on. Soon he'd see the road. But when he did, his heart sank. The cloud of dust down there was the khaki Land Cruiser. Driving out wasn't an option anymore.

Up ahead came the high growl of a trail bike. They'd cut him off. Without pausing Seth turned and raced down to the valley floor. It took twenty-five minutes for him to cross it and run a few steps up the slope of the next ridge. In the meagre shade of an ironbark, he flung himself down and sucked in air while his heart knocked out an endless drum-solo.

Listening hard over the ringing in his ears for the sounds of pursuit, he heard no snap-crackle of leaves and branches or thud of boots. He checked the Python, refilled the speed loader and took stock. Topographical map, compass, Buck knife and binoculars; the loaded gun plus three reloads, a little torch he'd got in Sydney – one of those new Maglites – and about ten centimetres of water.

He drank it. With a groan, he got himself up and started

moving again. It was a real effort getting up the ridge, but when he got to the top and looked down into the next valley he almost shouted in relief. Glistening below him was the Mitchell. He watched patiently for a minute, scanning its banks; listening for trail bikes, before jogging shakily down to the wide shallow river.

White moths fluttered in small bushes by the river's edge and metallic-blue dragonflies hovered over the water. Seth got down, drank deeply – then put his head under. Oh man, it was utter cool bliss; crystal-clear with pure white sand sifted over dark greenish rock. With real reluctance, he lifted his head back into a hot, harsh world.

Looking at his shoulder he saw that two shotgun pellets, likely oo-SG shot, had each torn a nasty furrow through the bicep; one deeper than the other. The wounds stung like a bastard, the pain peaking when he carefully washed them. Tearing off a piece of his t-shirt, he tied it around his arm.

He'd lost his hat and sunnies and that wasn't good. The sun now ruled the empty blue sky, the river rocks already radiating heat. With the map, compass and sun, he worked out a course east that would eventually come onto the Cape York Development Road. He should be able to hitch a ride back to Kuranda from there.

After another lovely cool drink, he filled his canteen and jogged on. He took a five-minute break every half hour to take a compass bearing, each time using the binoculars to check for any pursuit.

By mid-day he had slowed to a walk, moving through a hard, heat-rippled landscape of low scrubby hills, gnarly trees and brooding termite mounds. Crows farked unseen, but he once saw a wedge-tailed eagle up high, effortlessly circling; straight-winged and free. What a sweet life, he thought, surfing on the wind up there with the shitty old world far below.

By the time afternoon started its turn to dusk, Seth had drunk all his water and was feeling tuckered out.

When he saw a dust cloud moving along far ahead, he knew it was Cape York Development Road. As he trudged closer another vehicle smudged the horizon and that was reassuring. It looked like this was the right time of the day to hitch a lift.

Finally getting to the two-lane road, he took his boots off and rubbed his seriously aching feet. It was flat all around, but across from him, about two hundred and fifty metres away, was an eroding escarpment with eucalyptus forest behind it. The falling sun was turning the treetops into gold lace, and making long pools of shadow out of the washout gullies at the base of the decaying cliff.

In the distance a dust cloud appeared, coming from the south; the wrong way for a ride. Seth badly needed a drink of water, so he put his boots back on, stood up and held out his water canteen. He was Gunnur, who'd got lost hiking, now hitching back to his car, and he needed a drink.

Moving hour after hour across a shadowless landscape without his sunnies had given his eyes a bit of a toasting and he had to squint to see if the car would stop. Fairly speeding along, it looked like the rotten bugger was going to pass him by. Damn it! His throat felt like sandpaper. Then to his intense relief, the car rapidly deaccelerated. Oh yeah, he thought. I can just about taste that water.

The vehicle pulled up, throwing off blinding reflections. Blinking away dust, Seth shaded his eyes and saw a khaki-coloured Landcruiser with the passenger window coming down and a rifle barrel coming out.

He ran at the Toyota, ducked below the questing barrel and dodged madly around the vehicle. Sprinting across the highway and onto the dirt he made for the washouts below the big escarpment. In a few seconds, one or more rifles would be zeroing in on him. It would take close to a minute of balls-out running to get to the cover of the washouts. These were bad odds. Pretty much no odds at all.

As he ran, he imagined himself as the shooter, smoothly swinging the rifle, leading the running man. At precisely the right moment he'd gently squeeze the trigger and allow the bullet and moving target to intersect in time and space.

Feeling the bullseye burning into his back, Seth abruptly changed direction – just as a first shot rang out. The bullet cracked past his head and there was a yell of frustration. Seth swerved again and another bullet split the air apart close by. Then with a dreadful clatter, some bastard opened up on him with a big calibre machine-gun.

To his right a line of dust erupted and he spun around and raced back towards the road. Like G.I. Joe dolls, three men stood against the pink and orange sky. One had a rifle with no scope, another a Thompson sub-machinegun with a stick magazine and the third, bless him, held a pistol.

Seth spun around and sprinted towards the escarpment again. The odds now felt a little better. There was only one rifle and the Tommy gun's range would make it just about useless in the next thirty or forty seconds.

He stopped in his tracks and the ground a metre ahead blew up in a flurry of .45 calibre bullets. It was like World War Two out here! Another rifle slug cracked through the air, while the pistol banged impotently, sounding like kids chucking stones at a corrugated iron roof.

Taking off again, he travelled parallel to the road, before swinging around, jigging back and forwards, getting closer and closer to the sanctuary of the wash-out gullies. Seconds passed. Seth felt the intense focus of the gunmen aiming with care. Then the Thompson rattled again, peppering his legs with dirt. Its magazine must be empty now and by the time it was changed – he'd be nearly out of its range.

Stopping hard, he crouched down. The air cracked by his head, the nearest shot yet, and the bullet tore up the dirt just ahead. A leap sideways spared him the next well-aimed shot. He sprung up and charged on. The gun-fire went fully automatic now – that bastard ArmaLite man again, and Seth zigged and zagged through the nasty zip of bullets knowing the rifle's magazine must run out any second. It did and a cry of rage rang out.

A mottled patch of ground at Seth's feet suddenly came alive and he instinctively leapt sideways. In a spray of dust, stones and claws, a big goanna raced away. The massive lizard, spooked by the running man, made its escape.

So did Seth. At the first washout now, he dropped down into its shadows and ran along with his head down. More gun-fire sounded, but the puffs of dust were five metres or more away. ArmaLite man was firing blind.

For the first time since he'd left the road, Seth knew he wasn't going to die out here.

He scrambled out of the washout. ArmaLite man picked him up for the last time with a long burst that sent up little spurts of sepia half a metre from his feet. Seth madly dived behind the eroded walls of a steep ravine that went to the top of the escarpment. It gave him cover and he scrambled up, his boots dislodging dirt and stones that rattled away in noisy little avalanches. Finally, he got to the top.

Panting in the dirt like a cattle dog on a big muster was fine; he could keep doing that, but when he turned on his belly and peered over the escarpment edge he saw – for crying out loud! – the two men with the automatic weapons running towards him. These bastards were not giving up.

Like a worm he squirmed away, out of sight he rose to his feet. Ahead of him was the eucalyptus forest. Very soon it would be too dark in there to be seen. His legs and feet were fit to burst but he had to run just a bit longer.

Amongst the trees were fallen branches, logs and drifts of slippery leaves; all traps to twist an ankle. In the failing light he tried to read the lay of the land ahead. To his right the forest floor decayed into more ravines. Good cover, but maybe too slow to climb in and out of. His pursuers could catch him in a gully like a wild pig – and kill him like one.

On the left was the slope of a hill, steep enough to slow him down. Those bastards might get a chance to shoot him before he made it over the crest.

It was better to die running, so he went for the hill. The slope was covered in waist-high molasses grass and the long greasy leaves slowed him down. Then he found a pad – an animal trail – and by using the sound and feel of the bare earth under his boots to guide him, he ran up it.

It was an absolute guts effort. Up on the hill's crest the highest trees were gold-tipped with the last sunlight, and birds trilled and sung sweetly. It was the bloody Promised Land with Seth rushing to its glory. In a final burst he made it to the top. He spun around; looked, but there was no one on the hillside below.

He ran a few metres down the other side and collapsed. Hidden in the molasses grass he hyperventilated; seeing stars. When his breathing began to normalise, he listened intently for voices, still half-deaf from the gunfight eleven hours ago. The forest was silent and he sat up with a moan of pain. All around the dusk had deepened, the trees now losing their colour.

His legs felt boned-out and he slowly scooted down the hill on his bum. At the bottom he saw through the trees the pale shape of a clearing, maybe twenty metres away. With darkness crowding in under the forest canopy, he rose to his feet and used tree trunks to stagger over. It was a big expanse of flat rock; a seam thrown up millions of years ago. Maybe there was water here.

But the nightfall was now complete. Searching for water, even with a torch, was an endurance test he did not have the strength for. He slowly lay down on the warm rock. For the first time in close to twelve hours he could just be still. Stringing together two thoughts that didn't involve water was too hard and he quickly fell into exhausted sleep.

The sound of something on the rocks nearby woke him to a massive thirst. His feet ached, his shoulder throbbed, and his ears still faintly rung. The Submariner's luminous dial told him that he'd slept for seven hours. He flicked the Maglite on and shone it into the darkness. Several pairs of curious silver eyes were observing him – a family of rock wallabies. They were totally harmless, so he killed the light and lay back again.

This was crazy. One o'clock in the morning and here he was laying on the ground like a tired old dog out in the middle of bloody nowhere. And Mick was dead.

His killer was dead too – but so what?

Movies, TV and paperbacks, blokes down the pub; they'd all made out that payback was worthy – what honourable men did. But what had gone down on that ridge yesterday morning wouldn't replace his friend. He was gone. Forever.

Truth was; he'd shot Smiley because he had to. Life or death. Simple really. It was Mick's death that was hard.

To think of something else, he pondered the morning. Should he trek to the east through thirty or forty kilometres of densely forested hills and deep gullies? Yeah right. If he wasn't gun-shot, badly dehydrated and totally lacking in water he would probably give it a whirl.

No, his choices were limited to one – go back to the road and hope those bastards weren't waiting.

He dozed fitfully, finally crashing and sleeping until the dawn woke him. With his energy levels pitifully low and a killing thirst pecking at his skull, he slowly retraced his steps, the Python ready in his hand.

The Cape York Development Road looked clear, but he spent a careful thirty minutes scanning the whole area with binoculars before gingerly climbing down the escarpment cliff. He shuffled through the dust to the road and waited two, long, thirsty hours for someone to come along. Finally, a beaten-up looking Toyota station-wagon appeared out of morning heat-haze and stopped.

An equally beaten-up old couple peered out at him, the woman giving him the evil eye. Stopping for the big, filthy bloke obviously hadn't been her idea

"We're going to Cairns," said the old fella.

"Drop me in Kuranda?" said Seth.

"Kuranda. Yeah that'd be right," sniffed the woman.

It's Just Pain

At the turn-off to Myola Road, he got out; the old lady's eye still as evil as when he'd first got in. A drink of water from the couple had helped, but he was feeling crook. He stood by the road's gravelled curve until a young bloke in a half-repainted Kingswood station-wagon gave him a lift to the overgrown cave of Les's driveway.

It took an age to walk down it, but Les was home, thank God, and while Seth guzzled water his mate got out a first-aid kit. In the laundry Seth carefully washed the meaty red grooves in his shoulder then let Les disinfect and dress them. Aside from a few directions, neither of them spoke.

With his shoulder out of the cubicle, Seth had a shower, lulled into an aching trance by the hot water as he slowly cleaned away the blood, sweat and dust. Towelling off, he was gratified to smell coffee brewing and bacon and eggs cooking; his hunger like a wild beast. An old t-shirt and a pair of shorts were in the doorway and he put them on.

Outside, he emptied out the pockets of his filthy clothes, putting the contents on top of his boots. The Python, speed loader and ammo went on the table inside.

His breakfast was laid out there and Seth gratefully ate. Les waved an empty shopping bag at him and put it by his stuff. Then he pottered about in his loading room, calling out at one point, "I'm going into Cairns soon. I'll give you a ride to your place."

When Seth finished eating, he sat staring at his empty plate, feeling as weathered as a granite knoll. A fresh coffee was put before him and he looked up into serious eyes.

"How did you go?" said Les.

"It was a bit of a shit fight."

"Python didn't scare them?"

Seth hesitated. Not because of the law, but because of the boss fella he'd met at Leafgold Weir Road. A flash of Mick's corpse, unburied in those lonely hills, rocked him.

"I see you used six rounds," said Les. "Was that before or after you copped the shotgun blast?"

"You kill anyone in the war?" said Seth, shocked by the wretched tone of his voice.

Then he jumped in the chair as Les put a consoling hand on the back of his neck. He didn't look up; he couldn't, and now his eyes stung worse than his shoulder.

The hand withdrew and bare feet whispered across the floor into the kitchen. Glass clinked on glass. Liquid was poured and his mate came back.

"Here."

Les had two glass tumblers half-filled with grappa and they knocked them back in silence. After a bit, Les sighed.

"I know what you're feeling mate. It's always bad, but I know you Seth. I know it would have been life or death."

"It's not just that, it's . . . the bastard killed him, Les! He killed my mate."

"Ah shit," said Les, who hated swearing.

Seth felt uncontrollable emotion welling up in his chest. Crush it down, he raged – it's just pain.

Les made a soft noise of encouragement.

"I know about that too, Seth. All I can tell you is that it *will* pass. It will be bloody hard, but it will pass."

Breathing deeply, Seth stared at the wall of green forest outside and his dreadful weakness began to seep away. What a big girl he was being. Les must have seen far worse.

"Ahhh, it's just one of those things," he finally said. "No-one's gonna be calling the cops over it anyway."

He grinned ruefully at Les like he'd missed out on a spot on the footy team. "Just forget this happened ay?"

Les stared at him, and then said, "Yeah, okay."

Seth concentrated on drinking the last of his coffee.

"So, we're set to go to Cairns?" said Les.

'Yeah, yeah – don't want to keep you." Seth got up and went towards the door.

"Seth," said Les. He nodded at the gun on the table, his face unreadable but the message clear.

Absolutely mortified, Seth got the gun, ammo and speed loader, took them to his stuff outside and put everything in the shopping bag.

Driving down the range to Cairns, Les kept his eyes on the road and his mouth shut, flicking on ABC local radio as if to forestall any talk.

I really hope I haven't mucked-up and lost another mate, thought Seth. But when they got to his place, Les made as if to slap him on his wounded shoulder, then burst into laughter instead.

Seth smiled gratefully but Les wasn't finished.

"What you're feeling, Seth? It'll pass. But you need to keep your head down now. Go fishing, find a girlfriend – but stay out of that business. For good. This is a lesson you cannot afford not to learn."

You're not bloody wrong, thought Seth as Les drove off.

As he went to get his house-keys, tucked up under a roof eave around the side, a voice called out to him. It sounded like his neighbour and he went to where a line of coconut palms and hibiscus bushes divided their blocks. A bearded face grinned through the foliage at him.

Rod Savage was a dozer driver who worked out west on the mines. Seth kept an eye on his place when he was away.

"Alright, Rod? When are you flying out again?"

"Yeah all good mate. Leaving Sunday, but listen, I saw something a bit dodgy here last night. Around nine, there's a torch in your carport and I see two fellas checking out your truck. I thought they were going to nick it but they were just looking at the tyres and sides."

"Is that right?" Seth knew what they were looking for.

The phone started to ring inside his house.

"You want to get that?" said Rod.

"Nah, it's alright. Tell me about these blokes."

"I kept quiet and one bloke goes, 'Nah it's all clean,' and the other bloke goes, 'But, where is he?' So, I sing out and ask them what the hell they're up to.

"They come over in a flash, shining the bloody torch in my eyes. Real cocky bastards, they ask me if I've seen you in the last twenty-four hours. Well, I said you got picked up by a girlfriend and you've stayed the night with her. Hope that's right with you but they gave me the creeps."

"Nah – good move Rod. What they look like?"

"Like cops mate. Plain-clothed cops."

When Seth got inside his place, he checked the doors and window for signs of forced entry. Everything was cool.

Grabbing a tea-towel, he quickly wrapped the Python, ammo and speed loader in it, put the package into a heavy plastic bag and sealed it tightly with gaffer tape. The pistol needed cleaning but he was getting a real funny vibe now.

Hiding the bag under his shirt, he quietly went outside into his back garden. Out of sight of both of his neighbour's windows, he sat down and scuffed around under a hibiscus bush. Locating the top of a sealed length of ten-inch PVC pipe sunk into the ground, he unscrewed its watertight lid. He took out the keys for the Pig and put the package into the pipe. Carefully screwing the lid back on, he re-hid the stash under dirt and leaves.

Inside he found a cold beer in the fridge and gratefully sprawled out on the sofa. Taking a big satisfying pull on the frosty, he thought about what Rod had just told him.

Dodgy cops looking for Mitchell River dust on his truck was bad news. They'd been sent by someone . . . and Seth smelt menthol cigarette smoke and perfume, and saw that man behind the flaking latticework screen.

But that was just too damn spooky to contemplate and he abruptly turned his thoughts to Arnold Jessop. Yeah, remember him? And the plan to steal his briefcase full of drugs? Sure, he did. He'd be onto that in the morning.

Taking another good refreshing swig, he mulled it over, wondering what the briefcase contents might be worth. Fifty grand? A hundred? Two? A lot of money anyway; a bloody fortune really. He could sell it down in Sydney and clean up big time . . .

But he flashed on Debbie's housemate Ella at the Great Northern and saw the skeletal kids selling themselves on the streets of the Cross.

No, fuck that! That money would rot his soul. He'd flush that shit down the toilet where it belonged.

He drank more beer, putting off the inevitable. When the stubbie ran dry, he got his address book and rang Peggy. Waiting for her to answer he wondered how many lies he would have to tell.

"Peggy, it's Seth."

"I thought you were going ring me every day!"

"Look I'm sorry about that but something happened that I just had to deal with."

"What – in a place with no phones?"

"Yeah. Yeah it was."

There was silence as Peggy took in this information and he could see where her thoughts might go. When she finally spoke, it was just as he'd thought – but a kick to the head nonetheless.

"I paid you, and you agreed, to spend every day looking for Melanie. Instead you're what . . . growing marijuana?"

Dog-tired and aching in his body and soul, he could have gone off like a full tank of Avgas – shouting, "My mate was murdered! I shot his killer in the face! Blokes with machine guns chased me!"

But he didn't and his secret life sucked on his heart like a giant leech.

"Peggy it was *nothing* like that. A very good mate was in real bad trouble and I had to help him." Please hear the truth in my voice, he prayed.

"I don't know Seth. I really don't know."

He heard her lighter as she fired up a cigarette.

"Peggy, listen. I'll give you back your money and I'll still find Melanie. I promised you I would, and that's just what happened over these last two days. I promised to help find somebody and it became very urgent. Life or death urgent."

He waited, wondering if he'd ever be able to keep all the darkness in his life from her.

"OK then," Peggy finally said. "I accept that whatever you had to do was very important but I need you to keep me informed in future. I'm under a lot of stress."

"Don't be stressed Peggy. Melanie's doing good and I've got a plan to put Arnold Jessop out of the picture."

"You do?"

"Sure do. I've put the police onto him. One of them is my uncle and he's looking into it right now."

Outside of the uncle bit, this was his first, and hopefully, only lie. Besides, he was going to make it true as soon as he could.

"You have an uncle in the police?"

"Yes. He'll sort Jessop out."

"You never told me that."

"He's been away, but he's back on Monday."

"Oh wow. . . that's great Seth. Look, I'm sorry I . . ."

"It's all fine Peggy. It's all going to work out. I'll ring you tomorrow and tell you how it's going. Alright?"

"You can tell me in person. I'm back tomorrow. I'll phone you then."

Before he could speak, she hung up and he banged down the receiver in response. What about some thanks? Or some compassion for what he'd gone through the last two days! Ahh yeah, that's right – she didn't know about that. Nobody did. All this pain and sadness was his alone.

It was all too bloody much and Seth nodded off on the lounge and slept like the dead. It was close to dark when a furious knocking on the front door woke him. Aware of his bandaged wound, he groggily put on a shirt before opening the door.

The two bastards Rod Savage had warned him about were standing there, their arrogant faces enough to tell him that they were indeed cops, Ds in fact. These plain-clothed pricks were used to getting their way by exercising the full force of the law – and then some.

"You Seth Kelly?"

The detective had nineteen-fifties rocker sideburns and a pisshead's swollen beak. His mean-lipped string-bean of a partner stared over his shoulder like a freshly awakened cadaver. They both smelt of grog, sweat and cigarettes.

"That's me and who are you?" said Seth.

"You gonna let us in or what?" said Sideburns.

"No, I'm not. Who are you and what do you want?"

Sideburns produced his I.D and stuck it in Seth's face.

"We'll talk right here," said Seth.

"You got something to hide?"

"Why don't you cut to it, mate?"

"Where were you yesterday and last night?"

"I was with a friend."

"Good root, was she?"

Seth kept quiet while Sideburns' mouth made laughing sounds. When this evil noise subsided they just stared at each other; the D's eyes full of inflamed veins and practised menace.

Feeling left out, his partner stepped to one side, posing with his .38 revolver in its clip-on holster. This pair were almost comical.

"So, you fancy yourself as a tough guy," said Sideburns. "You got no record – a cleanskin, but we know you're dirty. Managed to buy a house with all the pot you've grown, hey? So, who's the dirty slut you spent last night with?"

Seth kept on saying nothing. These two bastards had no leverage short of bashing him and he wasn't scared of that. He'd sing out to Rod Savage if the fists started flying and have a straight-up witness for the courtroom.

"Where's your mate Mick Lovett?" said Sideburns.

That threw Seth, but he let nothing show. It looked like these cops had been sent round here to tie up loose ends. But how tight were they going to tie up the loose end that was him?

"Let's not piss around," said Sideburns. "You and your dumb mate are marijuana growers and dealers. We know all about you fellas. So, where the fuck is Mick Lovett?"

Seth didn't want to talk about Mick and he went on the offensive.

"Well if you really know everything about me," he said, "Then you'll know I've worked and saved and bought this house without any of the bullshit you're hanging on me."

"Pig's arse you did."

"If I was a detective, I'd check with the tax department and my bank before jumping to conclusions."

The D frowned like the big meanie he was.

"I hope you didn't get stung for too much money by the dog who put you onto me," Seth continued. "I'm old news."

"Oh, it wasn't no dog, but you'll fucking wish it was."

Fear flopped about in his gut, but Seth smiled pleasantly.

"Look, you seem like nice fellas so I'll save you a bit of bother," he said. "I've been interstate the last few years and those blokes I used to hang with? I've moved on from them. I've caught up with family, bought this place, and I'll be off real soon to work interstate again."

"Is that right?" said Sideburns.

"Yeah, so if you have nothing . . ." Seth began to close the door. The D halted it with a big shoe.

"I couldn't give a shit how you got this dump," he said. "Right now, you're a person of interest and we might have to search this house. You savvy?"

I savvy all right, thought Seth. You rotten bastards will plant something in here and force me into making a dodgy statement or worse.

"You better be quick, boys," he said. "I'll have this place rented in a jiffy."

"We might be quicker than you think." Sideburns knew it was bullshit, but he still said it.

"Gentlemen." Seth cranked out a polite smile and put his

weight into forcefully pushing the D's shoe back until the door-lock clicked home. From the other side of the door, Sideburns' partner put in his five-cents worth.

"You fuckin' cunt, Kelly."

Seth closed his tired eyes and listened to the Ds spit and swear as they stomped off. Ohhhh mate, he thought. The shit was piling up faster than at a stockyard on auction day.

Chasing the Dragon

The big sleep-in was what he needed, but it still felt like he'd played three footy matches in a row. The wounds in his shoulder throbbed, but an inspection in the bathroom mirror showed none of the puffy redness of infection. What wasn't so good was the trepidation on his face.

The dirty Ds little visit yesterday evening was more than unsettling. Their brash demeanour in coming right up to his door meant they hadn't got the full story yet – the one where the Mafia killer gets a hollow-point bullet in the eye. They'd obviously been on a fishing trip in coming here.

The machine-gun boys on the Cape York Development Road had got a good look at him though. How long before the man from Leafgold Weir Road sent someone around to avenge his man?

Feeling like a zombie, he made breakfast. The sounds of sipping tea and crunching toast were hollow in his skull. His little place felt like a doll-house about to be kicked over.

And when it happened, as he knew it would, he pushed Mick into that black box of misery inside, slamming the lid down tight. Man, it was getting full in there.

So, what were today's plans? He grinned mirthlessly. Yeah, that's right — he was ripping off a heroin dealer.

He got the Python out of the stash, and after cleaning and oiling it, he checked the action and reloaded it. He'd take it with him. Just in case. And a bandanna for a mask.

It was Sunday, so Edge Hill was quiet. He parked on the next street over from the Jessop place and sat quietly in the Pig, just listening and watching for a few minutes. Seeing no movement in any houses or gardens, he got his burglary bag, quietly locked up and slipped into a vacant block that was too steep to comfortably build on.

The dark rain forest, buzzing with insects, looked heat-stressed from months of minimal rain, and the ground crackled underfoot as he went up the slope. He moved in an arc towards the Jessop house, and within ten minutes was just above it. He found a good vantage point and after checking for biting ants, centipedes and spiders, sat down. Secure in the shadows, he got out his binoculars and took a good look at the property below.

The Jessop compound came right up to the side of the hill. Surrounded on two sides by rainforest it comprised a couple of levels. The big old mansion and gardens he'd seen from the street occupied the lower level. Above them was a second tier with three separate houses on it.

The closest one to Seth was in a corner right by the back boundary of jungle, mostly hidden by a whopper of a black bean tree and surrounded on three sides by smaller trees.

In their shadows lay piles of overgrown junk and rubbish.

About twenty metres from this house, a decrepit open-sided shed leaned into oblivion. Next to it was the wreck of a fruit orchard, the wild and unpruned trees home to wasp's nests, their trunks pocked with gnarly burls. Beyond this dilapidated grove was a shaggy stretch of overgrown lawn. On the other side of that; the two other houses.

These buildings adjoined a battered cement parking slab riven with mossy cracks. From it, an equally dilapidated driveway curved past the mansion down onto the street. This was the driveway he'd come up the other night.

Parked on the concrete slab was Briefcase Boy's Holden HX, next to it a sporty red Datsun Fairlady in the shabbiest condition; the bonnet and soft-top stained with bird shit.

One of the dwellings, a red brick single-story job, looked fairly new, maybe late sixties, and Seth saw movement next to it. One side of the house was floor-to-ceiling concertina doors; all pulled back and open. Next to this open wall, in nothing but sunglasses and shorts, was Briefcase Boy.

Jumping, spinning and kicking, throwing out multiple punches and strikes; he was practising martial arts moves. Though not really that big in his arms and torso, he rippled with muscle and looked bloody strong. And he was quick. Real quick.

But what was this? Briefcase Boy's ears were big bulges, and something cord-like whipped around behind him.

Seth snorted, half in approval. What a smart-arse!

The kid was wearing headphones and listening to music while he trained, looking like a full-colour, double-page ad in an expensive magazine. Suddenly stopping mid-kick, he looked up at the hillside; his sunnies catching the morning sun.

Although he was absolutely invisible in the rainforest gloom, Seth's instincts insisted otherwise. As though in the presence of a lethal predator, he stayed completely still. Closing his eyes, he willed his presence, his very sentience, to dissolve into the deep shadow around him.

When he opened his eyes a minute later, Briefcase Boy had gone back to his training. Seth didn't feel foolish like he'd over-reacted or anything. Animal instincts were real. In a life full of risk-taking, they'd kept him from being caught out. A couple of times they'd kept him alive.

Now he scanned the ground around the two buildings, searching for water bowls, gnawed bones and dog turds. Relieved to find none, he turned his attention to the next house.

Looking like a renovated shed, the two-floor building was done up with six big windows that looked out onto the hill – sets of potential eyes watching for trespassers. He looked at the house for a while, but no one moved inside.

With Briefcase Boy still going at it like a wind-up toy, Seth re-examined the ratty place under the massive black bean tree. Not as old as the main house but still pre-war, it was oddly placed so close to the hillside. The run-off from Mt. Whitfield would make it damp and fetid most of the year round, and it would be mosquito city there in the wet.

The house was badly run-down; the tin roof furred red with rust; the timber walls roughly feathered with flakes of paint. He tried to observe the windows for movement, but the angle was too acute and the trees too close.

He turned his attention to the big house – the beautiful mansion he'd seen from the street. It was also in bad shape, looking a good deal worse from this viewpoint: roofs and downpipes eaten and pitted with corrosion, sills and eaves cracked and blackened with rot, windows pale and opaque with grime; a few sporting cracks. It was a damn shame.

A whopper mango tree nudged the second-floor roofs. Beneath its high branches the roof was stained and rusted. Every mango season, mobs of flying-foxes would hang in that tree feeding on the fruit and dropping litres of liquid shit and loud mango seeds on the pitched tin roofs below.

Checking on the kung fu kid again, Seth saw he was gone. The red brick house was still wide open, so he slowly came down the hillside and crept behind the high buttress roots of a big fig tree. From this cover he looked into the house.

He saw one large room with a kitchen, table, and chairs at one end and a black leather lounge, large television and stereo system at the other.

Briefcase Boy appeared from a door, now in jeans, drying his chest and head with a towel. He put on a long-sleeved shirt, slipped on a pair of good-looking loafers, sauntered outside and called out to the converted shed next door. His backup bloke from the other day came out, and they stood in the sunshine talking.

Seth remembered Johnny Pep's request, watching as — here we go – Briefcase Boy gave an envelope-sized plastic bag to his mate. The bag was lumpy with individual bulges, obviously smack deals packaged up ready for sale.

If only he had a camera with a telephoto lens right now. Uncle Don and a judge and jury would love that.

The two men got in the HX Holden and drove off. This is starting to look good, thought Seth. The drugs in Briefcase Boy's place would be hidden, but with enough time he'd find them. The question was – were other blokes around?

He had to see if the house under the black bean tree was occupied. If it wasn't, he'd nip across the lawn into the red brick house and ransack the joint. Coming down out of the rainforest, he crouched low and scurried into the grove of smaller trees surrounding the house.

Under their branches was a dumping ground of decades. There was stuff chucked everywhere. A dressing table, its mirror pocked with spots from the lost silvering. Corroded milk-powder tins embalmed in weeds. An old open-top washing machine, its drum loaded with dead leaves, and the rubber wringer rollers cracked, grey and perished.

He went around an ancient car body, its edges rusted to brown lace, and side-stepped a slew of crumbling car-tires and corroding auto batteries slowly poisoning the ground. Up ahead amongst a drift of dead leaves he saw something bright and new. He went over and looked down.

What the hell? Laying on top of decaying black and gray leaves was a pair of woman's panties – unmarked, delicate, purple, and indescribably wrong. It gave Seth the willies.

With a sudden sense of being watched, he looked over at the mansion. Empty windows stared back, but the house itself felt observant. Keep moving he told himself.

Under the black bean tree, he approached the house, one eye on its windows, the other on all the hazards underfoot. Lichen-frosted wood piles hinted at dozing eastern brown snakes. Begrimed china plates begged to be loudly broken.

As he came up to the house, he heard a TV going inside. He stopped and listened, but heard no other sounds. By the veranda stairs were milkcrates filled with empty bottles, all top-shelf whisky, and next to them, many weather-melted stacks of once-bright magazines. The open veranda doors revealed filthy, latched insect-screens peppered with bullseyes of green and white mould. Seth crouched below the veranda's floor level, and carefully went past the doors and down the side of the house.

It was dark and damp there. Mosquitoes whined, and the dank stink of the mildewed house was strong. Golden Orb spiderwebs joined the roof to the trees, the bodies of small birds hanging cocooned in the great nets. More rubbish lay scattered beneath the house: decaying tea chests, broken records that he hoped were Val Doonican and his ilk, stacks of derelict aluminium and copper cookware freckled with cockroach shit. Amongst all this human decay and entropy, the revved-up cheeriness of a morning TV show coming from a corner window was most incongruous.

Seth stopped under the open window. The blue light of the telly flickered on the window panes, and a rank, pissy smell wafted through the air. Over the trebly chatter of the TV he heard the occasional clink of glass. Like an old man with arthritis, he crept away from the house and up the slope so he could take a look into the room.

As he squatted down and raised his binoculars, he heard a booming noise. It was a dense, low-frequency sound like a didgeridoo playing or a big, empty water tank being hit. It was behind him and close too. He turned and scanned the forest, seeing nothing but trunks, creepers, and leaves.

Turning back, he looked into the corner room. Propped up in a double bed was a grossly overweight and very pale woman. She had a great mass of uncombed, frizzy hair, and when she moved, liquor bottles rolled and clinked in the stained sheets around her.

The floor was covered in garishly coloured supermarket magazines and slim paperbacks emblazoned with the Mills & Boon rose. Empty chocolate boxes and discarded lolly packets quivered with flies. Right by the bed, in easy arm's reach, was a small bar fridge. My God, thought Seth. This must be Sandra Jessop, the ailing sister that Desmond Croaker had mentioned.

Completely horrified, he snatched the binoculars from his eyes. All the money she'd inherited hadn't led to the sort of life he might have imagined it would. This seemed like hell actually, and he didn't look into the room again.

He very much doubted she'd notice him crossing the open ground to the red brick house, so he got up and moved through the rainforest shadows.

Making his way to where he could go across the lawn, he heard a low rumble – the deep sub-sonic sound he'd heard before. This time it was so bloody loud he felt it vibrate his bones. Adrenaline exploded through him as a monster bird jumped out from behind a tree and ran straight at him.

With its wattles glowing bright red, the cassowary was big – two metres high, and hissing like a busted steam pipe. Breeding season had just finished; the eggs must be close by, and big daddy cassowary was going to use the twelve-centimetre-long daggers of his claws to rip the living shit out of the intruding human. Seth ran for his bloody life.

Bursting out of the forest, he sprinted across the lawn onto the concrete parking slab, heading for the driveway. The freaky hissing followed, those killing feet thudding and clicking on the concrete behind him. With the binoculars and duffle bag swinging madly and the Python jumping in his pocket, Seth raced past the mansion and down onto Everknell Street, nearly slipping over on the mushy slick of dead frangipani flowers there.

Hearing his boots on the road, but not the cassowary's claws, he threw a wild glance over his shoulder. The street was empty and he came to a halt.

In medium shock he shook with silent laughter. A bloody cassowary had just had a go at him! Suppressing bubbles of manic mirth, he walked back to the Pig.

At his truck he drank some water and faced the facts. No one had been killed by a cassowary in fifty years. Blokes had been injured though, and dogs had died, but cassowary or not – he had to go back. Briefcase Boy was out. The place was wide open. A chance like this might not come again.

He'd wear the bandanna, nip up the driveway and search the red brick house. After locking up the Pig, he went back, and as he got closer to Jessop's place, he saw a flash of white on the second-floor veranda of the house. He got off the road quick-smart and peeped around the plump trunk of a flame tree. Arnold Jessop was standing up there.

Of all the rotten luck. The dodgy bastard would see him coming up the driveway and that would really muck it up. Jessop would call for help, even ring the cops, and besides, it was Briefcase Boy Seth wanted blamed for the missing drugs – not him. Time for a change of plan.

Keeping low, he scurried to the house next door. There was no car in the open garage, no windows open, no lights on. He jumped the low hedge and ran to the house. Staying below window height he slunk down the back, eyes peeled for dogs and people. Fortunately the backyard was empty, and seeing no movement in the back windows, he went to the fence and looked over into the Jessop compound.

On a steep bank above him was the crumbling cement corner of the parking slab, beyond it the red brick house. The mansion loomed over it all; half a dozen of its windows looking down over the slope. Bugger it. Getting up there would take at least a minute and Arnold Jessop might spot him and – there he was!

Seth jumped behind a Datura bush and looked through its trumpet-like flowers at the old mansion. But there was no face at any of the windows. He was seeing things.

Now something really was moving. Up on the parking slab a cassowary head bobbed with suspicion. Seth stifled an angry cry. The stupid bird was still there.

He jumped in shock as a toilet flushed inside the house beside him. Footsteps sounded, coming towards the rear of the house. The back door was close. You're kidding me, thought Seth. Absolutely fuming, he turned to go.

The cassowary saw this movement and ran to the edge of the slab. It glared down at him like a murderous dinosaur. Up yours too, thought Seth. He crouched down below the fence line and scuttled away like a bandicoot.

There was no traffic in the street, no one at the front of the house, so he jumped the hedge and, as hopeful as a fool, pussyfooted it back to the Jessop compound.

Up there on the high veranda, lurking like an egret in the mangroves, was the white-garbed figure of Jessop. Feeling truly shat off, Seth trudged back to the Pig.

The Dirty Lowdown

Parked near the entrance of Everknell Street, Seth now waited. It was all he could bloody do. Maybe Arnold Jessop would get the urge to go hitch-hiking, maybe a lime-green Kombi Van would pull up. Three hours of neither of these things happening basted him with slow exasperation. When the HX Holden returned, he went home, hoping a shower and a cold beer would cure his crankiness.

Getting out of the Pig, he heard the phone ringing. He popped the Python into the stash under the dash and ran to get it. It was Peggy, back in Cairns. He resisted asking her to come over, instead arranging to meet for a drink at Hides lounge bar in an hour's time.

In the shower he went through what he'd actually tell her. Well, Melanie looked fine and he was pretty sure she'd be home for her exams. No, make that damn sure.

And yes, he'd met Arnold Jessop, suspected bad things were afoot in Edge Hill, and had spent many, many hours watching the place. And that was it really.

While he was getting dressed the phone started up its racket again. He dashed into the lounge and picked up the receiver.

"Hey, it's me," said Mick.

It took a moment for Seth to take that in.

"You there mate? I'm not gonna talk long."

"Jesus, I thought you were dead," said Seth.

"So did I. Those blokes were getting set to do the dirty on each other out there. One lot was going to rip off the other lot. Something nasty was coming and I stupidly got caught listening. I had to do a runner. They chased me to Mareeba and nearly got me there."

"You all right now?"

"I'm on my way to . . . you know. Don't expect to see me around for a long, long time."

"I reckon."

"Look, I'm gonna get off the line now. Just wanted you to know I'm good."

"Yeah mate, I fully appreciate that."

"But you watch yourself. Your uncle . . . not him, but his mob are in it up to their necks."

"Yeah, I had a visit."

"Oh, shit. I'm sorry."

"Have you talked to . . . y'know . . ."

"Yeah, yeah. She said she asked you to look for me. I've been ringing you for the last two days. You didn't go out there did you?"

"One day over a few beers I'll tell you all about it."

Mick groaned. "Oh man, I'm so sorry."

"Forget it. We live to tell the tale."

"Mate, I . . . better go. We'll talk again when the dust settles, and hey – I love you brother."

"Same to you mate, same to you."

Seth carefully replaced the receiver then raced outside where he shouted wildly at the sky, surfing a giant wave of emotion. When it peaked, he went back in to the fridge and chugged down cold water.

Stone the fucking crows – Mick was alive! His corpse wasn't being pulled apart by wedge-tails and dingos out west. There were going to be little Micks and Pams running around WA after all! It was bloody marvellous.

Except he'd now made himself a target for the most dangerous bastards in the whole of the north. Seth stared at the plates and cutlery in the dish-rack.

Killing Smiley, who was probably from the old country, had called down a vendetta on him that wouldn't stop until someone shot-gunned him in his bed one balmy night. Going back to Sydney wouldn't save him either. They'd catch up with him in a quiet laneway in Kings Cross and put a couple of .22 rounds into his head.

He closed his eyes and smelt the ocean air blowing into his house. Scarlet hibiscus flowers nodded at the windows and a speckled native gecko ran up a wall.

Drowning in remorse, he thought about his father. The poor bastard had suffered enough, but the front-page news of his son's execution-style murder would finish him off for sure. Overpowered by sorrow, Seth stood there, clenching his fists and trying so very hard not to fall apart.

When he was sure that he wouldn't, he opened his eyes

and looked across the kitchen counter into the living room.

His records were stacked against the wall and an album cover caught his eye; a side-on photograph of a man in a black suit, grinning faintly and sitting on a green and white park bench next to an endless blue sea.

In a daze he shuffled over and picked up the album. At the far side of the picture, almost out of shot, a woman's hand was draped over the back of the bench, her fingers crossed for luck. He slid out the vinyl, took the record from its inner sleeve, and put on side two.

As the heartbeat-bass pluck and rolled gold drums of the first track started, he smiled from tips of his toes to the top of his head. How cool was this song?

Flopping down on the couch, he once again listened to the story of The Lowdown. By the time it had finished he was cool again and hipped to the truth.

He'd heard his own story in the song like he always did, but now he absolutely knew that it was *just* a story, and that there'd been a million equally cool and screwed-up stories before his, and there'd be a million more.

His situation right now wasn't particularly special in the grand scheme of things, but his motive was. Keeping his promise to Pam and looking for his mate were about the only important things that had happened. If he had to die for that – so be it. It was worth it.

There was no use in getting freaked out. Better to just go along for the ride and have a real good time while it lasted. If he was meant to be shot to pieces in this lovely house, he wasn't going to worry about it.

But he sure as hell would put up a fight.

Number One Smile

"So, you think Melanie is coming back for her exams and graduation?" Peggy filled with hope was wonderful.

"Yes, I do. But right now, she needs to know that Jessop is no good. I think she's smart enough to get it."

Seth wore a confident smile; happy it was working.

"And that's where your uncle comes in?"

"That's it. He's back at work tomorrow and we'll have a good sit down with him. Uncle Don will be up for talking to Melanie – no problems at all. This is going to work."

Peggy's face relaxed a little more and she almost smiled. Around them the afternoon crowd softly talked, drank and laughed; everyone lazily hanging loose, waiting to see what the evening might bring.

"And it wouldn't be coming from her mum, or from the bloke she's employing either," he said. "A policeman telling her? She'll listen."

Seth took a pull on his gin and tonic, hoping she wouldn't ask why his Uncle Don, a sympathetic and trustworthy cop, hadn't been brought in earlier. The briefcase full of smack was the reason, but he wasn't going to tell her that.

"It's going to turn out fine. I'll keep patrolling Jessop's place while Uncle Don gets his boys on look-out for her.

Cairns is small, it won't take long. He'll give her the dirty lowdown on Jessop and she'll drop him like a green ant's nest. She'll enjoy herself up here for a few weeks and then come back down and ace her exams. This will be something to tell her friends in uni next year."

Nodding slowly, Peggy ventured a smile.

"You had an adventure like that yourself," he said. Peggy began to loudly rattle the ice in her glass.

"Your girlfriends in Sydney must've got a thrill hearing about your wild time up here. Down the track it's a great little yarn. It's character building."

"Character building? You broke my fucking heart."

A screwed-up mix of elation and despair blasted him.

"I didn't know you'd felt that."

"It doesn't matter now."

"No, no, Peggy – it does. I feel just that way about you."

Peggy tried for amusement but her eyes were all wrong.

"I blew it with you Peggy – I really did." He lowered his voice. "I really mucked up, because I really want to be with you Peggy. You are so special."

"Yeah?" Her voice sounded loud and rough over the ice jingling in her glass. "What makes me so special?"

"Oh, there's so much. Like, you are really smart but you don't push it in my face. And you're strong and you're independent . . ."

"Well, the thing about independent women is that they don't *need* a man," Peggy cut through. "Friends sure, lovers maybe – but we don't need a man to feel complete. I began learning that with Graham and finally understood it with you."

Seth blinked, lost for words. He'd been so honest it had hurt, gushing like crazy junior kid, and here she was – right up him, laying down her truth with no quarter given. But with marvellous surprise, he felt no shame – just relief, and the release of speaking from the heart.

"Why did you run out on me, Seth?" said Peggy.

Seth held onto that feeling of relief, clutching like a baby to it. He drew a love heart in the condensation on his drink and watched it slide away. When he looked up, Peggy's eyes were chips of emerald. There was nowhere to go.

"My brother and my mum died in a car accident. They came off the Gillies Highway in a thunderstorm. It was a sixty-metre drop and . . . I . . . ran away."

Peggy's mouth fell open in shock.

"I'm sorry Peggy." It was a whisper so he said it again. This was as hard as he'd thought it would be – worse, but it was better than continuously running.

"Oh Seth – that's so awful! You should have told me! I would have helped you."

Yeah that's right, he thought. She would have helped me. We'd probably be still together.

Peggy took his hand, her eyes full of real love and care. It was everything he needed, but he ruined it. Seeing the idiot hope in his eyes, she squeezed his hand, let it go, and gave him a heartbreaker of a smile.

"It wouldn't work, Seth. Even if I wanted it to."

"I'll move down to Sydney. We'll take it slowly."

Peggy slid out a long mentholated cigarette, lit it up, and told him what he knew already, but didn't want to believe.

"Seth – we're from two almost opposite worlds. Most of

my friends are women. We talk about clothes and fabrics. I practise yoga, I meditate. I have lunches and dinners with gentle, creative people and I go to art openings, the theatre. I help organise fundraisers. That's me."

She took a big hit, held it, then blew out the smoke.

"You're an amazing person, but . . . you're scary. I don't mean you're a bad person or that you'd ever hurt me, but you're a dangerous man, Seth. I knew that and for a while I liked it, but in reality that's not for me."

"I'm changing Peggy. I really am."

"You'll never change. You like it, that's part of who you are. I'm not judging you at all, and I truly believe you're a good man – but you're too heavy for me."

"I feel too heavy for myself sometimes," said Seth.

"Well if you can change, do it, but I don't think you'll really be you."

"Oh, the psychiatrist is in," said Seth.

Peggy laughed. "Well, if I'm Lucy – who are you?"

"Woodstock. Definitely Woodstock."

Peggy laughed some more and so did he, luxuriating in this happiness. Then with total clarity he realised that this was the moment for him to really let go of her. With love. With laughter. And just like that, he did. Simultaneously the hardest and easiest thing to do, it was a paradox so absurdly right – he got it in one.

Peggy sensed this and her laughter faded. Her eyes raked him with intense curiosity and he really saw Melanie in her now.

"So how is your father nowadays?" said Peggy.

Guilt ripped through him.

"Not so good. I've been slack since I got back."

"You must go see him. He needs you."

"I've got to find Melanie first."

"Yes, but you must find time to see him. Like today."

Seth nodded and tried to push back the sky.

"Oh right – I get it now," said a woman's voice and there was Debbie, looking better than good in pink canvas shoes, a long-sleeved white shirt and short shorts.

For crying out loud, thought Seth. What the hell next?

He jumped up and made as if to walk her away, but she smartly ducked around him – and stood next to Peggy.

"No, don't touch me," she said. "It wasn't my damn fault. I didn't know what Ella was up to. You just left me there."

Seth sighed silently, cringing at the interest on Peggy's face. Debbie waved at her with her fingers.

"Hi, I'm Debbie. I was Seth's fuck before you. Don't make a single mistake though – he's got very high standards."

"C'mon Debbie, I'm having a business meeting."

Debbie gave Peggy a mad grin. "You've known Seth for long?"

"A little while," said Peggy.

"How long is a little while?"

"Four months I suppose."

"Wow – same here. Did you meet him when he got back from Sydney?"

"No, it was over three years ago."

Debbie's nervy smile began to fade.

"Please sit down with us," said Peggy.

She took Debbie's hand, pulled her to the table and down into a seat. Seth groaned softly.

"I'm Peggy. I'm not with Seth now. He's working for me doing something very important."

Seth sat back down. Be cool, he told himself. Be polite.

"Are you Seth's girlfriend?" said Peggy.

"Yeah . . . for a while anyway," said Debbie.

"How old are you?"

"Nineteen."

"Really?" Peggy flashed Seth a look. "You're a year older than my daughter."

"Wow – you must have had her very young."

"I was the same age as you."

"True? I would never have picked that looking at you."

The two women smiled at each other.

"Would you like a drink?" said Peggy. "We're having gin and tonics. Seth, why don't you get us all one?"

No way, he thought. This is bullshit.

A sudden vision changed his mind. He was waking up in bed, in his house – with some bastard pointing a shotgun at his face.

Flashing Debbie and Peggy his number one smile, Seth sprang to his feet. "Yeah, I'd love to."

At the bar it had got busy and he waited patiently before ordering. In the gents he had a meditative leak, thinking what a bloody roller-coaster life was. Just keep moving and keep smiling, he told himself. That's enough for now.

After washing his hands and combing his hair, he went and collected the gin and tonics. Back at the table, Peggy was leaning forward and attentively listening to Debbie; an unlit cigarette between two fingers, a lighter clasped in her hand.

"I reckon Melanie is just stressed out," Debbie explained. "School is about to finish for good and university is coming. She's freaking about the future so she's taking it out on you. I did that kind of thing to my mum too. She couldn't wait for me to leave home."

"That's so sad."

"No, it's great," laughed Debbie. "We were driving each other crazy! Nowadays we can have a drink and a laugh."

"You left home this year?"

"When I was fifteen."

"Fifteen! Where did you go?"

"Well, Dad had gone inside again and I went and stayed at Aunt Mary's. But she's real churchie, so when grade twelve started I moved in with Janis, who's a nurse – she's real clever – and Ella, who is, well, a party girl."

"A party girl?"

"Y'know, guys pay her. For sex. Not at the house, but."

"Oh." Peggy looked alarmed. The cigarette came up to her mouth, stopped.

"What made you angry with your mum?" she said.

"The main thing was constantly treating me like I was still a kid, like I couldn't work things out for myself. I get on real good with Dad too and that pissed her off – though she'd never admit it."

Peggy sat back; cigarette unlit, eyes unfocused. Debbie used the straw on her G and T, then looked at them.

"You know what's weird?" she said. "I hated school but now I miss it. You think when you graduate that the world will be all different but it's not. It's the same old Cairns, the same stupid friends, the same dickheads shouting at you from cars." She smiled sourly. "At least at school I thought I was going somewhere."

I know just what you mean, thought Seth. But it must be worse for girls who had seen and felt a little bit more; who didn't want to be nice and straight. Marrying a bloke and being the obedient housewife and proper mum would destroy Debbie.

But running around with dodgy older blokes, the ten-quid rebels and small-time crims – like himself – wasn't much better.

Debbie looked at him and he gave her a tentative smile. The sympathy in her eyes was a surprise. So was his feeling of gratitude.

Peggy abruptly stood, put her sunnies on and swung her bag over her shoulder. She flashed them a brittle smile.

"Look I've got to go, but thank you. Thank you both. You are helping me so much. And so good to meet you Debbie. Thank you for talking to me. I'll ring you, Seth."

"Are you OK?" said Debbie.

Peggy nodded firmly and before Seth could get up, she quickly headed to the door.

"Oh shit, Seth, was that me?" said Debbie. "I didn't mean to freak her out. She's cool."

They watched her step out into Shields Street, her hair a sudden flash of copper in the sunlight.

"You and her would have been perfect," said Debbie.

Seth rubbed his face. "You think so?"

"I know so. If you mucked it up, then you're a fool."

"I used to think life had mucked it up, but now I know I *was* a fool."

"Ohhh, Seth," Debbie frowned in disgust. "Really?"

"Yeah well, no-one's perfect."

"What? Hello everybody!" Debbie leapt up, calling out to the lounge and waving her hands. "Excuse me everybody! News flash! Seth Kelly has just said he's not perfect!"

People turned, grinning, and in another life Seth would have verbally slapped her down. Now he just laughed. She was being a goose, but she was funny. And full of spirit. He'd missed seeing all that.

She sat back down with a devilish smirk.

"You're funny," he said.

"Is that right? Well enjoy me while you can because I'm getting out of this dump of a town."

That made him felt strange. Debbie caught this.

"You look like you cared for a moment there," she said.

Now he recognised the feeling. Alex and Mum dead and Dad a haunted shell. Mick and Pam on the other side of the country, Jeffyman gone south, and Peggy just his employer after all. And now Debbie wasn't going to be around much longer. It was strange. He had many good friends in Cairns but right now he felt alone.

"No, seriously, where are you off to?" he said.

"Brisbane. I'm going to enrol at nursing college. Janis is helping me get my application together."

"That's great Deb. You're going to do well."

"I reckon. I'm going down next month to get a place to live first. College starts in February so it'll give me time to check out the big smoke."

Oh yeah, dirty old Brisbane, thought Seth. The jacaranda trees, big department stores, stone cathedrals, and cricket fields made it look nice and straight, but underneath it was as crooked as fuck. He felt afraid for Debbie there, and he thought of Melanie and of all the young women making their way through a world full of bastard men.

With a jolt of liquid fear, he remembered the pair of purple women's panties laying on the dead leaves out the back at the Jessop compound.

"Hey, how's your friend Ella?" he said. Debbie looked at him in hurt and consternation.

"No, it's nothing like that," said Seth. "Look, I feel like a real grub for the other night. I apologise for running out on you, and for pushing you around too. It was pretty low."

Debbie stared at him.

"And at Mick and Pam's too," he said. "I'm sorry."

"Oh, you remembered that? Wow."

Feeling an uneasy mix of shame and candour, he nodded ruefully, searching for honesty, looking to make amends. But fresh pangs of trepidation spooked him anew.

"Listen Deb, I'm actually worried about Ella."

"You don't even know her."

"Does she wear purple panties? Lacey ones?"

"Are you right there?"

"Please Debbie – I'm serious."

"What, like the ones she was wearing the other night?"

Seth racked his brains but he'd been too out of it.

"Was that what she was wearing?"

"Purple, black, red – I don't remember either."

"Have you seen her in the last few days?"

"No, but she comes and goes all the time. We don't see her for days sometimes. She always pays her rent, but."

"She ever talk about scoring heroin at a big old place up at Edge Hill?"

"We don't talk about that stuff."

"Have you seen her with a fit young bloke; well dressed, good haircut, gold bracelet, drives a HX Holden?"

"Umm, maybe. She's always got guys with her."

"Young fit guy. Handsome. Speaks well."

"I don't know, Seth. What's this about?"

"When you see her next – ring me. I wanna know."

"Is she in trouble?"

"I bloody well hope not," said Seth. "And if *you* see that guy – ring me."

"Ooo, he sounds like trouble."

"You better believe it."

A Man

Seth drove up the driveway like he'd done five hundred times before; through the remnant rainforest and past the overgrown paddocks. The coastal range loomed up ahead, Mount Peter and the surrounding peaks all capped with thick white cloud; the moisture drawn up there from the Coral Sea.

There were no animals here anymore, so the gates were all open, one sagging on its hinges. With tyres skidding and bucking on dried mud ruts, Seth gunned it over the creek-bed that flooded in the wet, before quietly gliding in on the flat up to the house. Killing the Pig's engine, he heard a dog barking far-off and the sound of the wind in the trees.

It was a bit of a hike down here from Cairns and then west at Edmonton for eighteen kilometres. Mum and Dad had bought the place after he and Alex left home. They'd made a go of it with chooks, geese and goats – even a couple of cows. They grew all sorts of things by the season and Mum had made pickles and preserves.

From time to time, between jobs and houses, Seth had stayed here, lobbing in the downstairs bedroom. After it all fell apart, he found coming here too hard. Dad should have sold up and come back to Cairns, but he wouldn't. Now he lived here with ghosts and memories.

"Cooee! Hey Dad it's me!" called Seth. He listened for a return coo-ee but it didn't come. The old bloke must be out back in the gardens.

He went up the stairs, took his boots off and went in. The family photographs were hard to look at, but he did, and he was glad he did.

There was Mum grinning away in a swimsuit at Fitzroy Island. Gosh, she looked so happy and beautiful. And here's one of Alex; always posing it up, but half joking because he really thought he was the leading man. Yep, his brother had been the handsome one.

He looked at a picture of them together, barely in their teens, both in swimming trunks and holding fishing spears. Alex was the one with a fat bream on his spear. The funny thing was – he'd actually caught the fish. Alex had bullied it off him for the photo.

And look at this one – Mum and Dad dancing next to the bandstand at Ellis Beach, the band name – 'The Fireflies', painted on the bass drum.

It was different looking at the photographs now. He felt he could cry, but with happiness, because this family had had so much fun together, shared so much laughter and joy. What he'd always despised about himself – being from a normal, average family, was something pretty damn cool after all. How lucky was he?

He looked at the photos for another minute; savouring memories, digging how they didn't hurt. Then he went to share some of this great feeling with Dad. The poor bugger sure needed it.

In the kitchen he looked out the windows at the gardens. There was no sign of him. Maybe he'd gone out. Seth went out the back door, looked over to the shed and saw Dad's car parked there. As he came down the back stairs he began to sprint, dread at his heels, and he pelted past the gardens and down to the little creek. Under the big kadagi tree his father was sitting on the ground, holding something up to his face. Something the wrong way around.

"Dad!" he yelled. His father lowered a .22 rifle to the ground and pushed it away. Seth ran up and his father turned to him with his beaten smile and tired eyes.

"Hello son, this is a surprise."

"What are you doing Dad?"

His father smiled vaguely, looked around.

"Jesus Dad, what's going on? What's with the gun?"

But he knew, and when his father stood up Seth couldn't look into his eyes at first. When he did, he saw bottomless grief and pure destruction.

It was like a big tree falling, its roots tearing up the soil, and pulling up smaller trees around it. Seth couldn't let the tree hit the ground and he rushed in to catch his father and stop his fall.

He threw his arms around the motionless man, hugged him close and a huge bubble of pain burst up through him, tearing deeply inside. Now he was crying, bloody howling his heart out, and unbelievably – it felt good.

Arms hugged back, squeezing him tight and he felt his father's own wrenching sobs against his chest. Under the big sky by a little creek next to a mountain, two men were hugging and crying like babies.

When they had calmed down, they blinked at each other shyly. Dad looked down at his shirt and then at Seth's. He began to laugh. Seth looked and saw that their shirt tops were wet with tears, and who'd ever seen anything like that before? He started to chuckle and next thing they were hugging again, both laughing fit to burst.

When they came down from that, Seth was alarmed to see the worn-out smile and absent gaze starting to reclaim his father's face. The old bloke was becoming the stoic man again, the good egg who didn't grumble or complain.

As a young man, Dad had seen his mates die in the bush and on the beaches of New Guinea, bayoneted and blasted apart by grenades and naval shells. Like everyone else he'd tamped it all back down – the fear, the grief, the horror. You might go quiet for a spell, but you just soldiered on.

Then three years ago he'd lost his best friend and their oldest son on a storm-lashed mountain highway. His other son had run away like a coward. But he didn't whinge or hit the grog. He was a man.

It was so bloody clear. Dad had built his protection to stay strong and he'd made a hard, armoured shell. Now he needed a bullet to escape it.

But honestly? – that was him too. He'd learnt well from Dad in his own quiet way, from his big brother Alex, from their mates and from their big brothers and fathers too. You fought the sea, the paddock and scrub for a crust, and you fought each other out of pride, prejudice and sheer bloody-mindedness.

But you never ever showed a scrap of weakness. Not one single fucking peep. What a joke.

Dad's return to quiet desperation was nearly complete and Seth said, "Mum and Alex want us to keep living."

His father's dull gaze turned hard, almost angry.

"I'm sorry Dad. I was scared – I ran away."

He got a curt nod, his father barely moving his head, but behind the numb pain in his eyes, Seth saw something else, something tiny and miniscule looking back. Maybe it was forgiveness but right now hope would do. He reached out and took his father's shoulders.

"We're back Dad. We did all that and now we're back. We're done with it. That's finished now. It's done with."

His father nodded, more forcefully now, his scientist's mind seeing the logic – and his soul finally jack of all the pain.

Seth thought of the beautiful laughter they'd shared just moments ago and he put some of it into his gaze. A faint twinkle appeared in his father's eyes. Seth winked and the twinkle grew.

"Listen Dad," he said. "Come and stay at my place for a bit. Help me with my garden. We'll have a roast on Sunday, a few beers, even listen to some Nat King Cole."

"Yeah?" His father was intrigued.

"You bet!"

"You sure? I mean . . . won't that put off your ladies?"

"Bugger that Dad. Besides – one of those ladies might have an older sister or mum who's single."

"You cheeky ratbag," said his father, the twinkle in his eyes solid gold now.

The Colour of Shadows

It felt different when Seth woke up, like there was more sunshine in the bedroom or something. Yesterday when he had gone to pick up the rifle, Dad had grabbed it first and the look in his eyes was plain. He was back in the land of the living – and for good.

Things were looking up. Mick was alive and he'd made his peace with Peggy – and young Debbie too. All he had to do now was find Melanie, and – he reached under his pillow and took out the Python – stay alive.

After a shower he had breakfast. Then he got Aunty Mary on the phone and was pleased to hear that Uncle Don was back at work. Seth rang the station but the old copper was out on a call, so he left the message that he'd go over there in a few hours and wait.

Driving to Edge Hill, he thought of the possibilities the morning might bring. He'd hang out in the Pig watching and if Melanie turned up, he'd try and talk to her. If she listened it would save getting Uncle Don involved. If she didn't rock up he'd go up around the back again. If the HX Holden was gone he'd ransack the red brick house for the briefcase and get the hell out. It was a lot of bloody ifs.

Turning into Everknell Street, shock radiated through him. A lime-green Kombi camper van was parked out front of Jessop's house. Resisting the urge to step on the gas, he slowed and parked down the street. He took the Colt out from the stash under the dash and grabbed the bandanna from the glovebox. When he got out, he hid the pistol under his shirt, the nickel-finished steel cool against his belly.

Alrighty, he thought, let's go show these bastards that sometimes guardian angels have fists not wings – Pythons instead of swords even.

With no idea what was going to happen next, he knew he had to just dominate – and prevail.

He ran up the street, stopped behind the flame tree and eyeballed the Jessop house. The second-floor veranda and sun-washed garden were empty, so he went to the gate, and alert for rusty squeaks, carefully opened it. He dashed up a long concrete path, panicking drowsing skinks, his eyes alert for Jessop and his boys.

On the front veranda he stepped softly, wary of creating vibrations. Looking around, he took in the artistry of the wrought-iron work and massive timber beams. Along the veranda's length was the row of glass-paned French doors, each pair opening on to a room.

Most rooms were dark, their interior doors closed, but one looked bright. Seth went over to it, stopping just out of sight, and pressed himself against the wall.

He smelt incense, but heard nothing. Inching his head along to the glass door, he peeped into the room. It was empty, opening onto a much larger space also devoid of furniture. This white-painted room had the feel of a chapel, with a lofty ceiling and sunlight streaming through a row of French windows along the opposite wall. Everything was painted white and the big room glowed with light.

Two motionless people sat cross-legged on the floor in there. Some metres apart, they sat on small woven mats, their eyes closed; both apparently meditating. The totally naked long-haired man with his back to the window was Arnold Jessop, and the equally naked woman facing the window was Melanie. Seth jerked his head back.

His instinct was to burst in, grab Melanie and get the hell out. Not a good idea. A big man dragging a naked young woman down the street? It was a call to the cops for sure.

Feeling nauseated by what he'd seen, Seth just waited. When a breeze stirred the branches of an overhanging tree, making it tap and screech on the tin roof, he used the noise as cover to slink along the long veranda. He looked into the other rooms before coming to a huge front door. Two of the rooms had made-up beds and rudimentary furniture in them, but thankfully not Melanie's shoes or clothes.

What he needed was a plan. What he wanted was to get Melanie out of there *and* stick it up Jessop and Briefcase Boy. He sneaked back to the French doors that looked into the big room and saw that Melanie was gone. Damn.

Jessop was still there, sitting on his stupid hippy mat. Seth hoped Melanie was getting dressed and leaving. He'd follow her and talk to her.

Then Arnold Jessop stood up and turned, his stiff dick bouncing as he went into the next front room.

Seth recoiled from the window. Aw, yuck! He didn't need to cop an eyeful of that! No bloody wonder Melanie had got up and left. But where?

The double French doors of the room Jessop had gone into creaked and opened onto the veranda. Seth pulled out the Python and aimed, but Jessop didn't appear.

He stood there for a few seconds, his nose wrinkled in disgust, then slipped over to the open door and looked in.

Jessop lay naked on a made-up bed with his hands on his chest and his filthy bone in the air. He had closed the other door, so Seth stuck the gun in his pocket, tied the bandanna across his nose and mouth, then stepped into the room.

"Keep your mouth shut," he said.

Jessop rapidly deflated. Seth putting the pistol's barrel against his forehead must have had something to do with it. But the creepy hairy bastard didn't even try to cover up. Instead he just looked up without a shred of shame or fear. Didn't this fool know that a squeeze of the trigger would blow all that new age shit right out of his head?

Seth's heart sank as recognition lit up Jessop's face. The naked man smiled at him in delight, his honest happiness just revolting.

"It's the rock'n'roll boxer," Jessop said happily. "I knew we'd meet again."

The bandanna turned out bloody useless, thought Seth. It hadn't disguised his height, shape, or voice.

"Shut up," he said, angry that he'd given Jessop a lift.

Jessop did, his smile burning like a malignant sun.

"Okay, Arnold Jessop, listen to me very carefully." He was pleased to see surprise in Jessop's eyes.

"The young woman out there is protected. Always. You are never going to have anything to do with her ever again."

"Why?"

"Why? Why? You fuckin' nong! You were all barred up a second ago. How's that for starters?"

"I will never allow my vulnerabilities to spoil her journey to enlightenment. That's wrong."

"My oath it's wrong!"

"I see her beauty, but I must work on seeing and loving her, as a sister. Can you understand that?"

Seth could, and when Jessop saw that, the freaky magic just poured out of his eyes.

"My brother, we all feel that temptation! All we can do is to try and resist it. And try again. Success comes after much failure, but the true failure is not to try. Don't get trapped by who you think you are. You are not your story."

Seth felt torn between punching Jessop and listening to him.

"Shut up," he said. "Great line in bullshit there, but the reality is – you sell heroin and you ruin young women's lives. You're pure evil."

Jessop grimaced and his eyes filled with pain, but when he spoke, Seth knew it was the truth and it totally threw him.

"I don't sell drugs. Everything I do is a fight against that. It's my work, my cross to bear – my shadow."

Seth felt the road skidding out from under him and he dug deep, pulling up hot, righteous rage.

"Yeah? So, you don't know the young bastard who lives here is selling heroin? You haven't noticed that? Organised it? You inherited a heap of dough and you're using smack to triple it."

Arnold Jessop shook his head, his face shining with fear and, weird as hell, relief.

"I knew this day would come. I was hoping it would," he said.

"You lying sack of shit," said Seth and he hammered a good punch into Jessop's head.

The bed springs cried out. Jessop's eyes and mouth flew open with shock. Holding the revolver firmly to the prone man's head, Seth let fly, his left fist repeatedly beating flesh and bone. Maggot naked, Jessop squirmed and yelped as flecks of red appeared on the pillowslip and sheet.

Suddenly noticing the agreeable weight of the gun in his hand, Seth stopped punching. Jessop gasped for breath.

"I'm sorry. I'm so sorry," he whimpered. "It wasn't me – it was Robbie."

"What? That young prick made you buy smack with your own money?"

"I don't have the money. Robbie's got it. He made Sandra and I give it to him."

"Aye? How does a little shit like him make a rich bastard like you give up his money?"

"Because he's my brother. Because he hurts us."

What? His brother? Seth felt like he'd taken a good jab to the head. Christ! He'd got it very wrong bashing Jessop and . . . nah, he bloody well had it coming! You could see it easy on his sleazy rotten face.

Unconsciously slipping his forefinger inside the Python's trigger-guard, he reached for justification. It wasn't far.

Ella. The purple panties. What Knoxie and Johnny Pep had told him. Teenage girls. Smack.

Grinding the pistol barrel in hard, he yelled, "Where is Ella? What did you do to those girls?"

Something monstrous happened to Jessop's face then. For one gooey second, it slipped into a filthy grin, inclusive of Seth, and of all men.

Seth reared back, repulsed by his own acquiescence in knowing just what he was seeing. But he was right on the bloody money – this evil bastard knew. With due sanction, Seth curled his finger around the trigger.

"It wasn't just me, Robbie does it now," Jessop cried. "And our father . . . but I've changed! You saw that!"

Seth grabbed Arnold Jessop's hair, pulled his head back and forced the pistol barrel into his mouth.

The big blonde man's mind went to murder. His finger squeezed the trigger. The long-haired man on the bed fell still, his eyes wide in realisation. A heavy silence filled the old mansion, the garden outside now hushed and still.

Then he remembered Melanie, and Peggy, and Dad and his little niece. They needed him.

Seth slowly eased his finger off the trigger and Jessop's terrified, bleeding face came back into focus. From within the walls of the house came a deep sound like a sigh.

The closed door of the room flew open and Briefcase Boy – Robbie Jessop – looked in.

For a long second, he took in the scene, a slight, quizzical smile forming on his lips, then he slammed the door shut.

Seth leapt towards it, hearing a key turn in the lock, and in stupid reflex rattled the doorknob anyway. From the other side of the solid wooden door came the sound of running, and that little horror calling out Melanie's name.

Ignoring Arnold Jessop, Seth tore the bandanna from his face and rushed onto the veranda. He tried the door of the next room. Locked. And so was every other bloody door on the veranda. Arriving at the main entrance, he skidded onto the tiled mosaic landing and twisted the big metal doorknob. The front door swung open and he ran down a high wood-panelled hallway that led to the huge, chapel-like room.

Pausing at the doorway, he listened for movement. The mansion brimmed with silence. Moving out into the great room he winced as long hardwood floorboards called out, creaking underfoot. He froze and listened again. It felt like the house was listening back.

Where in this spook of a place was Melanie? He had to find her fast. To the left, a staircase with ornately carved wooden rails rose to the second floor. Maybe up there?

Across the main room was a hall. At the end of it was a big kitchen flooded with light, its rows of built-in shelves bare. Motes of dust swam in the sunlight and on a window-sill sat a row of empty amber-coloured bottles.

Though the kitchen windows were closed, a line of small, coloured, triangular flags hanging on the curtain rail were fluttering as if in a breeze. The back door was open.

Damn it, thought Seth. Robbie Jessop must have taken Melanie up to the red brick house. If he harms her or tries to use her as a hostage, I'll put him down like a dog.

As he went towards the kitchen he moved across a vast faded carpet of Asian design. Good, this might muffle any floorboard sounds, he thought. Now he saw four doorways lining the hallway to the kitchen; two on either side. They were all open and he didn't like that at all. Trying to watch four different points of attack while in the confined space of the hall was iffy in the extreme.

He ghosted forward, the Python good and solid in his hand. Bright sunshine poured in through skylights and the wall of French windows. On the right-hand side of the big room, he saw an open door and he quietly slipped over to it. Outside, there was a side veranda that opened on to the remains of a kitchen garden. Beyond the decaying garden borders and the rusty brown skeletons of outdoor furniture was the concrete driveway that went to the houses up the back.

Seth quietly crossed the side veranda and moved down well-worn concrete steps into the abandoned garden. With the Python held two-handed out in front, he looked along its sights as he weaved through crumbling raised garden-beds and the branches of stunted fruit trees.

As he came to the corner of the house, a wasp buzzed into his face. Dodging forwards, he saw the HX Falcon parked up on the concrete slab. Behind it was the red brick house. He began moving up towards it, and as he did, something rocketed into his left arm and sent the Python flying.

He spun around. A couple of metres away, Robbie Jessop was lowering his leg back down to the ground, a smile of genuine welcome on his face.

Everknell

"Fuck," said Seth, his arm gone totally numb.

"You think I broke it?" said Jessop.

Seth, with the uneven mess of the ruined garden behind him, darted forward, trying to anticipate the next attack. Instead of following him, Jessop jogged to the driveway, blocking any escape down it.

"Where's Melanie?" said Seth, waiting for the pain.

"She's hiding from the bad man with the gun and she's keeping very quiet like I told her to."

"Where is she?" said Seth. He looked down towards the garden, trying to see the Python in the long grass.

Jessop read his look and flowed in, throwing a head-high kick. Seth ducked it, turned and ran up to the parking slab. From behind him came a peal of laughter.

Out on the expanse of cracked concrete, Seth raised his arm and moved the muscles. Agony came in a fierce wave now. Robbie Jessop scampered up to the slab and regarded him with pleasure.

"I'm giving you time to recover because you look like you might be a decent opponent," he said.

Seth looked around at the other houses.

"It's just you and me," Jessop grinned. "My brother and sister will keep right out of this and my associate isn't here today."

Seth worked his arm, trying to ignore the sickening pain flooding through it.

"Do you practice martial arts?" asked Jessop. "I studied in Hong Kong and also in Thailand. There's a dojo here in Cairns – Matsumoto, but nobody there wants a real fight. They're all too nice."

"You don't live in Cairns?" said Seth.

"This hick town? I couldn't wait to get out."

"So why are you here?"

"Some business. Seeing the family."

"Buying and selling heroin and keeping your brother and sister in line. You control the inheritance, right?"

"You're too smart for Cairns. You should work for me."

"Nah, I don't like rich kids or evil bastards, so that's a double up-your-clacker from me."

"Ohhh, that's a bit hypocritical. I see a man like you with his mask and gun and I just know he's a villain. Yet he gets all moral when recognised as such. Aren't you old enough to have learnt how to be honest with yourself?"

"Fuck you," said Seth, angry at being preached to. "You know bugger-all about me."

"On the contrary. I look at you and I see a dozen men I've known – violent criminals all. You can fool yourself but you can't fool me."

"Where's Melanie?"

"It doesn't matter now. I've decided to kill you."

In his years of security work Seth had heard this threat dozens of times, always spoken by blokes soon subdued. This time he believed it.

"There's witnesses – Melanie, your brother. You going to kill them too?"

"Arnold will do just what I say and the little lady won't see a thing. She's a yummy young thing, isn't she? I don't want her seeing a corpse any more than you do, so I think I'll put you down under the trees over there."

"Fuck's sake – you think I'm a cow?"

"Let's find out."

Robbie Jessop gleefully darted in. Seth threw one of his block-busters but the little shit spun sideways under it and kicked him in the ribs. It bloody hurt but he didn't have time to whinge about it, as Jessop came in fast again, crowding in under his punches, jabbing short hard hits to his ribs, targeting the same spot. Trying to find some room to fight, he spun and charged across the slab, but the rotten bastard was right behind him, pummelling his kidneys.

Seth abruptly stopped, pumping the hard piston of his elbow backwards. He felt it connect, just, and he whirled around to exploit the blow.

Jessop was near the ground, not grimacing in pain, but down on his hands like a gymnast on the horse. His legs were swinging in a blurred arc at Seth's ankles.

A manic knees-up leap cleared the sweep. Landing hard, Seth scrambled for balance – then threw his fists up. With unbelievable speed, Jessop leapt to his feet and bored in.

Seth dodged two kicks, turned and absorbed another on his backside as he raced across the slab. At its edge he spun around, Jessop right there of course, and they exchanged a flurry of punches that tested his ribs anew. Making a shield of flesh and bone with his forearms, he smashed the bugger back, twisted at the hips and threw a jaw-breaker punch, his arm at full stretch. Jessop kicked him in the head. Pin-pricks of white starred his vision and he nearly fell. Jessop paused and raised his eyebrows in mock concern.

With his every punch evaded, his every ploy seemingly anticipated, Seth could see no way to overcome this horrid fighting machine. I'm going to die here, he thought.

On the grass of the lawn now, close to the edge of the rain forest, Seth recognised the big tree he'd hidden behind and watched from yesterday. It seemed a few years ago now.

His legs quivered and his shoulders sagged. He gave in to it, blinking at the ground and rolling his head. Jessop grunted in satisfaction and came in for the kill.

Seth held the pose; then came to life with a jack-knife feint and dodge, managing to skid a bloody good punch off Jessop's ribs. The little shit felt it, squeaking like a rat as he fell back. Seth capitalised on this opening, going in hard with a slew of desperate left and rights.

This relentless offensive made Jessop run backwards across the lawn and Seth saw a chance opening up. Robbie Jessop's concentration was now split between avoiding his attack and not slamming into the approaching tree-line.

Keeping up the fierce momentum, Seth put on a spurt of speed, leapt off the ground and stamped down hard on Jessop's foot, making him wail like a drunken lead singer.

This was it. Even as he brought his boot down he was slotting in the follow-up hit. While the little bastard's mind registered pain, Seth had a crucial half second to change this one-sided contest.

Ahead of his brain already, his fist sailed through the air right towards Jessop's throat. It was too late now to change the end result of this. His fist was going to crush the larynx, choke off Jessop's air, and very probably kill him.

But the kid had called it; it was on him. Like with Smiley on that ridge out at the Mitchell – it was kill or die.

Seth's fist hit thin air. Jessop had intuitively snapped his head away. A second later he freed his foot, a second after that he laid the other one against the side of Seth's skull – which rang in surprise more than anything else. Over the buzzing in his head Seth heard a deep booming noise.

Standing by the rainforest's edge, Jessop looked down at his foot. Lifting it off the ground, he grinned boyishly and moved it around. I hope I broke bones, thought Seth.

The low frequency sound came again. Jessop turned and frowned at the rainforest shadows. With a shrug he turned back, waggled his foot and winked at Seth.

"Nice try, but I think we'll play on," he said.

From behind him the papa cassowary came crashing out of the jungle, its tall casque bobbing with anger, its wattles crimson with rage.

Robbie Jessop wheeled around.

"Not this stupid fucking animal again!" he yelled, going into a fighting stance.

Seth stared in total disbelief. It must be all those years in Hong Kong, he thought, but this idiot has no idea.

Jessop spun on one foot and unleashed a lightning bolt of a kick. At the same instant the cassowary kicked back, its immense power knocking the man over. Then it was on top of him, stamping with its big feet and claws.

Shouting with surprise, Jessop thrashed about like a bug on its back, his legs frantically pedalling in the air. From between them spurted a geyser of blood.

Supremely stunned with shock, Seth stood stock still, too shit-scared to step in.

A big pale figure came into the sunlight at the edge of the lawn. It was Sandra Jessop, rousted by their fighting from her bed. She stared at her brother squirming in a widening red puddle, his body jumping every time a kick connected.

Throwing up her arms, she started shouting. Alerted, the cassowary looked around and then ran towards the noise and movement with hellish speed. Sandra Jessop bolted back into the gloom. Footsteps thudded on a veranda floor and a door slammed. The cassowary ran into the shadows and empty whisky bottles bounced and burst.

Robbie Jessop sat up, wet flaps of skin hanging off his face, and looked in horror at his thigh. Seth looked too and his heart just about stopped. The bird's big kick hadn't just punctured the femoral artery – it had slashed it wide open. An absolute sheet of blood was foaming over the green and gray concrete slab.

With eyes bulging in horrible realisation, Robbie Jessop took a deep whooping breath and began screaming. It was an awful sound – a demonic wail of petulant fury. Then he flopped back wetly onto the slab, made a freaky growling noise and began to die.

Seth heard yelling now – coming from the mansion. A woman's voice. Melanie.

Sprinting back to the kitchen garden, he spent frantic moments looking for the Python. Head down, his back to the slab, he listened for the cassowary's return as he clawed through the grass. A glint of nickel-plating alerted him to the gun and after quickly checking it, he ran through the overgrown garden, across the side veranda and into the mansion.

He kept an eye out for Arnold Jessop, the Python in his hand jumping from doorway to doorway. Melanie's yelling was coming from the next floor and he ran to the staircase. Seeing no-one, he thumped up the polished wooden stairs, his arms tingling with adrenaline, his mind jumping like a frog.

At the top Seth followed her voice, watching closed doors as he ran down a long hallway to a big bedroom door.

"Arnold! Robbie! What's going on! Let me out!"

The anger was good, but fear lurked in her voice. Robbie Jessop's screams had freaked her out, and man, he could totally understand that. What he'd just seen happen began to replay in his head. Nah, nah, nah, forget that, he ordered himself. Focus on what you have to do.

He tried the door. Locked. He took a run at it with his good shoulder; bounced off. Melanie went silent, listening as he thumped into the door again. It was pointless – the wood was as solid as a gravestone.

Seth stared at the Python – it was trembling in his hand. It's called delayed shock, he told himself. He had to tamp down the heebie-jeebies before he could speak. Putting his mouth close to the door, he called out nice and calm.

"Hey Melanie. It's Seth here. Stasia's friend. I met you at Wangetti Beach. I'm your mum Peggy's friend too."

Silence filled the hallway and Seth looked around. The light was weird – all granulated like an old photograph.

"Melanie, listen to me. Move away from the door to the other side of the room. Get on the floor. I'm going to shoot the lock off with a gun. Do you understand?"

"Why? Where's the key? What's happened to Arnold and his brother?"

"Please just do it. Move away from the door now."

"Not until you tell me what's going on."

Damn it, thought Seth. We have to get out of here!

"Melanie, you trusted me before. When we went to VW Empire. We talked about it – about how you knew who the bad men were. Remember?"

"Yes, I remember."

"Well trust me now. Please."

He waited in silence and it grew into a sickly hum. The hallway felt like a trap; the high painted white walls moving in. He felt an overwhelming urge to run.

"I saw you and Arnold Jessop sitting naked before," he said. "Were you cool with that?"

"Um . . . no. I thought it was weird," said Melanie.

"Well I'm not like him Melanie. I care about you and I care about your mother."

"Are you the man Mum met in Cairns when she ran off a few years ago?"

"Yep. That's me."

"I thought so."

"Can I shoot the lock off now?"

"I think you better."

At full arm's length he aimed down at the lock, counted loudly to five, averted his face and squeezed off a booming shot. The magnum round blew the lock to pieces.

Inside, Melanie was standing by the far wall, dressed and holding a bag. Unsurprisingly, she looked scared. He gave her a reassuring smile and quickly looked around.

They were in a magnificent master bedroom of good size. Intricate wood parquetry lined the edges of the floor and went halfway up walls crafted from fine tongue and groove planks. The high ceiling was made of delicately pressed and patterned tin. Framed floral etchings on the white walls, a made-up four-poster bed with an elaborately carved headboard, and a beautiful bedside table complete with porcelain wash bowl and jug, made the room look like a museum exhibit.

"OK, let's go," said Seth.

"Why do you have that gun?" said Melanie. "And there's blood on your hand."

"I'll explain it all when . . ."

He couldn't go on. The air in the brown and white room was suddenly foul, clogging his nostrils and throat. He looked around again and felt the piss go cold inside him.

The wooden parquetry work on the walls and floor had changed, the various inlaid tones of wood now looking like streaks and smears of sweat and blood and shit, the fine interlocked patterns no longer the exquisitely decorative leaves and flowers the craftsmen had created.

Now he saw bones. Human bones. Boatloads of bones.

Plantations of bones. Bones to build a town on. Bones of men and boys, girl's bones and mum's bones. Everybody stolen, everybody used and used up; everybody done for. All to make a fortune, all to build an empire, all to make a country.

Seth felt nausea and pain. A rotten worm squirmed in his groin, in his guts and head. This room, this mansion, this whole compound rotting away on the side of Mt. Whitfield was soaked in misery and degradation; reeking of slavery and brutal violence.

But what on God's good earth was this? There were other people in the room! A bearded man, red-necked and white-skinned, holding something vicious and thin like a sword or a whip, but made of cruel, changing things: razor sharp metal, plaited leather, and then pink and red like a muscle stripped off the bone.

And a young woman, frizzy-haired and dark skinned, kneeling down, rigid with fear. Seth knew her mother had been right here before her. He shouted out at this hideous hallucination and felt an excruciating blade of recognition pass through his heart.

The putrid stinking dam of the Jessops, their past and present, broke its banks and absolute filth filled his eyes, mouth, nose and heart. Some of it was his.

Sinking, suffocating, going down, he felt a hand on his arm and a voice in his ear. Surfacing in the mire he looked into Melanie's face just centimetres from his. The concern in her eyes wasn't even close to absolution, but right now it was what he needed.

"Are you okay?" she said. "What are you looking at?"

Absolutely reeling, Seth shrugged wildly, but Melanie, sharp and awake, knew.

"It's this house," she said. "It gives me the creeps too. So do Arnold and his brother. I made a big mistake."

Seth felt unglued; his wits blown. Come on, come on, he railed at himself – this kid needs you!

Melanie's hand, small and firm, took his.

"Let's go," she said.

God Really Loves You

A Ulysses butterfly, neon-bright against the green of the garden, surfed in on the off-shore breeze and fluttered past the head of the man sitting at the outside table. It soared up towards the morning sun, over the roof of the house and disappeared behind the big mango tree out the front.

Seth smiled softly at this display of effortless grace. He leant forward to get his cuppa and – ow, it hurt. His ribs and head ached from the beating he'd taken yesterday and he had a bonza collection of bruises in shades that would put Estee Lauder to shame. It was only fighters' luck that he hadn't taken any hard blows on the shotgun wounds.

Taking a mouthful of tea, he looked at the cheque on the table and happily re-read the amount it was made out for. Five thousand dollars. Maaate!

He'd protested but Peggy insisted, saying that Graham made that in just a few days. Well, he could live on that for months without working, but would you believe it? He had another job lined up already – another investigation.

Twenty minutes ago, Peggy's friend Rita had rung him.

After first congratulating him again for bringing Melanie back to her mother, she'd got down to the nitty gritty. Speaking on behalf of her husband she explained that someone on his extensive payroll was stealing from one of the businesses.

Could Seth find out who? If he did, he'd get a hefty bonus on top of the bloody good weekly wage on offer. Of course, he could.

This job, and Peggy's money, had got him all fired up. Why not get a licence and set himself up as a fair-dinkum private investigator? Phone calls, petrol, servicing the Pig, mango Weis bars – even the occasional client lunch at Tawny's – could all be claimed as expenses if he played it legit. He'd get an accountant and an answering machine too! Dad was going to love this.

From inside came the ringing of the phone. He hopped up with a grunt of pain then smiled. This was probably Rita's husband Michael, keen to organise a meeting.

"Hello Seth, it's me."

Debbie's voice made him smile even more.

"Ella's back. She was out on Fitzroy Island for a few days. Met a tourist with money so she didn't get a tan of course."

Seth felt relief. And pity and sadness too. In the long run this wasn't going to end well. Ella, barely out of her teens, was starting a life that was going to be one big battle of not just staying alive, but also dealing with real bastards. It made him feel like knocking heads. Hard.

"And she never met that fella – the handsome one you said was trouble. He still around?"

"Nah – he's gone now."

Seth suddenly thought of the blue shirt he'd bought at Tom Hull's Man's World hanging unworn in his wardrobe.

"So, Deb – what are you doing tonight?"

"Me? Nothing much. Why?"

"You wanna have dinner at Tawny's with me?"

"I'm going to Brisbane, Seth. You can't make me change my mind."

"No, it's not like that. I want to celebrate your new career and your move down south."

"Yeah? Aw, Seth, I'd love to!"

"Put on your best frock babe. Let's wow 'em," he said, sounding like some twit in an American movie. The sound of Debbie's delighted laughter was just about the best bloody thing he'd heard in ages.

In the Commonwealth Bank, Seth stood patiently in the queue enjoying the air-conditioning while idly tapping his deposit book and Peggy's cheque against his thigh.

His thoughts went to what had gone down yesterday, and he involuntarily shivered in fear. A lot of crazy things had happened to him in his life but that fifteen minutes at Everknell Street had to be right up there near the top of the list.

Beyond being nearly beaten to death, he'd come within a whisker of killing a man for nothing, and then watched a man horribly die. But what he'd seen and felt in the awful bedroom upstairs had really taken the cake – then stomped it into mush.

He'd felt a despicable truth there. Cairns would never be the same now. Hell, neither would he.

When he and Melanie had left that madhouse, the street was tranquil and hopefully devoid of potential witnesses. Melanie in her Kombi had followed him to a phone box on Sheridan Street where he rang Peggy to get the address.

At Rita's house, mother and daughter had hugged, both of them ambushed by emotion. There were tears and Peggy hugged Seth too, a huge thank you in her eyes.

That had felt bloody good. Actually, better than good. The realisation had washed through him – this is what I do. This is who I am.

Then Peggy and Melanie sat down by the pool and while they talked, he asked Rita if he could use her phone.

He was in luck ringing the copshop. Uncle Don was there and Seth told him where to go and what to look for. And yeah, he'd also find a dead bloke there who'd been killed by a cassowary. The old cop made him repeat that bit and Seth made him swear that this was an anonymous tip-off.

Around tea-time last night Uncle Don had rung him at home. It had taken him and his boys a few hours of serious searching but they'd found a briefcase full of heroin. They arrested Arnold Jessop, who looked like somebody had given him a good hiding, he didn't know who, and crikey! – how was his brother, all ripped up, his body circled by cassowary tracks in blood? In all his years on the force Uncle Don had never seen anything like it.

At the end of the call Seth got a heart-felt 'good on ya son.' It was a top way for the old cop to retire; a major drug bust with an incredible yarn attached to it.

Then a smell shook Seth out of his reverie, alerting him like a dangerous-looking face at a gig.

It was the fragrance of a man's perfume mixed with the scent of menthol cigarettes. Trying to match the smell to memory, he looked around the bank; his eyes settling on two men. They were standing at a back counter, one filling out a banking slip. Both fellas were sun-tanned, in nicely pressed slacks and short-sleeved shirts. They looked like Tableland farmers down in Cairns on business. One was tubby, with a strong nose and Seth recognised him.

It was the man from behind the latticework screen at Leafgold Weir Road. The man who was going to have him killed.

Black paranoia and terrible despair tore at him and he quickly turned away, loathing how he felt. Would this ever end?

He stared at the back of the head of the woman in front of him for a few seconds. How could he slip out of the bank without being noticed? Should he . . . ah bugger it. He left the queue and went over to the two men.

The tubby bloke saw him first and grunted in surprise. The other man frowned, moved forward; his hands turning into fists.

"Mr. Richard," said Seth. "May I speak to you?"

The tubby man held his arm out in front of his mate.

"Oh ho – it's you," he said to Seth.

"Yeah it's me. Look, I want you to know that both Mick and I listened to what you told us – that it's nobody else's business and that no-one talks about it. Well, we've done that and we will keep doing that. And Mick – he's gone forever. You'll never hear from him again."

The tubby man laughed with genuine good humour.

"How was it out there?" he said. "You must have run for sixty fuckin' miles."

"I don't know what you mean," said Seth. The man fairly hooted, and then came in close.

"Listen, my job offer is still open. You are bloody good."

What the hell? thought Seth. The man responsible for his imminent murder was treating him like his new best mate.

"I don't know what you mean," he repeated.

"OK, no worries, but I gotta thank you. You solved a big problem for me." The man snapped his fingers together like a trap.

"You killed a rat out there – a thieving rat. You keep your mouth shut too. I respect that and I won't forget it."

Seth couldn't believe what he was hearing.

Then he remembered Mick's phone-call and what this man was saying now became crystal clear.

Sweet Jesus, thought Seth. I'm not going to be killed.

The cunning old bastard saw the expression on his face and burst out laughing again. Feeling almost weightless with relief, Seth joined in and the whole bank turned to look at them.

"I tell you," chuckled the man. "God really loves you."

Soundtrack

Like Seth Kelly, I love music. Here is some of the music from
the book, plus complimentary tracks that speak of the place and
era – the times, latitude and attitude.

Just a Little Bit – The Purple Hearts
Precious – The Pretenders
I Love the Sound of Breaking Glass – Nick Lowe
Money – Dan Sultan
Young Man Blues – The Who
The Cisco Kid – War
Black Crow – Joni Mitchell
You Don't Love Me – The Allman Brothers Band
Vision is a Naked Sword – Mahavishnu Orchestra
Oh! Tengo Suerte – Masayoshi Takanaka
Alabama Electric Circus – Link Wray
Zoot Allures – Frank Zappa
One Way . . . or Another – Cactus
The Lowdown – Boz Scaggs
Blind Alley – Fanny
Woke Up This Morning – Lightnin' Hopkins
Situation – Jeff Beck

Author's Note

Far North Queensland is full of characters. Over the years I've been lucky enough to meet and become friends with a few of them. So, this is where I tell you that the 'resemblance to anyone living or deceased in this book is entirely coincidental.'

The Colour of Shadows is the first novel in a trilogy featuring Seth Kelly, set in Far North Queensland, and taking place in the 1970s and 1980s.

Acknowledgements

Mighty big thanks to Michael 'Gonzo' Gompert for his editorial diligence, unstinting encouragement, crucial logic and technical knowledge.

A huge acknowledgement and heart-felt thank you to my beta-readers and graphics mavens for their invaluable feedback. You know who you are.

And undying love and eternal gratitude to my best friend Jan Brown for her savvy advice, continuing support, and keen eye for both facts and emotions.